PRAISE FOR

MAÑANA MEANS HEAVEN

"Hernandez's intimate knowledge of life amid the agricultural fields of central California and his ability to conjure the thoughts and emotions of the young Bea Franco make for a graceful and melancholy tale."

—*Associated Press*

"A beautifully realized portrait of Bea Franco."

—*Los Angeles Times*

"Based on extensive research and investigation, part fact, mostly fiction, and years in the making, this novel will thrill the millions of readers who have read Kerouac's book and/or seen the movie adaptation. But no prior knowledge of Kerouac or his works is required: this is an entirely fascinating, stand-alone story in its own right."

—*Booklist*

"Hernandez gives incredible depth and dimensionality to the love story of Jack Kerouac and Bea Franco."

—*Los Angeles Review of Books*

"Seductive and fascinating."

—*The Fresno Bee*

"Hernandez's choice to write [Bea's] story as fiction is gutsy, inspired, and does honor to Kerouac, who fictionalized the real-life characters he met in *On the Road*. The result is an earthy and soulful tale, a version of their improbable love affair that feels as true as Kerouac's."

—*Catch & Release*

"We become more savvy readers of Kerouac through the eyes of Hernandez's muse."

—*Los Angeles Review of Books*

MAÑANA
MEANS
HEAVEN

Camino del Sol

A Latina and Latino Literary Series

MAÑANA MEANS HEAVEN

TIM Z. HERNANDEZ

THE UNIVERSITY OF
ARIZONA PRESS

TUCSON

The University of Arizona
www.uapress.arizona.edu

Printed in the United States of America

ISBN-13: 978-0-8165-3035-9 (cloth)
ISBN-13: 978-0-8165-3393-0 (paper)

Cover design by Leigh McDonald
Cover photo adapted from *Bea and little Albert, Los Angeles, 1942* © Al Franco

Bea Franco's letters to Jack Kerouac (which appear on pages 172, 178, 190, and 191) courtesy of the Henry W. and Albert A. Berg Collection of English and American Literature, The New York Public Library, Astor, Lenox, and Tilden Foundations.

Publication of this book is made possible in part by the proceeds of a permanent endowment created with the assistance of a Challenge Grant from the National Endowment for the Humanities, a federal agency.

Library of Congress Cataloguing-in-Publication Data
Hernandez, Tim Z.
  Mañana Means Heaven / Tim Z. Hernandez.
    pages cm. — (Camino del Sol: A Latina and Latino Literary Series)
  ISBN 978-0-8165-3035-9 (cloth : acid-free paper)
  I. Title.
  PS3608.E768M36 2013
  813'.6—dc23
                    2013000966

∞ This paper meets the requirements of ANSI/NISO Z39.48-1992 (Permanence of Paper).

For Dayanna, In Lak'ech, Ala K'in

THE LAST INTERVIEW

Wednesday, October 13, 2010

It was almost nine o'clock in the evening, and we had now reached the point when it seemed like there was nothing left to talk about. Silence filled the small dining room. Outside a car whisked past, and a dog barked after it. It was the sound of east-central Fresno. She was tired, that much was obvious. But there was still the one question I had not asked. It had been on my mind since our first meeting, but timing was everything. Sitting across the table from her, I wondered how to ask it. Or if I should. What right did I have to pry into the intimate matters of Bea's past? I couldn't help right then to think about the events that had brought me here, to this house, at this moment.

Three years ago I was standing in the snow in Boulder, Colorado. I had just walked out of a classroom at Naropa University where the topic was lineage. I left with a feeling of skepticism, wondering what exactly I was doing in this school, a place built upon the reputations of the very outcasts that the author Jack Kerouac himself dubbed *the Beats*—as in rundown, tired, beat.

Standing there on that curb, I did something that I had done several times before: I cracked open Jack's most famous book, *On the Road*. But this time, without really knowing why, I was looking for something of myself within those pages. I flipped straight to the chapter about a farmworker woman called "Terry," whom Kerouac referred to as "the Mexican girl." She was from the San Joaquin Valley, the town of Selma. A speck about twelve miles south of Fresno. Selma, *Raisin Capital of the World*—I remembered the billboard sign on Highway 99. I read on with a renewed sense of interest. Kerouac's description of California's agricultural region, the central valley, though only partly accurate, took me there, to that place I knew so well. Reading his depiction of Terry reminded me of my own grandmother. A woman who, much like Terry, also lived a good part of her life among the labor camps of the valley, or, as they're known locally, *los campos*. The cold air fell away and a warmth settled on the backs of my hands and against my neck; for a brief moment I had forgotten that I was standing outside in Colorado's coldest month.

When I was done reading the chapter, I closed the book and thought of Terry. The real Terry. That is, Bea Franco, the Mexican girl. I wondered what ever became of her. This was the beginning. Or at least my beginning. Her beginning was elsewhere, as I would soon discover. A separate reality. A different time and place altogether.

"Bea," I finally said to her. She lifted her tired gaze up at me. "Do you remember a man, a friend of yours named Jack?"

She rubbed and blinked her eyes several times, angled her face away from the light, and thought for a moment. When the answer did not come quickly enough, Albert, her son, nodded at me and pointed his eyes at the photograph that was sitting on the table.

"Do you think a picture of him would help you remember?" I asked.

"Maybe," she said.

I lifted the photograph and passed it to her. She took it from my hand and stared blankly at it for a second, then rubbed her eyes some more.

"I need my magnifying glass," she said, rising up from her seat.

She slowly tucked the loose end of her sweater under her arm and shuffled to her china cabinet, and from the drawer she pulled out a large round lens. She gripped its black handle, flicked on a small desk lamp, and lifted the thick magnifying glass inches above the photograph. Her back was to the table where Albert and I sat studying her closely. She maneuvered the photo until she'd found the right angle, and then held it as still as she could. Her hand trembled. She fixed her eyes on the image of Jack for a few seconds, and looked back over her shoulder at me. Albert fidgeted with his moustache.

"Do you remember him, Mom?" he asked, growing impatient.

She turned the photograph toward the light and stood motionless, fixated on the details of Jack's face. Her breathing was audible but soft. Her chin lifted slightly. She hesitated, and then stared at the photo another minute. Finally, she turned toward Albert, little Al, her son. The weight of her gaze was distant, hazy almost. She rubbed her eyes again with the back of her hand, and lowered the magnifying glass. "My eyes are bad today," she said, placing the photo facedown on the table. "Feels like I'm looking through cotton balls." And with that, she turned and quietly shuffled her way into the kitchen.

Turn and listen; not only in my eyes is Paradise.

—Beatrice, Dante's *Divine Comedy*

I

The Mexican Girl, 1947

1

When Bea was just an impressionable and melancholic ten-year-old, her first real memory—that is, the kind that lingers all years down the track no matter where or in what condition you find yourself—was brought about by an important delineation in the dirt. It began at a train station in Indio, California, and the year was 1930. The memory itself was of a thousand brown faces crowded onto the platform of the station, each one clutching a meager and most prized belonging. Some toted flour sacks woven shut with clothes, bursting at the seams, while others had boxes slung with rope across their shoulders. The men fumbled their dusty bowler hats, and the women clinched their ill-fitted dresses and lined up, or tried to, but the line turned into a frenzy of bodies once the steam engine came roaring into sight at the far end of the tracks. From the open mouth of each boxcar door emerged two armed immigration officers. They were carrying clipboards with important matters pinned down. Their brown suits were pressed to blades, and their moustaches were made of golden tufts of hay. They stood above the people so that the tips of their slick boots gleamed at the blunt noses of the men and at the sunburnt foreheads of the women. From their high roost they consulted their clipboards and began calling out names. Quickly, the people who belonged to those names were ushered aboard, family by family. Even then, as a shy yet somewhat defiant ten-year-old, Bea thought it curious that most of these people, these Mexicanos with proud faces and humble rags, had managed to shape their mouths into something that resembled a smile. They wore these peculiar masks as they boarded and took their spots inside the boxcar. Even when one of the officers swiped a piece of luggage from a husband's clutches and flung it onto the dirt, Bea found it unusual that the husband did not jump up and punch the man on the mouth. He only nodded politely and went with his family and was thankful. Of course, how could she know that the reason that husband did not rise up was because he had been promised, guaranteed, five hundred greenbacks for voluntary deportation, so whatever they did to him, to them, was okay, for now. The names went down alphabetically, and Bea knew they did because if there was one thing Ascot Elementary prided itself in, it was teaching little brown children early on about the English language, so she had memorized her alphabet. When a family of Quevedos and then Quintanas and then Ramoses were called, she watched her father Jesus take his hat off and knew it was their turn to move forward. He looked back at the oldest two, Epi and Maggie, and then at Bea's mother Jessie, and saw that her face was a statue of disdain, but nothing could be done about it. When one of the golden moustaches called out "Renteria," a block of bodies crowded up to the foot of the boxcar and angled their heads up at the officers. They called out the name Ignacio Renteria, and Ignacio and his three kids climbed aboard, except that Ignacio, with his stubby legs and round body had to be helped on, so they yanked him up by his overall straps. Once on the boxcar Ignacio turned his back to the people and quickly disappeared into the shadows. The next name called was Jesus Renteria. Jesus stepped up and reached back for Jessie, and she took her husband's hand and rose up onto the boxcar. All seven kids went on up after her, and together they found a spot inside, but not before Jesus managed to get a kick in the seat of his pants by one of the officers. When he fell forward he said nothing and could not look in the faces of his family, especially not Jessie. Of course, she said nothing about it, just looked away. Bea noticed this too. When all the people were on board and the floors and walls were cluttered with bodies, sweating profusely each of them, right down to the few infants who were suckling from their mamas' wilted breasts, Bea wondered why all the mahogany faces had the same wary and complacent look, like they were all going home after a long and disappointing vacation. Truth was, some were going home, but hell if California was any vacation. A good number of those wary faces stared at Bea and couldn't help but wonder why a girl with a complexion like that— her face the pale color of nectarine meat and big green lettuce-leaf eyes—was riding in their boxcar. But of course they all knew that no matter what the skin suggests, as long your last name is Mexican, sounds Mexican, or even looks Mexican, you get tossed in with the rest—damn the possibility that you might not be Mexican at all. Because this train ride was her first real adventure, Bea hadn't a clue what to do, so she followed what the other kids did, and pasted her little body against the wall of the boxcar and peeked her eyes out through the slats of wood. And just like the other kids, she too stuck her thin fingers through those slats and bent them at the knuckle and waved good-bye to California. She watched the lower end of the Golden State scroll past the slats—the mountains of San Jacinto, Sun City's white deserts, and the shores of Encinitas, all of it. *Adios*, the kids said, and some of the parents did too. To pass the time, a few of them sang songs, tunes from the old country, which for Bea was the new country. And she listened closely to those songs as she looked out the slats and, in her own mind, a part of her wished she knew the words. When they finally crossed over that important line in the dirt and the train rose up a hill, she could see a piece of America vanishing in the distance, and this was her first view of it from afar. Some of the children clapped at the sight, while others spoke giddily about returning home to Mexico, and still other children didn't speak at all. Instead, they cuddled up to their mothers and wondered if they'd ever return to the place they had been born, the streets they'd played in, the only home they'd ever known. Some of them actually believed they would return to California one day, and that it wouldn't be long at all, and others didn't. Though both did agree on one thing. It was the one thing they all knew and knew well. And that one thing was that plans rarely, mostly never, work out, and no one knows what tomorrow will bring. They said this to one another constantly, or else they hummed it in their minds, like a lullaby, until the hypnotic clacking of the train rocked them to sleep. And then finally, three days later, after most of the people had been let off at their respective pueblitos, the train skirted around a massive gorge and pulled along the green mountainside of the Arandas, flecked with orange and red, its soil raked to near perfection. When Bea looked out the slats, there before her eyes, spread out like the small Eden her father had promised them, was Irapuato, Guanajuato. Jesus knelt down beside his daughter and angled his eyes too through the slats, and she saw the way his dark brows lifted and his whole bronze face shone. But the one thing Bea did not foresee back then, even as a keenly observant ten-year-old, was that this sublime image would become that one memory she would return to time and again, and eventually dismiss as a dream. It was the memory of her father, Jesus Renteria, smiling, in that magnificent, particular way.

2

It's common knowledge that if a person cries when cutting an onion it's because they're jealous. Bea rarely cries. She's chopped onion nearly every day of her life and can count on one hand how many times she's shed tears. Her oldest sister Maggie used to tell her it's not normal. That she's not normal. She used to believe this when she was younger, but now she just laughs at the idea. Once the onion is diced she moves to the lemons. Pulls one from the basket and rolls her palm against it until it softens, quarters it, and places it in a bowl. Next come the serrano peppers. She cups them in her hands and blows a warm gust of breath onto them and rubs each one until it heats up, dices those too, and folds them in with the onion and cilantro. Finally, she drops the hominy into the pot. The scalding juice splashes up onto her wrists and hands, but she's no stranger to its blistering heat so she thinks nothing of it.

The meat's been set to boil since the night before. The pig's feet, tripe, huesos, all of it. She lifts a bone out with a blue ladle, and its brown translucent marrow jiggles in place. She blows on it and then puts the ladle to her lips, considers it for a second, and slurps the gelatinous brown from its casing.

Her mother, Jessie, swore by the marrow's potency.

"It has everything you need," she'd say.

"But it's so ugly."

"The uglier it looks the better," she'd claim. And all Bea had to do was look at her father to know that the poor woman wholeheartedly subscribed to this idea.

Jesus is a weather-bitten man, slender and thick skinned. His square face bears the kind of pockmarks people can only get three ways: either they are born with it, they've earned it through years of pickling the gut, or they've worked a lifetime beneath the sun's merciless spears. In Jesus's case it's all three. During the harvest season his moustache is unkempt and runs down to his chin and zigzags to his earlobes. Anyone who doesn't know him, and the few who do, usually keep their distance while out in the fields. As a mayordomo, he's the kind of callous son-of-a-bitch every farmer keeps at least two of. Quick to jump on a worker's back, if need be. A voice so colossal that it can be heard over a hundred acres if the moment calls for it. He could often be seen pacing the rows and pointing out the missed fruit—though hardly ever seen hunched over, doing the real work. And had Bea not observed these little curiosities about her father since the day she was born, she might've subscribed to her mother's theory herself, but as it was, she just couldn't get herself to relish the marrow as her mother did.

She adds a sprinkle of pepper and some salt, and then watches each ingredient disintegrate into the boiling red. Its spicy steam wafts across her face and opens her pores. She lowers the heat and dunks the ladle into the pot again, and then pulls her hair back into a bun and waits.

It's early still, the roosters have not begun to sing, and Beto isn't home yet. Standing in the kitchen, she crosses her arms and leans against the sink and wonders why she puts up with him. She feels stupid whenever she pictures him off in some bar, El Molino Rojo, with the rest of the mujeriegos, draining away more than their paychecks. The worst part is she's known this about him since day one. He's a bum. This is the word that comes to mind. At that moment the menudo bubbles and spills onto the hot stove and hisses. She turns the fire off and begins to fix herself a bowl.

While ladling the red broth and staring down into the fresh vat of ancient goodness she knows that there's nothing more a man yearns for than a steaming bowl of that savory stew to remedy his hangover. And then a flash goes off in her mind, an idea. No, she thinks to herself, I couldn't. It's too wicked, foolish even. It scares her to know she's capable of such absurdity. But then she gives the idea another minute, just to be sure. And then the corner of her mouth lifts slightly and she knows it has to be done.

She prepares her own bowl. She ladles in several scoops of menudo and fixes it to her liking—lots of lemon, onion, a spoonful of chopped serrano and a sprinkle of cilantro. She places her bowl on the dining table next to the stack of tortillas to let it cool. She reaches into the cabinet and pulls a large sack of sugar out and sets it on the counter. She opens the sack but then hesitates. She stares down once more into the simmering pot of her labors, and again worries if what she's about to do is nothing short of an abomination, a sin of unredeemable proportion. Through the small kitchen window she can now see the glowing purple of the eastern sky, and she senses Beto will be home soon. God, she prays to herself, let him be hungover like never before, and may his appetite be such that he salivates at roadkill along the way home. So hungry, that when he gets out of his truck and catches the scent of stewed tripe and pig's foot lassoing him toward the front door, he'll rush in with the expectations of a sick man at a holy revival. And with no longer an ounce of doubt itching in her skull, she heaves the sack of sugar up onto her shoulder and tilts the opening toward the pot. She watches a thick stream of white crystals spill into the menudo and dissolve into a red molasses. She sticks the ladle in and gives it a good stir so that the layer of syrup is unnoticeable. She knows Beto's attention to detail is uncanny, a trait he picked up in the army. After returning the sack to its shelf, she unties her apron, pours herself a glass of water, and sits at the table and begins to eat.

Right around the time the last golden knot of hominy makes its way down her throat, she hears Beto's rickety truck approaching. She peeks through the curtains and spots him slumped with his forehead against the steering wheel. She knows he's okay when his head rolls side to side rhythmically, a song still lingering in his mind. A minute later he stumbles to the front door. His keys jingle, and when he enters and sees Bea standing there, over the kitchen stove, ladling menudo into a bowl, a boyish grin slides across his ruddy face. He kisses her on the crown of her head, squeezes her ass tenderly, and she catches the hot stink of liquor emanating from his pores. He tosses his keys onto the table and pulls a chair out and flops his body onto it.

"This is why I love you," he says, "porque me echas a perder." He draws in a deep breath. When Bea sets his bowl down in front of him, he hangs his moustache over the greasy redness and waves the steam into his face and whiffs deeply, and then lets out a moan that rises up from the sour pit of his stomach.

She sits down at the table across from him and is quiet, almost too quiet, and he glances up at her from beneath the veil of his eyebrows. "You wanna know where I been?" he says, spooning condiments into his bowl. He looks at her, his lids half shut over his red eyes. He grabs a tortilla and rolls it in the palm of his hand and takes a bite. "Or you just gonna sit there all night, así, muda?"

"It's morning, Beto," she reminds him.

He bobs his head drearily and lifts a spoonful of stew to his lips and blows off the steam. A part of her feels like she might burst into laughter, and she has to look away from him, down at the floor, anywhere but across the table. He eyes her curiously.

"Is Patsy asleep?" he asks, trilling his spoon and blowing into the stew. Bea nods. "And little Albert?"

"Sleeping."

He drags his gaze across the kitchen, and the look on his face is pure exhaustion. A part of her almost feels sorry for him right then. "You gonna eat?"

"I already had mine."

He lifts the spoon to his lips and moves to take a bite, but then puts it down and takes a fistful of oregano and grinds it in his hands. She watches the small gray flakes go sailing into the bowl. "Know who I saw tonight?" he says, blending the oregano into the stew and blowing again.

She shakes her head, wonders how long he'll go on blowing. "Who?"

"Panzón."

She fidgets nervously with a lock of hair behind her ear.

"He was with some vieja from the hoover, una gabacha."

"Good for him," she replies, taking a sip of her water.

"Says he's working on a deal selling fertilizer to this rico from Madera. S'posed to be good money. The guy's a real pendejo I guess." He looks down into his bowl and brings a spoonful of hominy to his lips. His eyes narrow and he squints and investigates the spoon.

"What the hell's this?"

Her palms grow clammy and she braces herself.

"Shit, Beatrice," he says, twirling the utensil in his fingertips. "How am I supposed to eat with this?"

She leaps up from her chair and fetches him a bigger spoon. Beto continues with his story. "He asked me if I wanted in on it. Just gotta pitch in thirty bucks is all."

"He's stupid."

"Said he was gonna ask your brothers if they want in too."

"Gilbert and Epi don't have money, and Alex knows better."

She watches closely as he drowns his wide spoon into the bowl and fishes out a steaming chunk of pig's foot with a heap of hominy. He looks down at it affectionately, takes a bite of his tortilla, and shovels the food into his mouth. His eyes shut and he moans with delight, and after a couple of chews the enormous spoon goes up and down twice more. He chews and smacks his jaws, and then licks his teeth clean, and then, again, as if uncertain about the curious tang that makes his cavity ache, he drowns his spoon once more. A wedge of tripe and tendons jiggle toward his moustache and he shovels it in and gnaws away. After a few chews he becomes aware that the savory pork gut sliding down the back of his tongue is laced with a mysterious tinge, a foul sweetness. The shape of his face changes. Bea puts her hand over her mouth to stifle a laugh. He stops chewing. An orange syrup dribbles from the corner of his mouth, onto his chin.

Little Albert had woken up to that sound before. The distant yet familiar pummeling sound that haunted his sleep. It was a soft and rhythmic thudding of flesh on flesh, punctuated with grunts and moans. He knew this disturbing reveille well, and most nights prayed he would not have to wake up to it. The wooden floors of the small house quaked with the shifting of weight and the bass boom of a body falling, followed thereafter with a crash of pots or utensils, or his mother's high muffled screech, or Beto's bear-like growls and heaving of curse words in two languages.

That morning little Albert buried his head beneath the pillow, two pillows stacked atop each other, made himself a cave of blankets and pasted both hands to his ears, but still the sound prevailed, as it always did, finding the tiny cracks and easing its way through. Patsy remained asleep. When Albert could no longer contain himself he threw the sheets off and ran to the door for a peek. There, in the middle of the kitchen, stood his father with one hand propped against the wall, catching his breath, while his mother was somewhere on the other side of the table, beyond his range of vision. He could hear her whimpering, soft puppy-like wails coming from deep inside her throat. He pulled his head back and stood petrified, waiting for what would certainly come next. But when he heard the front door open and his father's truck peel away, the sensation of fire ants that had gathered on his neck and face dissolved, and after a minute he ran to find her.

She was standing with her head over the sink, pulling bits of hominy and tripe out of her hair when she heard his small footsteps approaching.

"Go to your room, mijo," she said, without looking in his direction.

"Mama."

"Do what I tell you, please, Albert."

Albert scurried to the bedroom, while Bea draped an apron over her head and hurried off to the restroom. He heard the bathtub filling with water and went to the door and timidly knocked. When he didn't get a response he stuck his ear against it and listened, but couldn't hear anything through the sound of running water. He knocked harder.

"I'll be out in a minute, Albert. Just wait."

He went into the kitchen and found pieces of tripe lodged in the cracks. He picked up the larger chunks of meat with his small hands, as well as clusters of hominy and set them in the sink. With a dishrag he sopped up the black flecks of oregano that dotted the walls, and cleaned up as best he could before sitting down at the table and waiting for his mom to come out, as she always did, hair wet, freshly bathed, grinning as though everything were right again with the world.

3

Somewhere, five or six miles east of Selma, there was a tickle in a rooster's gullet. The bird clicked its tongue to scratch it, but it didn't let up. There was only one thing to do. The rooster released a pre-dawn yawp, loud and ragged, and then again. It leapt onto the hood of an old truck carcass and flapped its wings and elongated its neck and wailed. Its sharp caw rose up and smashed against the foothills of the Sierra Nevadas and bounced back over Selma, in a fading rope of vibration that, by the time it reached Bea's ears, was hardly a thread, but she heard it. She opened her eyes just then and realized she had been dreaming. It was a haunting memory, one she was forced to relive time and again, but only in her sleep. So real was this particular dream that she would often wake up with her skin sheathed in sweat.

She let her eyes adjust to the dark before peeling her blanket off and sitting at the edge of the bed, quietly. For the hundredth time she thought about her decision. Little Al would have to stay behind. It was just how it had to be. If Patsy, who had been staying at her sister Angie's now for two weeks, was alright, then little Al would do just fine. She reached down and felt around for her slacks. When she located them she inched them over her narrow legs, and then reached for her shoes. She slipped them on, laced them tightly. She checked the clock and saw that it read four-fifty. Moving quickly but quietly, she pulled her coat over her shoulders and hurried toward the back door, a purse in one hand and a bag of clothes slung over the other. Slipping through the living room she found little Albert asleep, with his head folded into the abyss of Beto's hairy armpit. She peered down affectionately at her son's face and took notice of how his blunt chin and wide nose resembled his father's. Especially the way his tiny nostrils flared open like cornucopias. Their features were identical, but she prayed that the similarities ended there.

Even though it had been ten years since the first raids began, for the campos that peppered the land between Sacramento and Bakersfield, they were still as seasonal as everything else in these parts. If there was one thing Beto had picked up in the army, it was preparedness. So, it was a matter of efficiency that a loaded rifle was kept tucked behind the sofa for when the inevitable came pounding down the doors. Bea recalled him saying one night, "Them maricónes touch that doorknob they're gonna think twice." And had he said this a few years ago, maybe even one year ago, she might've thought it a joke. But lately she wasn't so sure. And as if that wasn't enough to keep her stomach in knots, now she had to worry about the way he placed the gun carelessly within little Albert's reach.

She thought of all this while standing at the back porch and glaring down at the old wooden boards. She knew that if she took one wrong step they'd let out a screech that was bound to wake him up. She looked around, flung her bags onto a patch of grass, and leapt down onto the soft dirt. She sprang to her feet and hurried out into the frigid morning.

The heady aroma of fresh bread hovered, and when she approached the alleyway behind La Estrella Bakery, she saw a pair of headlights cut across the street and knew it was her brother. Alex pulled the truck to the curb and flung the door open, and she tossed her bags into the back.

"Everything okay?"

She nodded, blowing warm air into her hands while Alex got busy grinding gears. He noticed the serious look on her face and thought he'd try erasing it with small talk, but it was obvious she wasn't interested. Her mind was rolling over the last conversation she'd had with Angie, how she was opposed to the whole idea. Not the part about leaving Beto, of course, but the matter of the kids.

"They're too young, Beatrice, you'll ruin them."

She couldn't believe that her sister refused to see her side of the matter. As the truck maneuvered passed the low buildings toward the tired vacant lots of downtown Selma, Alex kept looking at her from the corner of his eye. He racked his brain thinking of something good to say before they reached the bus station, some seed of brotherly advice for the road. After a few minutes he cocked his head. "Wanna know what I think?" And even though she really didn't, she knew her brother wasn't capable of tossing daggers and so she nodded. "Well, I think you should get out of here, I mean permanently. Move to a city like Philly or Chicago." He slapped the steering wheel, "Man! Chicago, now there's a city. For the two seconds I was in the army we stopped in Chicago, did I ever tell you that?" Bea sat motionless. "Well, let me tell you, if that was the only thing I took from the whole experience, it was worth it. There's a heap of money waiting to be made in a city like that." He looked at her. "Start fresh, you know?" She rolled her eyes at him. "The kids would do good in a place like that." He paused. "Plus, they'd get a white Christmas. Imagine! What kid don't want a white Christmas, huh? Man, I always thought the sight of snow falling would be something else." His eyes beamed straight ahead.

She noticed the sun was quickly illuminating the Sierra Nevadas. "Could you speed it up, Alex?"

He was happy to hear her say something finally. He put more weight on the gas pedal and the old truck rattled and nudged along faster. She began gnawing at the web of skin between her thumb and index finger; it was a habit she'd had since childhood. He remembered the time back in Irapuato when their father tried ridding her of it by rubbing raw habañero peppers on the flesh. Of course, that only worked for a few days, until, at the ripe age of ten, Bea had acquired a taste for chile.

Alex swung the truck left on the corner of H and Tulare Avenue and curbed it across the street from the station.

"Have you talked to Dad?" Bea asked.

He pulled his cap off and scratched his head.

"And?"

"He don't know nothing."

She turned her gaze out the window. "He'll find out soon enough, I guess."

"So what? He ain't gotta live your life."

She didn't have a reply. She got out of the truck and grabbed her bags, then looked across the street at the row of buses. She walked over to her brother's window and stood there, aware that she hadn't said much to him, not in the drive and not in the last few days. She rested her hand on his door.

"Look, Alex, I don't know how this'll work out." She glanced back at the station again. "All I know is . . . well, that I'm sick of Beto. I can't do it anymore. And I'm scared of being around him. Scared and pissed off."

"Ain't nothing to be scared over."

"You don't know him, Alex, not like I know him." She averted her eyes. "But hell if I'm gonna be his esclava anymore." He wrung the steering wheel in both fists. "I'll call you from Angie's," she said, backing away. "Watch over little Al for me, would you?"

He angled his head at her and replied the only thing he could.

"You know I will."

She stared into her brother's face and knew he meant it. Alex waved and then threw the truck into drive. As he pulled away he adjusted the rearview mirror and watched his sister fling her bags over her shoulder and dart across the street before disappearing into a small crowd of bodies.

4

The bus was an aged Greyhound Silverside, made from the last scraps of metal off the assembly line in the years before the war. She scrambled up onto it and looked for an empty window seat, but quickly realized she'd have to settle for an aisle. She began setting her bags down, but a haggardly woman seated by the window shooed her away.

"Is this taken?"

The old woman nodded. "I need room to stretch, mija, my legs are bad," she said, gripping her knees apologetically.

Bea glanced up the aisle and then back at her. She leaned over the woman and whispered. "Please don't make me sit in the back, next to all them solteros." The woman looked over the seat, and turned back to Bea and made a sour face before breaking out in a gentle smile.

"A dónde vas?" the woman asked, unwrapping a piece of hard candy.

"To Los Angeles, señora. You?"

The woman lifted her trembling hand and plopped the candy into her mouth. "Bakersfield," she said, stuffing the wrapper back into her purse. She rubbed her gnarled fingers together and bound her coat tightly over her chest, while Bea looked past her and out the window.

"You cold, señora?"

"Un poquito."

Bea leaned over and pressed her hand flat against the window. "The glass is practically frozen, no wonder you're cold."

The woman sucked on her candy and watched Bea from the corner of her cloudy eyes. For a moment, it was as if she caught a glimpse of herself fifty years prior. She rubbed her fingers together once more, and after a few long seconds she gripped her purse and motioned for Bea to trade seats.

Cars began to creep along the streets as the sky grew more luminous by the minute. After what felt like an eternity to Bea, the bus finally pulled out of the lot and lugged itself between the short buildings and iron street lamps that lined downtown Selma. It continued on past the cramped houses of Gaynor Street, out past the packing shed and train tracks, blowing dust at the long line of palm trees that ran along Hadinger's property and slouched toward Fresno. When the great silver vessel passed Nebraska Avenue and then reached the outskirts of Selma, she could see the silhouettes of the campo tents jutting among the grape fields, and she followed them with her eyes until they disappeared on the rose-colored dawn. She propped her head against the window and tried hard not to think about anything.

In the few minutes it took for her to doze off, her memory leapt to the tangled streets of Boyle Heights—that mean concrete bluff of dilapidated fences and corrugated tin where houses were stacked atop one another like the folds of an accordion. She could hear the dinkey clanking up First Street, hauling workers across the sad strip of river that divided the brown patch of Los Angeles from the rest of the city. And then there were the children, neighborhood kids, gathering at Antonio's Market for floats and frozen Milky Way bars, while on the front porch, her mother and their neighbor Rosalyn sat peeling potatoes for dinner and discussing family business.

"I was born here, I told Jesus," Bea could overhear her mother saying to Rosalyn. "And he looked at me like he wanted to kill me for saying it, but it's true. He wanted to go to Irapuato and I told him, what for? Everything we need is here."

"Mija, what's in Irapuato?" replied Rosalyn.

"Nothing but pigs and grapes. Same as in Selma," Jessie said with a chuckle. Her face turned serious. "His mother's there, too, I guess." A short silence fell between them. "He's just scared of everything that's been going on. Thinks they're gonna kill him."

"Who?"

"Everyone. The cops, his boss, some crazy gringo with a chip on his shoulder; I tell him he's paranoid. He hates when I say this. Says I can talk like that porque soy pocha. But it don't matter, Mexican or pocha or not, estamos igual de jodidos."

Rosalyn nodded. "You're right about that," she said, tossing a freshly peeled potato into a bucket and grabbing another, "We're all screwed." She hesitated. "Unless you look like Beatrice," she said, winking from beneath her sweaty brow. "With those green eyes y tan blanquita, parece hija de la Joan Crawford." They looked at one another and broke out in laughter, and Bea could see clearly the silver-lined crowns that beamed from Rosalyn's wide mouth like a comet.

While the kids on her block saw summer as that coveted golden carrot dangling at the end of each school year, for Bea it was the other way around. School was an escape from the torturous work of la pisca. Every May, Jesus and Jessie crammed the kids into the DeSoto and aimed it at the center of California, and in a matter of hours, two-word tags like City Terrace and Boyle Heights were replaced with hiccups like Selma and Fresno. As a result, Bea's formative years were divided into two halves—the valley and the city.

While the city was familiar terra, the valley was nothing but a cruel tierra of initiation.

Returning to the great San Joaquin meant a backache that would last as long as people still found an excuse for cotton. It wasn't all bad, though. Being at the campo was a lot like camping in the wilderness, Bea often thought when she was younger. Cooking on an outdoor stove, the smell of chorizo mixing with the aroma from the eucalyptus thicket that crowded the edge of the Kings River, where each summer they stayed at the squatter's camp, Reedley Beach. Of course the beach itself was a modest sandbank flanked with cardboard hovels and driftwood and whatever else found its way onto the shore. Even her parents had to admit then, that sleeping with the hush of that wide and thrashing river flowing past was a nice change from the incessant bickering of pachucos that cluttered Whittier Boulevard. Besides the occasional bobcat, the only thing a campesino had to worry about out there was whether or not he'd still be around when those first headlights came bouncing up the dirt road in the middle of the night, la Migra charging in like Custer's Seventh Calvary, looking to put an exclamation point on the last harvest.

Every half hour the bus would pull into a small depot and Bea would open her eyes and watch as more sagged faces would climb on with their luggage, squeeze into a seat, and say nothing the rest of the way. When the bus slipped past Delano and chugged down the wide bluff that settles into Bakersfield, she sat up from her comfortable slouch and looked out the window and saw the sun burning through a thin layer of fog. When they reached the station, the driver announced that the bus would continue on to Los Angeles in an hour.

She fumbled for her bags and waited for the old lady to gather her belongings from beneath the seat. The woman clutched her bags and hobbled up the aisle tortoise-like. When she stepped off, there waiting for her was a young man, a fresh grin stretched across his face. They embraced and Bea slipped past them and moved away from the station. She lifted her hand to her forehead and squinted her eyes in all directions. It was still morning, and there was a chill in the air, so she zipped her coat up and started across the street in a hurry.

Catty-corner from where she stood was Hank's Place, and she made her way to it. She took a seat by the window and cupped her fingers and blew into them. A small radio sat on the counter and belted out a country jangle—*Smoke, Smoke, Smoke That Cigarette*, the voice crooned. After a few seconds it came to an end, and then another voice flooded the tiny speakers. *Kern County—looks like we got a freeze coming on, tonight's down to twelve degrees, light up those oil heaters, boys.*

A few patrons erupted into a soft chatter.

"What'll it be?" a voice blurted from behind her.

Bea looked up and saw an older woman with tired eyes staring down at her. The name tag pinned to her chest said Gloria. A pungent combination of burnt grease and plastic gardenias emanated from her soiled apron. Gloria tapped her pencil against her notepad.

"Coffee, please."

A bell clanged in the kitchen and Gloria looked over her shoulder. A short, surly looking man poked his head out from behind the stove and angled his dark eyes down at a plate of steaming biscuits.

"Will that be all?"

Bea nodded, and before she could utter another word, Gloria jammed the pencil behind her ear and was gone.

She looked at the faces of the few people who occupied the seats and saw that they all held the same weariness. It was a mask she'd come to know well over the last year. Concern over anything had a way of shaping a person's face into something that resembled a raisin. The eyes bunched up in the middle and the mouth puckered and their heads arched forward like a damp bulb of unpicked cotton. Outside, along the sidewalks and atop the telephone wires, pigeons communed with crows as they looked down at the moist patches of grass and along the gutters for something wriggling up that would make for a good breakfast. Gloria came with the coffee and set it down at the edge of the table and was off again. While taking a sip of that tepid bitterness, Bea looked past the rim of the mug and watched her make her rounds. She glanced down at Gloria's exposed calves and saw a web of blue veins sprawled beneath her speckled skin like a map, and couldn't help but wonder just how many years it took for poor ol' Gloria to grow such vines. And then, as if her sympathy for Gloria cracked open another door altogether, she found herself worrying about little Al. She wondered if leaving him with Beto was really the only option.

"He'd be better off with us in L.A. too, Beatrice, at least for now," Angie had said.

"It's bad enough I'm letting you take Patsy. No way. I can't be without the kids too long Angie, I just can't."

Angie's face turned bitter.

"You can't brush off little Al's questions forever, you know," her sister pressed. "He's growing up, and pretty soon, he's gonna start seeing everything for what it really is."

She remembered clearly the scowl on Angie's face, each word punctuated with frustration.

Beto was now awake. She was sure of it. Probably hadn't realized yet that she was gone. She pictured him fumbling about the kitchen, scratching his crotch, hovering over the sink, splashing water on his face. Unalarmed that she wasn't in bed this morning. Must be at her parents' house, or the bakery. But no way in hell she's in Bakersfield—if he even gave it that much thought. That was the thing. As long as she was within eye-reach, he didn't pay her much attention. But give her two seconds out of his range and he'd lose his mind. She wondered how long before he'd realize she wasn't coming back. She took a sip of coffee and just then caught a faint whiff of cigarette in the air. She turned her head around to see where it was coming from. A young white man sat at the counter puffing away. He was scribbling something on a sheet of paper. He pulled the cigarette from his mouth and tapped the ash onto his plate and stuck it between his teeth again without ever looking up. She contemplated going over and asking for a smoke, but judging by the way both eyes aimed downward and nowhere else, she figured he was best left undisturbed. But then the man looked up and they made eye contact. She turned away quickly, looking out the window. At the station she saw the driver was letting people back on the bus. It had hardly been thirty minutes. Slowly each passenger stepped up onto the platform, one by one, grimacing in the cold open air. Behind her, she heard the man's voice.

"Miss," he was saying in a hurried tone, "I have to get on my way." He dug around in his pocket. "I'll go ahead and pay for this now." He set a nickel on the counter and lifted his duffel bag and started out.

Bea could see that the driver was sitting behind the wheel now. She reached into her purse for some change, and when she found it, she dropped a coin down onto the table too, then gathered her things and hurried out, across the street, making it onto the platform seconds before the door swung shut.

5

The bus bounded south along the highway, and through the fog she could faintly see the colossal heads of oilrigs bowing. They were spread out across the flat land every hundred yards, and they quietly went about their business. Their ceaseless bending motion reminded her of that one summer a few years back, when her father landed them a job pulling onions in nearby Lamont. A time when the sun peeked over the Tehachapi Mountains and came down like a devil's saber, and no handkerchief or hat or piece of garment could fend off the spikes that stabbed the flesh. She recalled how, for the better part of that harvest, her father had stood beneath the blue shade of a fig tree, sipping water from the canal, busying himself with small matters, refusing to hear the gripes of his children, or any other worker for that matter. Like the first time Beto had left her, and all the ol' man could say was, "The only sure thing is work and death, Beatrice." She could hear his callous voice, and it put a fire in her chest that took an hour to settle.

She placed her purse against the window and put her head on it, then slumped down into her seat and shut her eyes. The drone of the engine lulled her to a near sleep, and a numbing tiredness gripped her. Her eyes felt as if they had swelled in their sockets, and the back of her tongue began dragging with each breath. She felt as if her entire body was shutting down. As if every last organ, nerve ending, and fold of brain had agreed finally to close up shop. She collapsed to her side and tucked her legs beneath her thighs and decided she would be happy if she never woke up again. Or if she did that it would be in the next life. But soon even these thoughts had faded. Her mind was slipping now into that black and utter silence of deep sleep.

"Excuse me," a voice prodded from behind. The words sounded fuzzy, distant. "Miss?" It came again. A man's voice. She refused to open her eyes. But there it was once more. "Miss, you can use my sweater . . . for a pillow, if you'd like?" Reluctantly she turned her face in the direction of the voice, and opening only one eye, she rolled her head slightly side to side before turning away and trying hard to get back to that place.

The bus rattled over the train tracks and she had to readjust her body a dozen times to get comfortable. But then, when she did, something else came over her. She could sense the man's restlessness in the seat behind. The air around her was uneasy. She could hear him shifting his belongings, whispering to himself. She grew worried and knew that as long as he was back there she'd never be able to rest. And then she wondered if he might be staring at the back of her head. She sat up in her seat and glanced over her shoulder. He was in fact staring at her. It was the man from the diner. He leaned forward again.

"Miss?" he whispered. "If you're cold, you can borrow my sweater."

"Listen," she began to say, attempting to give him a proper rejection. The man tilted his head to the side and gazed up at her from two great blue orbs. A young white girl sitting across the aisle looked over at Bea and then diverted her eyes to the man. He held the sweater up once more, and this time lifted one corner of his mouth into a half smile.

"I know how these buses can be," he interrupted, "like sleeping on rocks. Hell, even a rock might be more comfortable than this." He lifted the wadded sweater over the seat for her to take. She hesitated. "Go on." He gently nudged her shoulder with it. She leveled her thin eyebrows at him and then slowly took it from his grip.

"That's awful nice of you," she uttered, wedging it between her head and the window. It reeked of cigarette smoke, just as Beto's clothes did, but she didn't mind. She rested her ear against it and watched the man from the corner of her eye.

She saw him lean back in his seat and could hear him mumbling to himself again. She wasn't sure whether to think it strange or funny. A minute later he hung his head over the back of her seat again.

"Is it always this cold around here?"

Bea turned toward him. "It's the fog," she mumbled.

"I just came in from Frisco myself, now there's a cold city. Not like here, I mean, just a whole other kind of cold altogether. A wet cold. I mean it gets into any bit of dry spot you have." The man hesitated. "Of course, if you've been traveling all night like I have, well, it's a tough way to go about things." He paused. "Can I tell you something?"

Bea hardly nodded.

"This is a little embarrassing now, but it's true. When I saw you back at that diner I thought to myself, she looks like a decent woman, and man, what I'd give to have a pleasant conversation with someone like her." He rubbed his eyes. "And then I step onto this bus and here you are, one seat in front of me."

The corners of her mouth lifted subtly.

"Would you mind if I sat with you? I'm harmless, really." The plump of his bottom lip protruded slightly and it reminded her of a little boy.

She took quick inventory of him before lifting her bags up from the seat and placing them on the floor. The man got up and maneuvered next to her.

"My name's Jack." He stuck his hand out and she took hold of his warm fingers.

"Bea."

"It's a pleasure, Bea."

She sat up and handed the man named Jack back his sweater.

"Where you headed?" he asked.

"L.A."

"I'm going there myself." He hung his right leg on his left kneecap, sitting like a man of dignity, and Bea took notice, for no macho she knew would be caught dead sitting in such a way.

"And where from, Bea?"

She looked out the window and hesitated to answer. She recalled the way her father used to claim that because he was from Mexico, "Mis hijos tambien son de Mexico!" But in his absence, their mother Jessie would shrug and assure them they were no less American than President Hoover himself. Of course there were only two real answers she could give, Selma or Los Angeles.

"It's a small town," she mumbled, "you probably never heard of it."

"I know just about every small town there ever was. Try me."

"How about Selma?"

"Of course! Passed through it just last night, around Fresno, isn't it?"

She raised her eyebrows. "What about you?"

He bent over and pulled a small notebook from his back pocket and leaned close to her. She could smell the rain and wind of highways in his clothes. He opened the tablet. "See there?" He pointed to a speck on a hand-drawn map. She leaned in for a look.

"Never heard of it."

"Well, that's me," he said, lingering on the picture a moment before cramming it back into his pocket. "It's a small place in Massachusetts. Sweet little town," he said, his gaze retreating to some long-forgotten memory. "Haven't been back there in years, though."

"Why not?"

He glanced in her direction. "Been traveling mostly, seeing friends, getting to know the land . . ."

"By yourself?"

"Yep."

"Must get awful lonely, don't it?"

"Naw. Solitary, but not lonely."

"Well, I don't see much difference between them. I mean, either way you're alone."

"Big difference. Loneliness is what a person runs from. Solitude, well, everyone can appreciate a little solitude. You ever done much traveling?"

"Naw, not me." She tugged on a strand of hair behind her ear. "When you're done traveling, where do you stay?"

"I got a bed in New York."

She waited, expecting him to continue, but he stopped there. A silence settled between them. The white girl across the aisle glanced over again and Bea couldn't help but grow self-conscious. She leaned subtly away from Jack and pressed her body closer to the window. From the corner of her eye she watched as the girl stole glances. Jack was aware of her too, but the look on his face was unassuming, almost naïve, light.

"Why'd you leave home?" she whispered to him.

He lifted a single brow. "College," he replied, turning his body in her direction. "At least in the beginning." His eyelashes stuttered. "I loved that little town, once upon a time." He scratched the shallow stubble on his neck. "But I landed a spot at Columbia. Ever hear of it?"

She thought about it a second.

"Well, it's a college, right in the gut of New York. Went there for a spell, took up writing, and after a year I decided I'd learned everything I was going to, so I hit out traveling. At first just to get away from all that," he paused. "But then once you get out and start to see your situation, I mean, from Godview, you know, when you can see the big picture, it kinda makes you wanna change things about yourself. Get intentional about life. Thought I'd be kidding myself forever if I didn't just get on with it. That's what I'm doing now, getting on with it."

There was something about the way he spoke that she couldn't put her finger on. Whether it was the certainty with which words spilled from his mouth, or the longing of elsewheres that took hold in his eyes whenever he spoke. Whatever it was, she found herself lured in by the undeniable tenderness in his voice. Also, it was the kind of talk she'd only heard in movies or on the radio, never at the campo. People at the campo only concerned themselves with words like *trabajo* or *raids*, and the ubiquitous *Dios*. *Dios aprieta pero no ahorca*—God tightens the noose but doesn't choke you. It might as well have been the official slogan of all campesinos.

"I don't know about you," Jack continued. "But I outgrew that small town pretty quick. One day I just woke up and it seemed my clothes didn't fit me right anymore. Hell, the whole damn wardrobe was wrong, and smelled like someone else entirely. Someone I was sick of. Thought I'd rather run around the world naked than wear those old drapes." He chuckled and patted his coat pocket for a cigarette.

In that moment, seated there beside this man, Bea felt as if she were looking into a mirror, and for the first time making sense of what it was she herself had been feeling for so long. "I've never met a writer before," she said, arching her back to stretch.

Jack grew modest, his face pinkened. "Yeah, well, I'm supposed to be anyway, nothing's worked out yet." He fidgeted with his shirt cuffs. "I send my work out and all I get back is letter after letter, the same noise. 'You've got talent.' 'Good writing, but what about plot?' Everything's about plot nowadays. Of course none of it really amounts to much." He looked at Bea. "You want to know what I do with those letters?"

She lifted her chin.

"I stick 'em up on the wall above my desk so I can look at them. Prove 'em wrong, that's what I'll do." A determination gathered on his face. He paused. "Of course, right now I've got more paper on my walls than in my wallet."

She turned toward the window and spotted the Kern River snaking in the distance. The sun had burned off the rest of the fog and was now illuminating the yellow tufts of grass along the side of the road. What should have been an awkward silence was not awkward at all. She was comfortable beside him now. From across the aisle the white girl continued to gawk at them. This time her eyes were unapologetically fixed on Jack's face, and she took in his handsome looks and square chest, hoping he'd offer a glance her way. When it didn't happen the girl peered over at the small strange bird at his side, the dark-haired one with pale skin and green eyes, and the girl's face turned sour. The look itself was familiar to Bea; she'd seen it on the faces of many a white girl, in Los Angeles and the valley, but as her mother had taught her early on, it's when you stop getting dirty looks that you have reason to worry.

Over the next few minutes Bea continued to steal glances at him from the corner of her eye. She couldn't help but think of how wrong her first impression of him had been. At the diner, slumped over the counter scratching into his paper, he came across awkward, troubled almost. But now, sitting here beside him she could see that he was nothing of the sort. There was a sensitivity about him, a timidity disguised beneath a layer of denim and tobacco smoke. Nothing like the men at the campo or in the fields, who, upon hearing of Bea's troubled marriage, often tried luring her with sweet talk of money and sexual escapades. Perros. The kind of men who bunked a dozen to a tent and stayed up late talking about the women they'd balled in their short and lonely lives.

The Silverside popped and leaned back on its haunches, now chugging up the steep incline, scaling out of the valley, entering the panoramic stone gates of the San Emigdio Mountains. Jack looked out the window and was taken by the sight of Grapevine Pass scrolling across the window, reaching back down to the valley floor and then curling into the pine woods of Tejon and Gorman.

From here on out it seemed that the two were inexhaustible. Their conversation unraveled in an uninterrupted stream that ran as rich and infinite as the Golden State Highway itself. The whole way, Jack's mood was of pure sincerity. It was a particular way of being that later, years later, Bea would recall experiencing only once before. It was reminiscent of the way that the Purépecha women in Irapuato carried themselves. Whenever she crossed their paths, she noticed that the women, on their way to or from the zócalo, averted their eyes in humble gesture, toward the earth. Por respeto, her father once explained. And this felt good to Bea back then, even as an aloof and free-spirited ten-year-old. When she told Jack about this story, about the Purépecha women she'd once lived among, deep in the lush lands of a Mexico she'd just as soon forget, he couldn't have been more eager to hear about it.

Plowing toward Mt. Pinos, skimming across the Tejon Pass floor, they sat up talking, waving their hands about, voices rising and hushing with the rolling hills.

Approaching Gorman, Bea pointed out to him the wooden relics, saloons wilted by time, where once her family stopped and caught a western shootout reenactment and sipped warm pop beneath the shade of an oak tree while the car's radiator cooled. And when the bus floated past the shanty abodes huddled in the crevice of Fort Tejon, Bea repeated to Jack something she'd once overheard a tourist say while at a rest stop, that the real-life Zorro, Joaquin Murrieta, had stashed his treasures there, never to be found again. Jack's eyes widened just like a child's, and she could see the excitement on his face as he relished each detail. He looked at the other passengers and saw nothing but drab faces staring back, and he ran his fingers through his hair and prodded Bea on until everything she knew, and even some things she didn't, had been spilt.

"I've crossed these mountains so many times, I swear, I must've heard every story by now," she said.

"I bet you have," Jack replied.

And then she noticed something else about him, something she hadn't seen until now. It was endearing and at the same time jarring. There was a heavy earnestness with which he stared at her, into her, as if he was witnessing something wonderful unfold before him. This scared her and she recoiled, and had to remind herself why she was on the bus in the first place.

A few minutes passed before Jack spoke again. "You married?"

She nodded, slightly.

"I was married once too." He scratched his head. "Not an easy gig is it?"

"Not at all."

"Kids?"

Her face shone. "A boy and girl. Little Al and Patsy." She folded her arms. "Al's six, but Patsy's just a baby."

He hesitated. "Where they at?"

"Patsy's with my sister, Angie. That's partly why I'm heading to L.A. I'll be staying with her for a little while. Al's with his father, back in Selma."

He pursed his lips and then pointed his eyes straight ahead. Bea could sense he wanted to ask her something, and she could almost see the question forming in his mind. She held her breath.

"I left my husband," she said.

Jack squinted. "It's none of my business."

The bus jerked and their bodies rocked forward. Without really knowing why, she needed him to know the reason for it.

"I got sick of his meanness, I guess." She fidgeted with her purse strap. "Just the kind of man hard to live with." She waited for a reply, but Jack remained quiet. She felt foolish almost, for bringing it up. "You probably don't care about any of this do you?"

"If you wanna tell it I'm listening."

She sat quiet for a moment. He could tell she was thinking.

"If he didn't drink so much he'd probably be a half decent guy," she said. "He wasn't always like that. Just started right up after the army. Guess you don't really see these kinds of things coming." She hesitated. He could see clearly that the scar was fresh. "I just hope little Al don't turn out like him."

She folded her hands over her lap and decided to stop there, figuring she'd said too much. She glanced at him, into the blue lakes of his eyes, and could see he was not the type to bring it up again. She wanted to trust him. In that moment, with the bus hurling along the open road, and her, basking in the light of a new friend, she suddenly felt liberated from Beto's clutches. Even if it was only temporary. But just as quickly, there was a slight needle-prick in her heart. She wondered what it meant.

"My old man died of drink," Jack uttered, leaning back in his seat. "What always got me was that he wasn't much of a drinker. I know what drinking men look like, I mean some of these places they have in the city, all hours of day and night you can walk right up a street, toss a pebble into the air and chances are the head it hits will be some poor ol' soul down on his luck sucking fumes from an invisible bottle he hasn't held in too long."

She let out a giggle. Jack looked at her curiously. She was well aware that every town, even Irapuato, Selma too, had its own kind of speak. But the way he rambled, and the words he chose, she suspected it was something a person could only get from college. When she asked him about it he slapped his knee and felt compelled to sum it up.

"Wouldn't that be the day! All college teaches a person is how to properly limber up for the big moment." He paused and thought about how to explain it.

"You ever see that rubber man in the circus? That poor half-gone soul whose rib bones are practically jutting through his flesh so that he don't have the meat or muscle to get in the way of folding himself in half?"

She flexed her eyes and followed along.

"Of course the big moment comes when he squeezes himself into that cigar box, and the customers hoot and clap, feeling like they got their dollar's worth. Well, see, that show might as well be called College."

She folded her legs and let herself be amused by his explanation. "What are you talking about?"

"I'll tell you." He sat up. "See, once the show is over the clowns get together with the trapeze artists, and they invite the muscle-man over. He brings the bearded lady and her friend Dog-boy," he said, his eyes wildly searching for words. "And they get to talking, and soon enough come to the decision that they no longer agree with the ringmaster. 'How come I gotta hang upside down for two hours justa collect a few measly bucks,' says the trapeze guy." Jack shifted his voice to a high squeak, "'And I'm just a sensitive soul,' the muscle-man confesses." Bea lit up at the sound of it. "'Why is it that if a man's got whiskers it's no big deal, but I got a few and suddenly things ain't right,' the bearded lady rationalizes." He couldn't contain himself and he laughed and went with it, "'It ain't my fault I'm half Persian.' She's got a point, they all agree."

Bea was invested now. "And what about Dog-boy?" she prodded.

Jack's voice turned serious. "Well, Dog-boy, see, he's outta luck, 'cause after all, he hasn't been house trained and the only reason the bearded lady puts up with him is 'cause he kindly licks her bunions at the end of each night."

Bea winced and slapped his arm playfully.

"Anyway, the whole gang of them decides that *they* aren't the freaks of the party, but the guy with the whip, the ringmaster, see, he's the real freak. And by extension, anyone who pays to see this little man's sick menagerie of good folks who've been dealt a gross hand is equally as deranged. I mean they should probably have their souls checked if they knew what was good for them." Jack cocked his head at her to see if she was getting it all. "So then and there, back stage of The Greatest Show on Earth, the gang makes a pact. Not some secret handshake or set of rules, because that would taint the whole purpose, right? But an unspoken pact. Well, they spoke it already and don't need to speak it any more. Now it's about moving on it."

A look of curiosity sprouted on Bea's face. "And how does that happen?"

Jack rubbed his chin. "Hell, who knows? The bearded lady might hafta return to Persia. The muscle-man'll probably visit his poor ma' back in Poughkeepsie. Point is they each gotta step along now that they see clearly the circus ain't for 'em!"

She rolled her eyes, and when they were done laughing about it, they spotted in the distance the sprawling skyline of Los Angeles and fell silent.

The Silverside downshifted and belched along Interstate 5, cruising down the spine of Hollywood. Jack leaned over to get a better view. In this position, their faces were now inches apart. From the corner of her eye she took in the details of his earlobe and neck. The steady breathing that seeped from his nose. All the tiny sounds of the human body, magnified. She could feel her heart palpitating in her throat.

Something about the arrival of the end took them both by surprise. They sat petrified for a moment, their eyes fixed on everything except each other. It was easier this way. And right then something occurred between them. Something that later on, years later, Bea would recall, only slightly. When Jack leaned back in his seat again, his bulky fingers slipped over hers, and in the time it took before the touch dissipated, he grasped her hand tenderly. The sudden gesture paralyzed her. It took all but two seconds for her to decide whether she wanted to leave it there or not. Bea Franco, wife of Alberto Franco and daughter of Jesus Renteria, would retract it out of fear alone. Bea Franco, a woman who just this morning made a final stand to flee Selma once and for all, would leave it.

They sat motionless, brimming with electricity. Her hand still, trembling almost, remained right where it was. And then, in a move that caught even an unbridled spirit like him off guard, she went one step further, rolled his hand over and pressed her palm flush against his, until the precise combination of all ten fingers locked into place.

6

When they got off at the bus station on Seventh Street, they cut across Alameda and found themselves smack dab in the gut of Lotusland. Walking up Central Avenue with Jack at her side, Bea's head was shrouded in a smog of paranoia. She remembered the last time she left Beto, and how it only took him half a day to find her. And when he did, he put such a dent in her psyche that it took almost two years for the effects of it to wear off. Even without her father pointing Beto the way, she was sure he knew just about everyone in L.A., and of course it didn't help that the streets were rampant with darting eyes.

It had been six years since the Japanese attacked Pearl Harbor, but for a city close enough to catch a tan from Hiroshima, it may as well have happened yesterday. Strains of resentment were still crusted in the cracks of the sidewalks, from Watts all the way up to Santa Monica Boulevard, and there wasn't enough rain in the entire Pacific Coast to wash it off of L.A. that easy. The blackouts too seemed like only yesterday. The whirring propellers of low-spying zeppelins, yesterday. The Zoot Suit beatings, yesterday. Every time the warm winds blew up from the Inland Empire and the palm trees whispered, all the eyes in the streets turned skyward to make sure something sinister wasn't unfolding yet again.

As they strolled along, their stomachs grumbled at the wall of aroma that sprung back from Little Tokyo and wound its ribbon down toward Jefferson High School. The entire stretch was an endless ebb and flow of flavors: grilled onion and deep-fried fish spewing from a rib shack, pollo rostizado and chop suey hung in a thick cloud just above the heads of the five- and six-story buildings that dotted the strip. The soundscape was punctuated with raw music: the scream of an engine, the sizzle of hot grease from an open window, a fed-up neighbor threatening to call cops on the hoodlums who lurked in the alleyways. Across the street, a band was loading up a car with chrome and brass musical instruments, their shirttails untucked and hats cocked, faces ragged after an all-nighter. Cars hummed past, and the noon hour buzzed with working stiffs tending to the incessant nag of life.

They entered Carmelina's Eatery, took a seat by the window, ordered two cups of coffee, and then folded their hands on the table and avoided eye contact for the first few minutes. He glanced over at a glass display shelf, where three fat whole cakes rotated slowly. At the counter, two plump men in greasy coveralls sat slumped over plates of ham and eggs and groaned about work until their faces were red.

In the next booth over, a black kid with a serious face sat bouncing the tip of his slick shoe up and down nervously. His hair was pasted to his scalp and a short metal chain dangled from his belt loops. Jack noticed him right off, and he saw that this kid with pulsing white eyes appeared to have a thing for Bea. She noticed it too. While they made small talk she glanced over periodically, hoping that the kid's interest had waned, or at least that he'd given his glare a rest from burning a hole through her blouse.

"Just ignore him," Jack said, pulling a cigarette from his coat pocket and lighting up. He passed it to Bea and she took it and stared out the window, sucking in a long drag. Through the reflection of the glass she could see that the kid had not let up.

"Something a matter?"

Bea passed Jack the cigarette. "He knows almost everyone around here."

"The kid?"

"No, my husband."

Jack nodded. He rolled his eyes toward the kid and held his gaze on him. He couldn't help but laugh.

"Well, the boy ain't nothing to worry about. Just some kid in his papa's pants. Cities like this are crazy with youth trying to prove themselves. Christ, it's L.A. after all—I bet you find one of these jokers on every corner."

Bea tried forgetting about it. She rested her chin on her hand.

"Told my sister I'd be there by tonight." She looked at the clock above the door and saw that it was half past noon. Jack looked at it too. He watched her eyes shift nervously over the small table, eyeing the patrons before turning toward the street.

He fiddled with the butt of his cigarette. He took one more drag and smashed it out in the ashtray. "I have a thought," he said.

She angled her eyes at him.

"It's crazy now, but, well . . ." He shifted in his seat, hesitantly. "Nah, forget it." He waved his hand in front of his face.

"You can't do that. You hafta tell me now," she replied, reaching across the table and touching his fingers.

"You'd think wrong of me . . ."

"Oh, just go on."

"Alright." He paused. "It's crazy. I'm warning you. So don't go running out into the streets when you hear it."

She folded her arms. "What is it?"

He sucked his gut in and a childish grin fell over his face. "What do you say about keeping me company a day or two?" he stammered. "I mean, I sure could use someone to show me around here." He lowered his eyes then raised them slightly. She sat motionless. "You see, didn't I tell you it was crazy? Forget about it."

Her expression was empty. He almost couldn't bear to look at her. He fidgeted in his seat. Bea smiled, or she wanted to. But mostly, she was angry with herself for giving a goddamn about the voices in her head. Beto's voice. Maybe this was the needle-prick she'd been feeling since this morning. Jack raised his eyebrows and exposed two of the bluest moons she'd ever seen. In that precise moment she knew making it to Angie's house that night was not going to happen. A decision, she assured herself, that any warm-blooded woman with a sincere man-soul like Jack nipping at her heels—a college boy with looks that would make Cary Grant throw his hands up—would have made ten times over.

"Sure," she replied, timidly. And even when it came from her mouth, it felt like an accident. Like she meant to say "Sorry." But she wasn't sorry.

"Really?"

"Sure," she said again, this time with all certainty. Her palms clammed up right then, and she felt something she hadn't in a long time. It was an unsettling joy in the pit of her stomach.

When their food arrived, two orders of meat and potatoes with a watered-down milk gravy, she glanced over at the black kid, and this time found him with his eyes closed and mouth agape, nodding off. She gestured at Jack and he turned to look, and they both had a good laugh over it.

"I do have to see Angie eventually," she said, taking a bite of her potatoes. "She's got Patsy, and I just gotta see my little girl."

Jack chewed his meat, and when he spoke he waved his fork in the air between them. "I don't want to be the cause of any problems," he said. "You sure about this?"

She tucked a strand of hair behind her ear and took a drink of water. "Of course, but I do gotta see her, maybe tomorrow. Yeah, tomorrow'll be good." She paused. "But Jack, you can't be with me when I go. I mean that just wouldn't look so good."

He took a drink of water and subtly investigated the lines of her face and neck, the shallow wave of her collarbone, right down to the folded knuckles of her small fingers. She noticed the way he stared at her, and the caress of his gaze alone was almost too much to bear. She found herself no longer able to eat. She pushed bits of meat around the plate with her fork. Meanwhile, Jack chewed his food and thought to himself, how much luckier can any son-of-a-bitch be. He knew right then that out here, west of the American West, the gods were smiling down upon him.

7

The Duke Hotel was a modest block of brown stone that sat on the corner of San Pedro and Fifth Street. Two palm trees stood crooked over the entranceway, and in the lobby was a pair of knockoff marble cherubs, spilling a cracked jug of water into a fountain.

They got their room key and started up the stairs. The air smelled like moldy clothes and body odor. She put her hand on the railing and felt the chipped wood grain sliding beneath her fingers. Down the hall a voice shouted out something indecipherable, and it sounded like an argument; two men were having it out in one of the rooms. Jack looked at Bea and then stuck the key into the hole and pushed the door open. It squeaked, and then rocked back on its own. The room was a modest box. Staring into it, Jack thought of that old Les Brown tune and sang a line: *My dreams are getting better all the time.* He flung the keys onto the dresser while Bea dropped her bags and collapsed onto the bed.

"Sure feels good to rest my feet."

"Ain't that the truth."

He made himself busy digging into his duffel. A short but welcomed silence gripped them. Bea checked her face in a small hand mirror and then realigned her lips. Jack pulled his notebook out and went over by the window and sat at the table.

"What do you got there?"

He bit the end of a pencil and glanced up at her.

"Just my notebook," he said, spitting out small shards of wood. He noticed a curious look on her face. "A writer's gotta have his notebook with him always. It's just how it's gotta be." She nodded. "Suppose I get an idea," he continued, "something great, original, you know, and there I am without a pencil or paper to get it down. What kind of writer would I be then?" He hesitated. "It's a habit by now. I've been at it since I was a boy. I used to draw in it mostly, back then, wrote a few things, kid stuff of course. Comics, that sort of thing." He let the pages flip in his fingers and he looked down at his words with a goofy sincerity. Bea giggled.

"You sure are a writer aren't you?" He scratched his head with his pencil. "Go ahead," she said, "I'm not stopping you."

His eyes fell to the open page and he began scribbling away. She opened the curtains and tried pulling the window up but it was jammed. She banged on it with the heel of her palm and tugged again, and this time it skidded open. A gush of cold air blew in and she inhaled deeply, the sharp perfume of L.A. She set her hands on the sill and leaned out over the edge and looked down at the street below.

"Gosh, I could stay up here forever, you know that?"

Jack mumbled something.

She went to the bed and began digging through her purse. She opened her thin red wallet and counted out what little money she had, a few bucks and some loose coins. Holding the change in her hand made her think about calling home to check on little Al. Maybe it was too soon. Besides, Alex had promised to watch after him.

After a few minutes Jack shut his notebook and went to the bathroom. She pulled a cigarette from his box and stood in front of the mirror and watched herself smoke. The bathroom door was left partly open, and from where she stood she could see through the narrow opening between the hinges. His back was turned to her but she could see him standing over the toilet with one hand propped against the wall. She looked once and then looked away. And then once more. She distracted herself by going to the radio and fiddling with the knobs. Alberta Hunter's staticky voice seeped through the small speakers. Bea relaxed and dropped her shoulders, kicked her shoes off. Jack zipped himself up, and when he came out of the bathroom the song ended and silence filled the room. They stood facing each other. There was no way around the awkwardness.

"How about I run out and get us a drink?" Jack ran his fingers through his hair.

"Good idea."

He grabbed his coat, and before she could speak another word, he was out the door, barreling down two steps at a time. She stuck her head out the window and called to him.

"I'll be right here, waiting for you," she said. He turned back and waved and she looked up the street, in both directions, to see if anyone was watching.

She went and turned the faucet on and ran a hot bath, peeled her clothes off and got in. On the radio Django tickled out a moody bolero against the fading light as she slunk her rump farther down into the tub and cupped water in her hands and spilled it over her face, careful not to wet her hair. It was a trick her oldest sister Maggie had once taught her. A body wash, she called it. When your hair is exactly how you like it, not one strand out of place, and you want to keep that look going, especially, Maggie gestured, right before a date, you keep your head above water.

She thought about Maggie, and how they'd grown apart over the years. Ever since Beto had come into her life, he was obsessive about how much time she'd spend with her sisters. He'd accuse her of being brainwashed with their *pendejadas*, as he put it.

"Just look at them," he'd remark. "Do their husbands look happy to you?" A question he'd answer on his own. "No! That's why they're like that."

"Like how?" Bea once dared ask.

He stumbled for words. And every time he did this his mouth would torque and switch to Spanish, curses mostly. "Tu sabes," he waved his hand in the air, "Pinches mujeriegos!" he'd say, narrowing his eyes.

Just thinking of him put her in a bad place, and when her thoughts returned to the bathtub, she realized she'd been soaking for thirty minutes. She climbed out, and just as she was slipping on her blouse, Jack walked through the door with an apologetic look. He was clutching a brown paper bag in one hand and a cigarette in the other.

"Sorry it took so long, baby," he said, pulling out a bottle of Tokay and setting it on the table.

"It's alright. It gave me a chance to freshen up."

He saw that the tips of her hair were damp and a faint smell of perfume hung in the air. He smiled and wedged the cigarette between his lips and walked over to the window and hung his head outside. Bea twisted the cap off the bottle and took a guzzle of it. When she leaned her head back, he stole a peek at the way her white blouse accentuated her chest. The neon bulbs snapped on somewhere atop the Duke Hotel and lit up the street below. She passed the bottle to him and he emptied an inch of that amber liquid. They could feel every last bit of lingering shyness finally begin to dissolve.

8

An hour had passed, or maybe it was five. Their brains were fuzzy with drink, and so all forms of measurement were off. Jack took a bath, and when he came out he was sopping wet with only a towel wrapped around his waist. Bea couldn't help but feel a stitch of modesty about it. He dropped his clammy body down onto the bed and lit a cigarette, while she sat up against the headboard staring at the white-tipped goose bumps that formed over his biceps and stomach. She had not been with another man before Beto. Not in that way at least. She had kissed many, and one even pawed her breasts, but to actually press her thin naked body to another man's, with his pulsing extremity deep inside her, as if to stake his claim—only Beto had landed that privilege.

Jack got up and went over to the window and dropped his cigarette to the street below. He grabbed his wrinkled pants from the floor, slid them on beneath his towel, and watched her roll over onto one side of the bed and yawn.

"I sure can't wait to see Patsy tomorrow," she said. It was nervous chatter.

The warm venom of the Tokay was seeping from Jack's head down past his stomach, settling between his thighs. He went and lay next to her, gently, his guts fluttered. She turned her back to him and the crescent arch of her hipbone rose like a wave. He lifted his hand, contemplating for a second, before resting it on her lowest rib. Though he could not see it, she smiled.

By morning she would not remember clearly if what happened in those dark minutes after would in fact be true, or else a delicious dream, filed somewhere among the sour ones.

When his touch landed, a sensation rose up and scattered in her pelvis like the branches of a tree. In the darkness their mouths found one another and refused to let go. His hard cold hand plowed under her blouse, her bra, kneading her warm breasts. Her slacks slid away to the floor. Underwear followed. She grabbed at the swell beneath his zipper and tugged and kissed his lips sloppily and sucked his earlobe. Their pupils darted wildly to gain their sight. Headlights slit the dark open and they caught a glimpse of each other's bodies. She climbed on top of him and her thighs quivered. He strained his eyes to get a good look at the landscape of her small frame. Her blue-bronze body arched, and the tiny rows of ribs sprawled like his own piece of fellaheen country, with its vast and fertile complexities, plains and valleys, peaks and ripples. She thrashed back and forth until her body, against his, was liquid, making its way down the pipeline, while he lifted his hips and dug deeper yet. His thick fingers scanned her body, touching all the parts that had forever been void of attention—the back of the ribs, wingspan of collarbone, tender flanks of calf muscle. More headlights cut the dark open. She could feel herself surrendering. She fought it, once more, before letting go entirely. Suddenly his fingers strummed the scar on her navel. She moaned and arched back. Again his hand stroked the soft tissue. This time she shrank and nudged his hand away, gently, then thrust her hips deeper onto him. He watched as the green of her eyes rolled like alfalfa in a harsh wind. She fell over and threw both hands against his bare chest to contain herself, gripping at the sparse patch of hair like she was tearing beets from the root. He uttered indecipherable words and they trickled on her neck, and she focused hard on holding back, for one last second. But then he took hold of her head and swallowed her mouth whole, and right then, all she could do was give way to the pressure that stemmed from all polar points on her body, imploding in her pelvis like a five-pointed star.

When it was over, they lay tangled in the sheets, legs and arms collapsed sloppily over one another. Jack folded his right arm under his head and lay still. She reached over the side of the bed and found her underwear and slid them on. She could feel his eyes on her backside as she sat up and slipped her breasts into the teacups of her bra. A cool gust drifted through the window and sirens raced down the street. A dog yelped and a woman yelled for it to shut up or else. Jack got up to close the window, and when he returned Bea had the sheet pulled up to her neck.

"Jack?" she whispered. "I was thinking earlier, it sure would be nice if we went to Santa Monica one of these days. They got this pier out there, you ever hear of it?"

"No." He lit a cigarette.

"Well, it's nice. The ocean's right there, everything smells like fish and buttered popcorn. I just love that place, haven't been there since I was a kid."

"We oughtta do it then." He wet his lips with the opening of the bottle.

"We should," she said, pausing. Right then she wondered if it was a stupid idea. Careless, really. Beto knew how much she loved the pier. He hated it. Wouldn't be caught dead there. "You know, I don't have much money. I mean, I got a little but it's chicken scratch. Guess I told you that already, huh? Can't do much in L.A. without money." She rolled onto her stomach and rested her cheek on the pillow, facing him. "I'm thinking I might stop by my old job at Hart's factory, see if I could get on there."

He took a swig. "Right," he said, puffing his smoke and pondering it for a minute. "Guess I could use some work too. Maybe we get us some jobs, nothing too sticky, just something to keep us afloat for awhile."

"That might not be such a bad idea." She leaned over and kissed him, and then rolled again onto her back. Jack put his cigarette out and reached over her and peeled the sheet away from her body.

"What're you doing?" she said, buckling over shyly.

"I wanna look at you . . . if that's alright."

She groaned and turned her spine to him.

"We already made it, baby."

A door slammed in the hallway and footsteps echoed down the staircase. She hushed Jack and he lay still for a few seconds. "What if I let you have a look at me first?"

He rolled over, flat on his back and rested both arms at his side like a corpse. She glanced over her shoulder and caught a glimpse of his pale flanks and burst into laughter. "Go on," he said, trying to contain himself. He adjusted his body and the mattress springs creaked. Bea giggled, and put her hand over her mouth.

"I'm not laughing at you, honey. I mean, it's funny, but not like you think."

"Go on," he said, shutting his eyes.

She turned to face him, then propped her cheek against her hand and peered across the gray length of his body. The hair on his chest was sparse and straight and lay down like felled wheat, trailing in a faint line toward the well of his naval. The bulk of his thighs were thick mounds that surrounded the black curls of his crotch, where a dark wad of foreskin rested like a deflated balloon. She wanted to say something but didn't know what it was she needed to express so she stayed quiet. She angled her gaze at his hips and put her hand out and let it rake over the mass of his thigh. She leaned forward and pulled the sheet slowly over his hips.

It was his turn.

He wasted no time and slid his hand across the jutting peaks of her bra, rolling his fingers down to where the underwire met her ribs. She tensed up as he slid his hand down farther still and, once again, strummed the rippling scar just beneath her belly button. She turned her eyes away but let his hand stay there.

"What happened?"

She reached for his fingers and clutched them. Her voice was barely audible. "Little Al was born early—they had to cut 'im out."

Jack rolled away and reached over the side of the bed and felt around for the bottle of Tokay. He lifted it to his mouth and took a deep swig. He passed it to her, and she leaned her head back and let the last of it go burning down her throat. She sensed he wanted to ask something. He adjusted himself and then bent to kiss the band of skin that ran from one hip to the other like a smooth pink vine. She trembled, and took his face in her hands, and quickly began speaking the first words that came to mind.

"I remember the smell of lemons," she said. He lowered his head onto her stomach and listened. "There was a lemon on the ground, and when I went to pick it up," she hesitated, "well, that's when it happened." She laughed abruptly and couldn't believe what she just said. She shrunk back. "I knew right then, I mean, what it was." His fingers continued to explore the scar.

"I never thought a baby could survive being born so early. I figured his skin must've been thin as this sheet." She turned the sheet over in her fingers. "Beto wasn't around. I had to go down the street a ways to this woman I knew. Henrietta was her name. A colored lady. Real nice. I knocked on the door and her little girl answered. I started thinking that the baby was probably suffocating inside me, but then Henrietta came to the door. I said to her, *I think my bag just broke, Henrietta*, and she looks down and sees me standing in a puddle. God, I was so embarrassed. She grabbed her keys and I swear we flew to the hospital because the next thing I know I'm laying down on a bed. Henrietta was so sweet. She kept saying, *It's gonna be alright Bea, you just see . . . it's gonna be fine.* I'd never been alone with her like that before. I only knew her from our high school days at Jefferson. We weren't friends or anything, just lived in the same neighborhood for a while. I remember thinking to myself that when this is all over I'm gonna do something nice for her." Bea paused and scanned her memory. "I kept expecting the doctor to give me some bad news, but then he tells me the baby's alive and doing fine. Says the bag isn't completely broke, it's just sprung a leak. I never heard of such a thing. I had to stay on my back and not move a muscle. I was like that for a few days, but then I couldn't feel the baby moving around anymore and when I told the doctor he said we had to get it out right away or else he wouldn't make it."

Jack stood up and walked over to his pants and pulled his cigarettes out of the pocket. "Go on," he said, lighting up and returning to bed.

"So they put me in one of those gowns and got me on that cold metal. The doctor goes down there again, and whatever he did it felt like the baby was gonna come out. God, I never been through anything like that before in my life. I'm pushing but little Al don't wanna come out. I feel like his body's stuck, like he's caught on something. The doctor thought the cord might be wrapped around his neck. Anyhow, next thing I know my stomach's flapped open and there's little Albert."

Jack puffed his cigarette and ran his hand through his hair. "And he's fine now?"

She stuck her hand out and he passed the cigarette to her. "He was born so tiny that I wasn't allowed to hold him that whole first week. He had hair all over his body, looked just like a little monkey," she said, shaking her head and wedging the cigarette between her teeth.

"Did his old man go see him?"

A cloud of smoke poured from her lips. She waved it away with one hand. When it cleared, she sat staring at Jack blankly, both eyelids on the verge of collapsing.

9

A grinding noise entered through the open window and woke him a few minutes shy of eight o'clock. A garbage truck yawned in the alleyway; the rattle of trash shook the walls of the hotel room, and Jack couldn't go back to sleep. He rolled over, expecting to stare into Bea's face and assure himself that all of yesterday was not a dream. He could still smell on his skin a musky sweetness entangled with bodily secretions. He wiped the sleep from his eyes, and when he opened them he found only a dent in the mattress. She was gone. He sat up, and the first thing he looked for were his clothes and his duffel. He spotted his pants lying dead beneath the table, pockets strangled outward like tongues. The duffel was nowhere. A panic flashed through his mind, and he leapt to his feet and searched the room. He slapped his forehead and mumbled aloud to himself, "Goddam idiot!" But then his shoulders dropped when he found the canvas bag tucked beneath the bed. On the floor was a page torn from his notebook.

> *Dear Jackie,*
> *I went to Hart's place. You know why. I took a quarter from*
> *your pocket for coffee and a cab. Be back soon.*
> *xoxo, Bea*

On her way to the factory she passed the downtown street vendors who were getting an early jump on the day. It was Saturday after all, a busy time in that slice of the city. A Japanese woman arranged bucketsful of gardenias. She primped them delicately, as if she was wiping a smudge from a child's face. Across the alleyway, a metal door scrolled up and out came a pushcart, maneuvered by a short dark-haired man with thick eyebrows. He smiled a big toothless grin at Bea as she crossed the street, deeper yet into the gut of warehouse row. Outside one of the buildings, a line of women wrapped around the corner of Dobb's Shoe Leathering factory. Each of them clutching documents, looking to land a job.

She knew it was a long shot, asking Hart for her place back on the line. The man was notoriously callous when it came to workers who abandoned their sewing posts, which is exactly what Bea did. Forget that it was Beto who forced her to quit—Hart could care less. Of course Mrs. Hart, on the other hand—a rotund Irish woman with small blue eyes and a crooked nose—took a liking to Bea. And what the missus lacked in physical beauty she made up for in compassion. She was a tender-hearted lady, once giving Bea an extra two bucks on the side just for remembering her birthday. No matter, even if the missus was there, it was still the old bastard who called the shots. As she approached the street where the factory stood, she waved at Hank, the old black man who sat on an apple crate and swung his wad of newspaper at flies. He called out to her, just as he used to do every morning.

"How you been, young lady?"

Bea shouted back, "Fine, Hank, just fine."

"Good to hear it," he said, saluting her with two fingers to his forehead.

She smiled contentedly, and she realized that as much as she'd been away, off and on, over the last few years, a part of her missed Los Angeles. When she turned the corner, expecting to see Hart's giant brass sign welded onto the front of the building, she found nothing. Only two iron posts jutted out from the brick wall where pigeons sat perched. She looked up at the street sign to make sure she was in the right place, and she was. She walked to the front of the building and then around the side, near the gates, where the workers once entered. She saw that the wide scrolling metal door was bolted shut. The gate was locked too. A big heap of trash was gathered in the middle of the parking lot, and from it a hobo poked his head out and startled Bea. She turned and started back up the road, rushing past Hank, threading a path through the vendors and the alleyways, searching for the nearest pay phone.

"Hi honey, it's me," she said, out of breath.

"Where've you been?" Jack replied.

"I came looking for work. Didn't you get my note?" She didn't wait for a response. "I can't believe it, Jackie, Hart's gone under. The whole place, I mean, it's a ghost town here."

"That's too bad," he said, breathing into the phone. "Now what?"

Bea thought about it a second. "Guess I'll come back to the hotel."

When she returned to the room, she found him at the window happily scribbling in his notebook. The ashtray had a dozen cigarette butts gathered in it, and still another hung from his bottom lip. He was shirtless, and a thin tail of steam trickled from behind the bathroom door. The smell of soap dangled in the air. He looked at her, then took the cigarette from his mouth and blew two perfect rings that sailed in her direction. She flung her coat onto the bed and, setting her purse down on the table, pulled out a short brown bag. He hooked the opening of the bag with his finger and peeked inside. It was a bottle of Tokay. He shut his notebook and sat grinning like a child who'd just been given a sweet.

"It's for you, honey."

Jack pulled it from the bag and held it to the light. "How'd you swing this?"

She sat on the bed.

He spun the cap off and took a whiff.

"Jackie, I really do gotta see my sister, before she starts calling half of L.A. looking for me."

"Of course, baby, but we got plenty of time. We'll go this afternoon. Let's have ourselves a few drinks first. What do you say?" And with that he threw back a guzzle and passed her the bottle.

The rest of that day passed languidly. Between fits of laughter and long kisses, within a permanent halo of cigarette smoke, they drank the hours away, until their eyes reddened and varnished over with a numb glee. All the while they slurred and touched each other affectionately, and at one point Jack reached beneath Bea's shirt; she wiggled out of his attempt, but no line had been crossed as far as she was concerned. Off and on, maybe once an hour, or every other hour, they peeked out the window, only to remind themselves that the world outside, the stiff and utterly square world, didn't apply to them. Not its rules or contradictions, not its streetlights or crosswalks, not its arbitrary neighborhoods quartered off by highways and byways, bridges and barrios. Deep into the afternoon, at the pearl hour, buzzing with invincibility, Bea stuck her head out the window and spread her arms as if embracing the sky. She blurted out, "Goddamn you L.A.!" A voice greeted her back, "Shut up!" She and Jack laughed and rolled on the bed. He pressed his thigh between her legs and nudged her body slightly. She moaned and kissed his neck and then rolled away quickly.

"Is that all you like me for, Jackie?" She pushed her bangs away from her eyes. He could see she was serious.

"C'mon, baby," he said, "I think you're an angel. Something wrong with that?"

She shifted her eyes toward the bottle of Tokay and saw that only two inches of that sweet topaz was left tinkling at the bottom.

"I just wanna take it slow, honey, is that alright?"

"Course it is," he replied. "Of course."

She threw herself back onto the bed, and Jack began asking her questions, making small talk, but it quickly turned into big talk. Her eyes beamed, and she was reminded again why she liked him so much. He wanted to hear "her story," as he put it. No one had ever asked for her story before. And put that way, she thought, she might've gone the rest of her life without ever knowing she had a story in the first place. But he meant what he said, and prodded her on.

"When I was a kid growing up here," she started, "L.A. was the biggest place on the planet, but it felt like home anyway. Sometimes I hated it but mostly it was alright. When I got older, around high school, I thought I'd seen the worst part of people by then, but then my dad took us to the valley. Man, I hated it. My mom hated it too. Her and I would talk about it whenever he wasn't around. I just couldn't stand the people there, the men especially. Of course they all had a thing for hillbilly girls. I just hated that about 'em. Then you had the farmers, even worse. Had us all breaking ourselves like fools." She paused and took a swig, then wiped her mouth. "You probably think I'm a lunatic, don't you? I really don't ever talk like this, honey, honest."

"Go on," he said.

She sat up and pulled her legs to her chest. "Now that I think about it, it's just so strange. Like something you hear about in another country. These guys, these farmers, would come out to the campo early sometimes, before sunrise, and all the men would line up, some of the women too, just like they were on an auction block. I'm not kidding you, Jackie. And they'd go around eyeing the best workers, the biggest, and the uglier the better too, 'cause they knew if they got some good-looking kid from the campo, well, they knew what their daughters were up to. Sure were a lot of good-looking boys out of work, let me tell you." Jack chuckled. "I guess it ain't such a big deal, I mean everyone knows what they're getting into. Guess the part I can't stand is seeing certain folks get rich, I mean stinkin' fat rich, for work they haven't done themselves. Just eats me up inside." She paused. "You guys got raids back East? Supposed to be everywhere, I guess, but I only heard about 'em here in California."

"Don't think we do."

"Well, when all the picking's done, the farmers call immigration on themselves so all the workers get deported, this way they don't have to pay 'em their last check. Sometimes, though, there isn't enough immigration around, so then he gets his buddies together, other farmers mostly, and they do the job themselves. They come around with shotguns and ax handles, like something out of the Wild West, if you can believe that. Of course, they're predictable nowadays, I mean the whole campo can see 'em coming a mile away." She swiped the bottle from his grip again and took a long guzzle. He could see the torches in her eyes. "My brother Alex told me about this one guy he used to work for, a fellow named Peters. Guess he had made a gold mine selling this certain kind of seed, I think it was a special type of cotton or something. I don't know too much about that stuff, but what he did, according to my brother, was took some formula from one farmer, and then a few ingredients from another, and he mixed it up and then sold it right back to them." She laughed and slapped her thigh. "Can you believe that? And then these guys would gather up when the Farm Show came around and they'd act like the greatest friends. I mean, really, that's just the kind of stuff that goes on down there."

Her head wobbled loosely on her neck and Jack could see that she was past drunk. He took the bottle from her and polished it off. He put his hand on the soft meat of her thigh and she took hold of his wrist and kissed him.

"Tell me about Mexico," he said.

She laid her body down and stared up at the ceiling.

"Not much to say really. We were only there a little while. If there's any place worse than the valley, it's probably Mexico. Well, Guanajuato, at least. We used to live in this little house with brick floors. And every night we'd have to check for scorpions under our bed. Haw! That's just crazy, isn't it? The bedposts were in bowls of water so that they couldn't climb up when we were asleep. Man, I can't believe I remember that stuff. That whole first summer we couldn't sleep because we could hear pigs squealing in the distance. And if it wasn't the pigs, it was the coyotes. Me and my sisters used to say—" she paused suddenly. "Fuck! What time is it, Jackie?" She sat up and scrambled around for her purse. "Angie . . . God, she's gonna kill me."

Jack lay motionless.

"We gotta go, c'mon. I gotta go." She found her shoes and attempted to put them on.

"It's too late now, baby. We'll go first thing tomorrow."

She fussed with her laces and couldn't get the shoe on, so she flung it across the room.

"C'mon, Bea, we aren't in any condition to be out in those streets right now. Not at this hour. Come and lay down." He got up and went over to her and took hold of her arm.

She was reluctant at first. But then she gave in and hobbled back to the bed.

"Don't worry," Jack said, "we'll see your sister first thing tomorrow, I promise."

"She's gonna be sore, I know it. I can already hear her."

They lay down, and he pulled the sheet up over both their bodies.

"She'll be fine, you'll see. It'll all be fine tomorrow. Now go on with your story. You were saying about Mexico."

She rolled on her side; it took her a few minutes to pick up where she'd left off. "We were only in Irapuato for a year, maybe." She yawned. "Hold me, honey, would you?" He adjusted his body so that she fit flush against him, and she buried her head into the nape of his neck.

"Go on."

"My brother Epi used to get bad stomach problems. He couldn't keep his food down. My mom thought it might be the water so she started boiling it, but that didn't work either. We had to help her collect rain in buckets, no kidding, and then she'd boil it but it was no use. I remember her saying to my dad once, 'Viejo, Irapuato's so foul that God won't even waste the good stuff on us.' He hated when she said stuff like that. She was only joking, but the way he acted you'd think she insulted his mother. After that my dad made us go to church. I remember it was this little chapel and all the indios went there. It was called, I never forget the name, El Templo del Hospitalito. What a name, huh? The Temple of the Small Hospital. You ever hear such a thing? It was an old place and the inside always smelled like burnt wax. Pigeons flew in and out of nests that were in the corners of the ceiling, and sometimes you'd find their eggs smashed on the ground. It was okay, the only problem was that the priest was an old man who delivered the sermons in Spanish, so we'd fall asleep on the pews and my dad would rap us on the head with his knuckle. We were miserable there. My mom especially. When we finally thought my brother Epi was gonna die from his stomach problems, that's when we left. It got pretty bad. Of course my dad just stopped coming home. Guess it all got to him. My mom and him fought a lot, and she didn't know what to do with herself either. She used to listen to this radio program, El Barco de la Ilusión, and this was the only thing that put a smile on her face. I think it had something to do with comedy or politics. All I know is that for one hour every day she was either laughing or else cursing at the radio. I think we all knew that being in Irapuato was wrong, even my dad." She turned to Jack, her eyes now barely slit open. He kissed the side of her head and held her tighter. She let out another yawn. "My dad stole my mom from a schoolyard, can you believe that? He used to park in front of her school and watch her to see if she was a good girl. Isn't that nuts? My mom says she only stays with him because she knows him so well. Says she can predict him, and so why would she go looking to start over again with someone else." Bea shut her eyes but continued speaking. "I don't see how any woman can be with a man who don't give her a home to settle down in. You know, he never once bought us a house, not once. We were always hopping from one place to another, like gypsies. I told myself a long time ago, if I ever have kids I won't do that to them. Turn 'em into gypsies. I want 'em to have a home. That ain't so much to ask for, right, Jackie-honey?" She yawned once more. Her voice trailed off. "I'll never forget poor Epi, gagging and belching, all sorts of ugly noises coming from his mouth." A light chuckle seeped from her lips. "Whenever I hear the name Irapuato, I swear it sounds just like Epi vomiting."

10

"Jackie?" Bea said, as soon as she awoke. "I gotta see Angie."

He moaned.

"I really got to see her. I can't go another day like this."

He rolled toward her.

"I couldn't sleep so well, just thinking about how somewhere inside, I bet Patsy just feels so alone, like maybe she thinks I abandoned her."

"That's a heavy word."

"Well, maybe, but that's what I'm feeling if I don't go see her."

She sat up in bed and rested her chin on her knees and stared toward the window.

"What do you say we poke around for some work this morning, only an hour or two, then head over to see your sis?"

"That's fine," Bea replied, numbly. "So long as we go today."

"Yeah, of course, we'll go, baby."

Standing on the corner of Hollywood Boulevard and Vine Street, Bea looked up at the surrounding buildings, and saw that each of them had a glaze of optimism that made them look important in ways that no building in Los Angeles had ever looked before. It was impossible to tell that this was the same cursed city that only a few months earlier had found Elizabeth Short sliced in half at the midsection and now had women and men alike becoming active members of the local gun club, looking over their shoulders at anyone who so much as hiccupped off-key. Red and white banners were tethered to unlit neon signs and strewn up and down the streets, flapping in the salty breeze that tumbled in from the Pacific Ocean a couple miles to the west. Delivery trucks honked their pardons at one another and parked wherever they pleased, and brawny drivers jumped out and carted off boxes of vegetables and meats to every restaurant on the block. A couple of city workers positioned a ladder, and one climbed up and tinkered with the delicate bulbs of an intricately sculpted street lamp. Below, dapper men in bowler hats and three-piece wool suits clicked their heels along the concrete, kept their gaze on the stretch of sidewalk ahead, and made sure they got to where they were going. Another block over, busloads of tourists yakked and gawked at the buzzing city, the inner parts of a Los Angeles that, while growing up, Bea had had no desire, or business, to be gallivanting around. But here she was now, peering up and down the strip like she belonged there. And for a moment she believed she did, that perhaps this shiny perch atop the golden shoulders of Los Angeles was where she was meant to be all along.

She took Jack's hand as they passed up Chi Chi's place and made a beeline for the first coffee shop they saw, Melody Lane. They took a seat by the window and shared a cup of coffee, and scanned the want ads of the *Examiner*. They found nothing except lame offers for hair-growth tonics and sewing machine repairs.

From their position by the window they spotted Owl's Drugstore across the way, and Bea thought they should both try getting jobs there. She could already see it. Jack working inventory, and her pouring drinks at the soda fountain. And since they had nothing else to go on, they paid for their coffee and went over to Owl's and asked to speak with the manager.

A black woman emerged from the back room. She sauntered to the counter and told them that no positions were open, but suggested they try Chi Chi's.

"That place is always looking for folks," she said, shrugging her shoulders. "Sorry, I just ain't got nothing for you."

Hand in hand, they walked over to Chi Chi's and found it closed, so they pounded on the front door. It was a massive slab of wood adorned with brass knobs, and so they had to kick it too, just to be sure they were heard. Which they weren't. Jack ran around the building and cut into the alleyway to see if there was a back door, but there were a million back doors and none of them marked, so he sat down on a small wooden crate and waited a few minutes to see if someone might come poking out of one. He didn't have to wait more than thirty seconds before a wiry kid did poke out. He was wearing a chef's apron, and it was bloodied with small bits of entrails. He lit a smoke and walked over when he noticed Jack staring at him.

"You ain't a cop, is ya?" the kid asked.

Jack laughed out loud. "Boy, you got me pegged wrong," he said. "Mind if I bum a smoke off you?"

The kid opened his pack of cigarettes and tossed one at Jack, and with it a box of matches. "You lookin' to score?"

Jack lit his smoke and swung his gaze up the alleyway. He could see people walking past, and wondered if Bea was alright waiting for him out front. He looked up at the kid from his place on the crate. "How much you selling for?"

"A nickel'll get you a few sticks."

Jack reached into his coat pocket and found a nickel and flipped it up at the kid. The kid fumbled with his cigarette and failed to catch the coin. He bent over for it and when he came up, there by Jack's shoe lay three thin joints. The kid rushed back inside and Jack grabbed them and stuck them in his sock, then stood up and hurried back to where Bea was waiting.

The rest of that morning bore no fruit. For the most part they dallied around holding hands and watching the world, as if on the other side of a panoramic window, go about its usual rhythm. Cars zipped by on their way home from a day at the beach—home being far from that glittering drag, in Torrance or Culver City. They watched women, brown-faced women, small clusters of them, cackling in Spanish as they boarded city buses, their faces elongated from a day of cleaning and managing unruly children not their own.

As they walked back to the hotel, they stopped every few yards to embrace, to feel the closeness of a body in that gargantuan city. And then they'd kiss good and sloppy. Hard kisses. Soft kisses. Pecks. And once in a while, in the midst of one of these kisses, Bea couldn't help but wonder if she was in fact kissing anyone at all, or if she was dreaming the whole thing up, and in a minute the sun would rise, and with it a rooster crow, and then Beto's fat hand would grip at her thigh, or else a breast, to wake her up for the day's work. But then Jack would speak and it all became real again, because they were the kind of words that Beto wouldn't be caught dead uttering. Sweet words. Tender little spells, about her ears, and how against his lips they were like oysters. Words comparing her shoulders to other soft things of the sea, like sand dollars or dunes. It must've been the smell in the air, or else the seagulls carving zeros in the sky, because his words did not end there. The entire route back to the hotel was paved with compliments that sounded like music, and they spilled from Jack's mouth endlessly.

They made love the instant they reached the hotel room, and then afterward they smoked one of the joints by the window and stared out at Los Angeles from their perch above the red dusk halo of the city.

Bea bit the skin of her thumb. "Honey," she whispered. "I didn't forget about seeing Angie, you know. I just don't think I'm ready." She lowered her hand away from her mouth. "All I care about is Patsy, anyway. If it wasn't for her, I could just as easy go another month before I deal with Angie. Does that make me a chicken?"

"No, it doesn't make you anything." He lit the joint again and puffed away.

Bea declined. She leaned forward and watched the slow purr of cars echoing down San Pedro Avenue. From their roost they could see all the lights of downtown, clear up to Little Tokyo.

At the corner, a trio of women stood around smoking cigarettes. One of them was Mexican, or appeared to be. Her face was done up like a peacock's plume, but her hair was black and straight and she spoke with an accent. The other two were white, and besides their street rags and jagged quaffs, they looked plain as any Van Nuys housewife. Like window-front mannequins, they kept to their post, waiting to snare a John. They guarded the corner like they owned it—and they probably did, thought Jack.

Bea took one more hit and Jack finished off the joint, then went to fiddle with the radio. Static crackled through and soon the warm guttural bellow of a baritone saxophone oozed over the room like hot piloncillo. He flopped back onto the bed and so did Bea, next to him. They kissed and their mouths pulsed like fragile sea anemones, and then they licked their lips and cradled one another, and they sipped some water and let the dryness of their eyes go on burning.

She lowered her eyelids and let the cool medicine have its way with her thoughts. Meanwhile, Jack scanned her body, investigating the details, the smallest ones. Her hands, for instance. He noticed they were petite, yet there was something robust about them, commanding. Like they could shell a hard-boiled egg and yet split a cedar log with a sledgehammer without cracking a fingernail. Her neck was a supple stem, a sapling, and when she swallowed air, the lean muscles that encased her throat rippled like pond water. The whole of her frame appeared to him as tender and complex as a rosebush, and he wanted to know more about her, so he asked. She was still a little embarrassed about some of the things she'd let slip the night before, wondering if maybe she'd said too much. This time she chose carefully what to reveal.

"Isn't much to tell," she said, shrugging her shoulders. "I haven't done anything special, really."

"Nonsense." His cherry eyes flickered. "You ever hear of a guy named Thoreau?"

Bea shook her head.

"As I drew fresher soil about the rows with my hoe, I disturbed the ashes of unchronicled nations who in primeval years lived under these heavens, and their small implements of war and hunting were brought to the light of this modern day."

Bea nodded. "Sounds almost like a prayer."

"That's right, holy without the Bible. But you see there, everything a person does, even the terrible little chores, play some role in the giant picture." She looked into his eyes and could see that he was serious. At that moment a trumpet machine-gunned from the radio and interrupted the conversation. Jack bobbed his head with the music and then got up to lower the volume. It seemed louder now than before.

"So your old man had you in the fields?"

She blinked and rubbed her eyes. "That's why after high school I begged my parents to let me take up sewing. I used to have to get up at four-thirty each morning and walk across the bridge just to get to the sewing academy, can you believe that? But I liked working there, having my own thing, you know, felt nice. It was probably the only time I can remember feeling like I was on my own. Even though I was living with my folks and all, it just felt like I was on my own. The bad part was that the academy was in Hart's warehouse so it didn't have windows, and boy did it get hot during summer. I used to feel especially bad for those women who had to bring their kids with them. They'd pile a stack of raw material and put their babies to sleep on it. Great big stacks of cotton or underwear, but they'd sleep there just fine. I used to love the smell of raw cotton. I can still smell it if I try real hard." She tugged on Jack's shirt and pressed her nose against it. "Naw, yours just smells like smoke," she said, slapping his chest.

An hour passed, maybe two. She tried coaxing Jack to talk about his life but he skirted around, except to say that his was a small family. A mother. One sister. A brother who'd passed on, a time he'd just as soon forget. When she pressed him about his father, his face glowered and his red eyes dimmed.

"I'm sorry, honey," she said, touching his leg.

He rolled his head side to side and raised his eyebrows up from the pit of his sullen gaze. "It's no big deal, really. Anyone with two eyes coulda seen it coming a hundred miles off." And that was the end of it.

Moments later, she heard a faint thudding, and wondered if it was the music. She listened closely. It was her own heart beating. She rolled away from Jack's clutches and shuffled to the bathroom. In the mirror she splashed water on her face and then had a good look at herself. She was naked and could not remember the last time she'd seen herself that way. Her father thought too many mirrors in the house was sacrilegious and so made it a point to only have one. A ten-inch vanity mirror he kept beneath his bed and carted out only for special occasions. In the worn yellow light her skin appeared sallow, porcelain almost. Her body wavered in front of the mirror, and she eyed carefully the shapely waif that stood before her. She patted down the mangle of thick hair that draped over her shoulders. Gawked at the two round knobs of her knees and saw how they were chafed from all the kneeling down on cold compacted earth. They were the blushed color of an armpit. And then she ran her fingers over the scar and thought of little Albert. Her mind filed through all the memories, the bad ones mostly, and she could hear the high pitch of his voice as if in the other room. It was clear as day. "I think you're the best mama in the whole world." He said this to her often. Especially after her and Beto argued. "You're the best ever," he would rattle on in his small voice, staring up at her. And then he'd lasso his little arms around her hips and hold on. She needed to know how he was getting along without her. She remembered Alex's words and instantly felt better. She glanced at herself once more, then wrapped a towel around her body and went back out.

Jack was standing in front of the radio with nothing but his underwear on, swaying to the music. A tired mask was pulled over his eyes and cheeks. She thought his smile looked sinister. He swung his head side to side and nodded Bea over. Her stomach churned. She went and sat on the edge of the bed. He tried luring her but she refused. "C'mon, baby," he said, "move with me!" She looked down and saw her clothes shriveled on the floor. She turned her back to him and timidly slid them on. He tried again to get her to dance but she refused. He figured she hadn't smoked enough, and so he lit up another bomber and waved it in front of her. She hesitated, at first, but then, looking up at him and the goofy, boyish way his head bobbled to the music, she felt at ease, and so she took a hit. He lifted his arms into the air and turned a full circle, shaking his hips side to side, teasingly, until finally a giggle spewed from her mouth. "C'mon, baby," he tried once more, grabbing her with both arms and forcing her up on her feet. She put up a limp smile, not wanting him to think her a complete square, and she forced herself to dance, just enough to prove to him that she was still alive. As the song ended, she rolled down onto the bed and sealed herself tightly beneath the blanket.

Later that night, or morning, in those immeasurable seconds right before a body gives itself to the dream world entirely, she whispered to him.

"Jackie," she said, "I really can dance you know."

"I bet," he mumbled.

"I'm pretty good too."

"I'm sure you are."

And that was it.

A silence sprang from the city, and not a single car or breeze could be heard. And then there it was again, her heartbeat. It was louder this time—like a tom-tom drum in the shell of her ear. Thump.

"When we were kids, my father never let us dance, you know. Not the girls anyway. Me, Angie, and Maggie, we had to sneak somewhere if we wanted to. Isn't that the saddest thing you ever heard? Once in awhile, if he was in a decent mood he'd let us dance a little, but it had to be in front of him, right there in the living room. He'd sit on a chair and watch every single gesture we'd make. If we smiled too big, or if we bent too low he'd clap his hands at us or snap. Or if we looked *atrevidas*—God, I hate that word—he'd shut the radio off and send us up to our room. And the song had to be something mild. Church music mostly. Guess he thought we'd turn evil or something. I just never understood it, really. Imagine that? All those great dances happening right here in L.A. Me and Angie used to walk down this very same street when we were kids and boy, places would be hoppin'. We used to peek inside the door and see how those people moved, then we'd come home and try those moves out on each other, whenever he wasn't around. Guess it was stupid."

And then she suddenly realized that she hadn't been saying any of this at all. Not out loud at least. But there was a conversation. Jack repositioned himself and his body rolled away from her. She could hear clearly now heavy breath skirting from his mouth.

She was still dizzy and could feel the rise and lull of the grass working through her. Her heartbeat returned. Thump. When her eyelids shut, the room spun, so she forced, muscled them, to stay open. Strange how things change so quickly and without reason. No des brinco sin huarache. Beto always says this. Never jump without sandals. Followed up by her father's scorn, Dime con quién andas y te diré quién eres. Who are you with, Bea? Whoever it is, this is who you are now. It was her own voice, echoing in her head. Music tinkled from the radio. In and out. Screw Beto and my father. She thought this. It was a strange darkness they were in. The two of them. Bea and Jack. Locked in a hotel room in the city of her birth. The earthen rank smell of old cotton deep within the threads of the sheets.

11

"Beto's got his uniform on and he's looking nice, clean cut. His mom's proud of him, you know, her son going away to serve the country." Bea let a few grains of sand sift through her fingers, before continuing. "I guess I felt a little proud then too, but I also had an idea things would be different, I mean when he returned home from it all. He put his hat on my head, I remember getting a little upset by it because I'd taken almost an hour that morning fixing my hair. But he was feeling good, and it didn't hurt anything. I don't hardly think I ever saw him as proud as he was right then. Guess that's what a uniform will do to you. I remember that day too, it was sunny and humid. A regular L.A. summer. His friends came over to see him off, and they were poking at one another and giving Beto a hard time, saying he was gonna come back queer, cause there weren't any women in the military. I hated when they talked like that, like I wasn't even there. Of course, Beto's mom, Julieta, didn't think twice about any of it. She was a mess that day, proud and worried. What a sweet lady she is too. Beto kept holding me is what I mostly remember. I don't think his arm wasn't around me for one second that whole afternoon. He wasn't usually that affectionate, not unless he was drinking, but that day, I do remember, he had a look on him. There's a photograph of that day that I used to keep in my purse, 'cause I wanted to remember it. Sure enough, all of that changed when he got home. He was turned off about everything. Said they kicked him out for misconduct, that's all the papers say, misconduct. But they don't say why. But I know it's 'cause he was sneaking out of his barracks to go with some women. He's fast, too fast for me. I can't stand fast men. But he'd always sorta been like that anyway. He acted like he didn't care about us anymore. Not me or little Al or Patsy." Bea paused. She leveled her eyes across the sandy shore and reached her hand out. Jack passed the half-empty bottle of wine to her. She continued. "Things just got worse so I left him." She took a small sip from the bottle and set it down in the sand.

Jack lifted his feet up from beneath a small mound and dusted them off. A fog rolled in over the hushing tides, and only a handful of people were left strewn about the shore. He took Bea's hand and the bottle and they stood up and started back to the hotel. They had been at the beach for the better part of the day.

That morning had been hardly more productive than previous mornings. It started out with both waking up at half past eleven. "What's the difference," Jack said at one point, while drinking their complimentary coffee in the hotel lobby. "Sometimes it's enough to be with someone. There are lots of lonely people in this world, and who are we to ignore that the universe put two people, two small souls like you and me on the same path?" Bea's eyes lit up every time he broke out into these small sermons, and she let him go on, a smile on her face, her small frame overshadowed by the wide arch of his words.

Earlier that day they'd caught wind of a pay-as-you-wish dive that was only a few blocks from their hotel. Having not eaten a single bite all day, and with the wine gnawing at their stomachs, they decided it was worth a shot. Clifton's Cafeteria was a gaudy joint, but damn if the food and service weren't tops, Jack would later say to Bea. She had never been to such a place, so fancy, so generous, nothing like the greasy dives in Boyle Heights, or Selma for that matter, those roach-infested burger shacks and foul diners that spotted the Golden State Highway. She ate until her stomach felt like it would burst, and so did Jack. They polished off their plates—two sodas apiece, a couple of slabs of meatloaf, and a slice of lemon meringue pie—and when they were done, Jack pulled a frail single dollar bill from his wallet and tested Clifton's policy by laying it flat on the table beside their dishes. He waved the waitress over and the woman took the single. She hesitated. "You know it's three bucks," she said. "I know," Jack replied. Bea shrunk in her seat. The woman eyed her, and then swiped the dollar from the table before hauling the dishes away.

Stepping out onto Broadway they felt weightless and unbridled, and they might've skipped all the way back to the hotel had they thought of it. They drifted toward Fifth Street coddling one another in a bed of cigarette smoke, gabbing the whole way with their hands in the air as if conducting a symphony. All thoughts of work or money dissolved with each drag and exhale, aloof to the world. She held Jack's arm and, for the first time, was unaware of anything or anybody. It was a type of simple anonymity she hadn't known until now. Even the stone that had formed in the pit of her stomach over the past few days seemed pebble-sized. Her shoulders dropped and her mood lightened.

"I think I wanna see my sister now, honey. I think it'll be fine."

"You sure?"

She gripped his arm tighter and nodded, and they continued toward Main Street.

Upon reaching the intersection, she stepped over the gutter and out onto the asphalt. A truck appeared from nowhere. It swerved and blared its horn, and it would've clipped her had Jack not yanked her onto the sidewalk. It sped off, the driver spitting curse words out the window.

"You alright?" Jack asked. He tried touching her face.

She pushed his hand away, gently, and could feel her heartbeat at the back of her tongue. She stared up the road and watched as the taillights of the truck disappeared in the traffic. She replayed the instant in her mind. The driver's face, she could see him. The cold expression. The square eyes. It became clearer with every replay. It was Beto. She was sure of it. Jack tried putting his arms around her again, and this time she let him. He kissed her forehead and she pretended to be fine with it. He took her hand and led her across the street. If Jack spoke at all in that moment she didn't hear it. Her mind was recalling Beto's image—blurring past, aiming.

12

At the hotel, she couldn't shake him from her mind. While Jack scribbled in his notebook, she sat on the bed and folded her legs beneath her. She could hear, on the other side of the door, two men walking up the hallway. Their words were stifled by the walls and by the way they spoke, their deep and resonant voices, a part of her worried: Was it possible he had followed her? When they passed she could hear them laughing—loud, hearty laughs—and when their door slammed shut and she was satisfied that it was not him, her mind returned again to Beto. But this time it was not the cabrón, poco hombre version that she was thinking of. Instead, it was the young Beto, the charming carita who once had eyes for her. The Beto who smelled of aftershave and La Habana pomade. Alberto, as he first introduced himself.

She stood outside of Rosenberg's Curios on Whittier Boulevard, dolled up in a newly hemmed dress that her mother had helped her stitch from an old set of drapes. There was a baby shower later that day, and she and her cousin Margarina had stopped by to pick up a gift. Margarina, in a hurry as she always was, had Bea wait outside while she rushed in to grab something, anything, just so they wouldn't show up empty-handed. Just then a crew of solteros came strutting up the block in a typical breeze of invincibility. They blew down the street in a whirlwind of high-fives and jabs, grinning from ear to ear, hair sculpted up like onyx bugles, trumpeting virility. Meanwhile, young Beatrice stood there like a virgin in waiting. Her shapely pale arms exposed, and thin puckered lips the succulent crimson of plums. Her sleek black hair was pulled back, and tight curls hung down above her forehead. Had Jesus known she was gallivanting around Boyle Heights looking as fresh as she did, he would've chained her to the front porch, or else taken her with him to Selma for an early start on the algodón.

Knowing what a sirena her daughter was, Jessie made Margarina promise she'd have Bea home by dinnertime. To which Margarina gained her tia's confidence by crossing her heart and kissing her fingers up to Diosito.

As the guys approached, they gawked at Bea, slowing their walk and winking ridiculously, all of them profusely opening and shutting their eyes at her, as if they were pushing against the headwinds of an invisible dust storm. And when she turned her back to them and stepped into the curios shop after Margarina, only one of them, Alberto, had the nerve to chase after her. He was handsome, and he strode right up to her, there among the short aisles of bubble gum and nylon pantyhose. Before she had a chance to hurry Margarina up, this young caballero with a chiseled face and deep painful eyes was standing at her side, winking. She couldn't help but laugh, and he mistook this for an invitation, so he asked her out on a date. Margarina could hear them, and she looked at her prima, and nodded her head, yes, go on, and so Bea said yes. The whole time certain that her father was spying on her, watching from behind some parked car, ready to pounce on her as soon as she exited the curios shop.

It wasn't long after that they married and had little Al. Of course, Beto was proud of his son, and he let everyone know it. In fact, when it came down to it, little Al was the reason Beto enlisted in the military in the first place. Or at least, so he claimed. The day he was to ship out, he held the boy in his arms and snapped off several photos, saying, "One day Junior can look at these and be proud of his old man." But when he returned from duty he wasn't the same. Nothing was. His thirst for booze was insatiable. There was a look in his eyes that she could only attribute to a good brainwashing. By the time she was pregnant with Patsy she thought it would be a miracle if he could stay sober long enough to welcome her into the world. This is how bad it had gotten. Still, she knew things could always be worse.

13

Late that night, when drunk voices were again heard echoing beneath the streetlamps, Jack found himself unable to sleep. He propped himself against the pillow, above Bea's motionless body, and called her name over and over. She awoke, startled, and her eyes rolled and slit open before resting shut again.

"Baby?" He kissed her cheek.

She lifted her hand to her forehead and rolled toward him.

They lay still for several seconds. He ran his fingers through her hair, then slid farther down onto the bed until he was eye level with her. In the darkness he could barely make out her face.

"Bea." His voice sounded light, careful. "I've been thinking."

She pretended to be more asleep than awake but could hear him perfectly.

"I've really been thinking . . ." He took another minute. "There's no way to put it." He hesitated. "You awake?"

She nodded, slightly.

"I'm thinkin' I oughtta get back to New York. I have some things, you see . . ." She could feel his warm breath ebbing against her neck. "Business really, things I gotta get back to." A sharp silence wedged itself between them. "Bea?"

She rolled her body away from him. "I understand." Her voice was like wool.

He searched for something meaningful to say. He didn't want to utter just anything. Especially not on a night like this, when the moon's lunacy had a way of forging promises that by morning were sure to lose their luster. He pulled the blanket back and exposed her shoulder. Kissed it tenderly and smelled her skin. She shrunk away. He fell back on his pillow and stared up at the ceiling for several minutes.

She mumbled. "Guess you gotta *get on with life*, huh?"

He had no reply.

"Forget it."

He lay still. "No, you're right." He shifted onto his side. "That's why I had this little question I wanted to ask you."

"I'm listening."

"What if you come with me?"

A short laughter burst from her lips. "Don't say that." She shut her eyes and her stomach tingled. She thought of Beto again, and of Selma. She could see the look on Angie's face too, the righteous scowl in her eyes. The city's silence pierced her nerves, and she pulled the blanket tighter over her body. Jack sat up in bed now, and she could feel him staring at her.

"I'm serious. What do you say?"

"About what?"

"New York. Come with me."

She turned her head toward him. Her gaze was steel.

"Hell, I wouldn't say it if I didn't mean it." He waited for her reply.

She searched for something in his face. An answer, possibly. Some hint of sincerity. Suddenly, the room appeared smaller to Bea, confining. Her eyes peered through him. She found herself looking clear out beyond the drab walls of the Duke Hotel, and past the cluttered skyline of Los Angeles. It was a vision of herself standing at the foot of a building that rose up and got lost in a cloud. Cabs and whistles spun around her, subway trains vibrated the souls of her feet. Somewhere close behind, little Al and Patsy trailed, a look of possibility on their faces, illuminated by the neon lights of a New York she'd only seen in movies. She thought of her brother Alex, and what he had said to her only a few mornings ago, about how there was a heap of money waiting to be made in big cities, and how in the end, it would be better for the kids. For the kids, she could hear his voice again. She could see the snow drifting, and pictured little Al sticking his tongue out and falling back into a mound of powder, his eyes free of that crease that had recently formed between them. And as if all that wasn't enough, she thought of that miserable campo, that sad den of discarded prayers, and of the wretched valley whole, its smells and moods, and finally, its people. That was all the thinking it took.

Her expression changed, and Jack could feel the electricity ebbing back once again. The answer, Bea's answer, had churned up from her depths and settled around her cheekbones. It lifted the ends of her mouth, and she didn't have to speak a word of it. He could see clearly that her answer was yes. Yes and yes. He threw himself onto her and, as they kissed and tousled, all sensations were heightened. The next ten minutes was a melding of separate worlds, universes in heated collision, atop a flimsy hotel mattress; their lives with all the certainty of a kite broken free of its strings.

Afterward, Bea lay on her back, catching her breath, thinking to herself, *Damn if everything don't feel perfect right now.* The window was cracked open and a cool blade of air sliced through the room. Jack got up to shut it. While lying there she felt a pinch in her stomach, a nervous fluttering, different from the stone. This one was light, limitless. She thought about the preparations. It wouldn't take much. Some clothes, a few conversations, maybe. Money, of course.

"Honey," she said, "we're gonna hafta scrape together a few bucks before we can get going."

"We will, baby," he assured her.

He lifted her arm and pecked at the inner part of her elbow. The stubble on his face tickled, and she liked it, but suddenly, there it was again. She found herself thinking of Beto. She wondered how he'd act once he caught wind that she'd split for good, kids and all. He'd come undone. She pictured the look on his face, the rigid curl of his moustache, the drape of his eyes, his desperation. She was sure it would kill him. So what. She could hear his loud voice sawing the air, how she was a worthless wife, a terrible lover. She couldn't wait to see that slow disintegration take over, his broad shoulders crumble like one of those big rusty abandoned plows sunk beneath mounds of dirt. Joy took over her face, and she kissed Jack on the mouth, and tasted him, the fat of his tongue on hers, and this time it tasted like silver, mercury, like the salt-spit of a vast and bottomless ocean. She pressed her skin against his and told herself she belonged there. But then again, only seconds later, a small part of her, just a freckle, smaller yet, was feeling sorry for that son-of-a-bitch. She was exhausted with thought. Her breath grew heavy, and her body twitched in place. When she was out, completely out, Jack wiggled from underneath her arm, pulled his notebook from his bag and went and sat near the window. Quietly, he folded open his notebook, rested his writing hand on the page, and let his thoughts come to him.

14

At seven thirty in the morning they walked to Clifton's for breakfast and took a booth by the window. A couple of hobos hovered over dim plates of eggs and potatoes; they sipped their coffee and, when they were done, got up and shuffled out without putting down a single dime. A waitress came around and cleaned up after them. She griped about the mess and was embarrassed when she turned to find Jack and Bea looking at her.

Jack worried about the last few bills that lingered in his wallet. They each ordered a coffee and agreed on sharing a single plate of eggs and ham.

While Bea chipped away at the eggs with her fork, Jack ran his fingers through his hair and looked out the window. He reached into his pocket for a smoke.

"Aren't you gonna eat, honey?" she asked.

He lit the cigarette and folded his hands on the table. "I've been up half the night trying to figure a way into some money." Frustration gathered between his eyes. "I got nothing."

She dropped a cube of sugar into her coffee and stirred it while looking at him. He lifted the smoke to his lips and took a drag, then scratched his forehead and pointed up at the ceiling. "You ever see anything like that?"

She turned her eyes upward and saw paddleboats dangling overhead, like odd chandeliers. Oars hung over the sides, and from them a massive fishing net was pulled across a part of the ceiling. The waitress came by and refilled their coffee. Before walking off she set the check on the table and they both eyed it.

"Least we don't have to pay it all," Bea said.

He lowered his eyes.

"Can I get a drag of that?"

He handed her the cigarette and she stuck it in her mouth and puffed. "I'm thinking of asking Angie for a loan." He folded his arms over his chest and leaned back in his seat. "I'm gonna have to see her anyway. Was thinking we might as well go after breakfast."

He agreed. Bea's mood lightened. "Can't believe I'm gonna get to see Patsy today." She raised her arms above her head and stretched and let out a deep sigh. "God, I hope she hasn't grown too much."

"How long's it been?"

"Almost four weeks now." She caught herself. "I can't hardly believe it." She covered her mouth with her hand and looked away.

"Why'd she get sent with her aunt?"

Bea took a drink of her coffee. "I was supposed to leave Selma a few weeks ago. It took a little longer than expected," she said, staring at him.

He sucked in a last drag of the cigarette and smashed it out on the empty plate. "I'm happy for you," he said, reaching beneath the table and touching her knee.

"Angie'll loan me something, not much probably, but anything's better than nothing."

He ate the last sliver of toast and nudged the plate to the edge of the table. He opened his wallet and pulled out a single dollar.

"If Alex was around I'd ask him too," Bea carried on. "He's not the type to ask a bunch of questions either." She looked up. "You think twenty-five bucks will get us far? I mean if we hitch mostly, and get a room here and there, eat like we're eating now. How far do you think that'll get us, honey?"

He crammed his wallet into his back pocket. "Have you ever done any traveling in the states?"

She shook her head.

"Nowhere?"

"Why are you asking?"

"Because twenty-five bucks isn't anything to sneeze at, but it'll only get us so far." He calculated in his mind. "But if we're smart about things, and do like you say, we might make Denver. There's plenty of work there. And we could scrape together a few bucks and that'll get us the rest of the way to New York."

The waitress swiped the single bill from the table and charged off without a word. Bea lifted the cup to her lips and drank the last of her coffee. "I swear that tastes like it's been strained through a boot." She pushed the cup to the edge of the table.

"Twenty-five would be something," Jack nodded. "I've made it farther on less."

After breakfast they trekked out toward the east side. They climbed aboard the dinkey that hobbled over the First Street bridge and got off at the Evergreen Cemetery. They trudged up the slope toward City Terrace, zigzagging the narrow roads, past the cramped houses on Boulder, then Malabar Street, until finally they reached Blanchard. Bougainvillea vines scaled the overhangs of front porches and clawed their way from fence to fence. In every yard a cactus and, tied to it, a dog of one kind or another.

On one corner was Antonio's Market. It was a hole-in-the-wall five-and-dime, painted adobe orange. A couple of mustachioed men stood out front, drinking their pop and eyeing them suspiciously. Bea and Jack stopped a few houses away from Angie's.

"You should wait over there," Bea said, shifting her eyes in the direction of the men. Jack glanced over and the men lifted their heads at him. She primped her hair with her fingertips. "How do I look?"

He nodded his approval. "I'll be right here," he said, pecking her cheek and starting off. From across the street he watched her enter the rickety front gate and saunter up the pathway to the steps of the house. Before she went on up she looked back at him and waved. The men got into their truck and sped away, stuttering up the road in a cloud of exhaust. After that the neighborhood was mostly quiet. Jack stood out front for a few minutes and smoked a cigarette. A German shepherd emerged from an alleyway and moseyed over to him and sniffed his leg. It was a big dog, and its ribs were almost visible through its fur. He clicked his tongue at the animal and it shrank back. He knelt low to the ground and tried calling it over, but it turned its nose away and bolted. Jack looked up and saw that Bea had entered the house. Down the street a radio blared and a black DeSoto came into sight. As it crept along toward him, he got a bad feeling, so he dropped his cigarette on the pavement and went into Antonio's.

The store was a matchbox. Nothing but two small aisles and a large, buzzing Frigidaire. The clerk behind the counter stood up from his chair.

"Something you need?"

Jack shook his head slightly and made his way to the Frigidaire. He opened the heavy door and had a look inside. The clerk leaned over and didn't let the stranger out of his sight. After a minute, Jack let the door slap shut. From the small window next to the Frigidaire, he could see Angie's house clearly. The clerk folded his arms.

"What're you looking for?"

Jack waved him off and kept his gaze out the window.

"You gonna buy something or you just come here to stand by my icebox?"

Jack made his way to the counter. "You Antonio?"

"Who wants to know?"

"Just making friendly conversation is all."

"No," he replied. "I'm his son. Antonio died."

Jack dug in his pocket for some loose change, and then poked his finger over the stacks of chewing gum. "And you got the place?"

"Something like that," the man replied. He sat down on his stool and scratched at a scab on his elbow. Jack pulled a stick of gum out and placed a penny on the counter. The man angled his eyes out the window and nodded.

Across the street they spotted Bea walking down the steps of the house with Angie nipping close behind. She was waving her arms furiously, and Bea slammed the gate shut behind her. She looked back and howled something at her sister, and Angie went stomping back into the house. Bea dashed across the street, and when she got to the sidewalk she stopped to adjust her blouse before entering the store. The man clicked a small radio on and messed with the tuner. Static spilled out; he smacked it with the butt of his hand and tried tuning it again.

Bea entered the store and took Jack by the arm. "Patsy ain't there, can you believe that?" The look in her eyes was panic.

He led her to the back of the store.

"She says Patsy's with her godmother, of all the people! Why would she leave her with Beto's sister?" She put her hand to her forehead and looked away. The man behind the counter smiled at Bea. "Hey, Junior," she said.

Junior looked down and continued messing with his radio.

"Where's the woman live?"

"She's way out in Long Beach. We can't get there on foot." Bea's breath grew short, and he could see the hue of blood draining from her face.

"Calm down," he said, pulling her body into him.

"She knows about you."

"How's that?"

She pulled away. "Said she saw us walking up the street together from her window."

Jack laughed.

"It ain't funny. She's mad at me. You shoulda heard what she was saying, acting like everything's my fault. Like I'm the one choosing this. I can't believe her."

Junior looked up from his radio and let out a phony cough. Bea glared over at him.

"Let's get outta here, honey."

They walked back through the Evergreen Cemetery and found an old marble bench and sat down. They didn't speak for several minutes.

Far to the east, hanging somewhere above the Mojave Desert, a sliver of day moon could be seen. Over toward the west, beyond the Los Angeles River, bearing down on the Pacific Ocean, the red sun wavered against a wall of blue clouds. They sat there, quiet. Each to their own thoughts. Jack watched the pigeons hopping across the lawn, pecking off insects and feasting on crumbs.

Nearby, a man and three children were knelt down over a small stone, wiping it off with their bare hands, whispering to the ground. Bea chewed on the web of skin between her thumb and index finger, and filed through a short list of friends she had in Los Angeles. She knew none of them were in any kind of position to loan her money. No one was. She stopped picking at her thumb and stared at Jack, who was now squatting beneath a tree, clicking his tongue at a few pigeons. He knelt down and tried enticing one over with a few pebbles in his hand. The bird waddled within a foot before catching on and turning away. Jack dusted his hands off on his thighs.

"I say we go to New York, Jackie, money or no money."

He glanced at Bea and then eyed the length of the cemetery.

"You said it yourself," she pressed. "We don't need money to hitch, right? I mean if folks are going a certain way anyhow it's not like we hafta put in on gas." She stood up. "You said it yourself, didn't you? The sooner we get on with it the better. Well, I'm dying to get on with it. I can't tell you how bad I wanna leave this town, I just can't stand it anymore. Everything's gone to hell." Her eyebrows flexed and she turned away. "I swear to God, if it weren't for the kids I would've left a long time ago. I would've. But I just can't do this anymore, Jackie. Do you know how that feels?" She waited for him to respond. "I know it ain't that easy, I know that, but you don't know me well enough yet. I mean I can handle myself pretty good."

He propped his hands on his belt and tried to get a good read on her.

"You're serious, aren't you?"

"We can hit Denver first, just like you said. Then New York. What do you say?"

He let out a sigh, and then threw both hands in the air. "Fine by me. You wanna hitch to New York, hell, let's go then."

She smiled, and a quiet certainty settled around her eyes. And the more he thought about it, the more it made sense. He took her hand and they started up the road together.

"We'll have to hurry before it gets dark. It's impossible to find a ride if they can't see you."

In less than an hour they raced through the narrow streets, away from the cemetery and back through Boyle Heights, over the bridge, and across Central Avenue, right on through the lobby of the Duke Hotel. The whole way, Bea rambled.

"Once we get to New York, honey, we'll have to find work right away. I can't live without my babies for too long, alright? I'll need to send for 'em soon as I have enough saved. I bet little Al's gonna love New York. I can see him already. He's gonna be crazy when I tell him about it. I can just see his little face."

"We gotta hit Denver, though, I mean a few days there is what we'll need."

"Sure, honey. I think I'll love Denver."

"Hand me those bags," he said, taking them from her grip and slinging them over his shoulder. They rushed down the stairs and stepped out into the waning light, hustling along until they could hear the whirr of traffic spinning out from the Golden State Freeway. To Jack it was an all-too-familiar sound, like the opening note of a favorite song. His eyes darted across the complex tangle of on and off ramps, looking for a good spot for a pick-up. Bea followed along closely, shadowing his every move, trying hard to hear his voice through the flood of a thousand engines blowing past. In the rapidly dimming light of a Tuesday evening rush hour, she stood next to him along the shoulder of the highway, entranced by the hum of unlimited directions.

15

They caught their first ride with a square couple who bickered about which way was the best route to Monrovia. The husband argued it was up through Pasadena, but the wife refused to believe it was quicker than El Monte.

"El Monty," the man sneered. "You gotta be kidding me!"

She slumped back in her seat and rolled her eyes at Bea and Jack.

They let them off in Arcadia, dropping the two right at the edge of the narrow shoulder. A delivery truck sounded its horn as it swerved past, and the husband gripped the steering wheel with both hands and shot off into the traffic.

Bea struggled with her bags while Jack shouted for her to back away from the road. The 210 freeway was chaotic. Jack grabbed their bags in both hands. "No one's going to stop for us here, we need to move further out." They treaded up the road, pushing against a stiff headwind pouring in from Mt. Baldy.

When they reached the Colorado Place turnoff, they slumped their bodies down for a rest and worked out a plan. Jack would stand off the shoulder, out of sight, while Bea acted as the lure. It seemed simple enough, and Bea agreed to it. She stayed put while he took the bags and hiked down a slope of shrubs. He found a spot about a hundred feet away and gave her a thumb's up. "Go on," he hollered. She could barely hear his voice over the noise. She put up her best smile and stuck her thumb out. A delivery truck moaned past, and the wind whipped her hair across her face and she pulled it away from her eyes. She lifted her hand again and up went her narrow thumb. Faces zipped past and eyes glanced back at her, curious to see a brown woman, alone and fearless in the American night. She leveled her small shoulders face-to-face with traffic and stood on her tiptoes and waved robustly. Jack delighted seeing her take to the road the way she did. She looked back at him, and he signaled for her to keep her eyes peeled.

"Back off a little," he hollered. His guts were in knots; as inexperienced as she was, he wondered if they should trade roles. He clenched his teeth. "Back off, Bea!" he shouted. He cursed himself for agreeing to this, but it was the only real shot they had. He pulled a cigarette from his coat pocket and struck a match and was silenced by the sight of Bea's small frame against the backdrop of a graying sky.

After thirty minutes had passed, they both felt sporadic droplets of water grow to a steady sprinkle. It was near dark now, and headlights flickered against a glowing veil of mist. Jack looked up and saw a sheet of heavy clouds laboring in from beyond the San Gabriel Mountains. He quickly hefted up the bags and hiked over to her.

"What's the problem, baby?"

He scratched at his ear. "This ain't gonna work. We gotta find shelter."

She looked up at the sky. "It's not too bad yet. Let me try a little more."

"You sure?"

She pulled her hair back with one hand. Her determination was unsettling.

"Alright then." He clutched the bags and retreated down the slope.

She stood once again, staring into the oncoming lights. "Geezus," she mumbled to herself, "One of you has gotta have heart enough to stop." She stuck both hands in the air and let the light rain have its way with her face. Thunder snapped in the distance, and a few minutes later both her arms glistened against the parade of headlights.

"Back off, Bea, you're standing too close," Jack shouted, gripping his temple. She ignored him. He ambled quickly up the incline after her. He grabbed her sleeve and pulled her away from the shoulder.

"Are you mad!"

She yanked her arm away and glared at him. He stood frozen for a second. "Listen," he said, "this rain isn't doing us any good. We'll try again later, once it's passed."

She stood defiantly. But only for a minute. Reluctantly, she followed him down the slope.

"How long you figure the rain'll last?"

"How the hell should I know? That's the thing about hitching."

"What's that?"

"You give up the privilege of knowing certain things. It's the knowing that makes a person feel like they got a grip on something. But, really, there's nothing to hold on to. I mean, what the hell does anyone know about anything?"

They sat beneath the freeway overpass waiting for the rain to stop. She rested her head on his shoulder, and they listened to the steady downpour. The clouds spilled in from over the mountain peaks and crawled out toward Los Angeles. An hour later the sky was black and flecked with the pinholes of a billion stars. Only a light sprinkling hovered. Jack's stomach grumbled, and he jammed his hand against his ribs to stifle the sound.

"You hungry?"

"I'll be alright," he replied, digging in his coat pocket for a smoke. He pulled the pack out and discovered it was empty. He crushed it in his fist and flung it to the ground.

"Know what I do whenever little Al's hungry and I don't have much for 'im?" Jack folded his arms over his knees.

"We play this little game, see," she lay back on the concrete, "where we lay ourselves face down, on a mattress of course, and then we take our fists and put 'em underneath our stomachs so it feels like we got something there." Jack watched her as she balled up both hands and placed them on her stomach. "Then I tell him to shut his eyes and imagine the best meal he's ever eaten in his whole life, his most favorite thing ever. He loves this part. I tell him, imagine a whole table full of whatever it is." Bea sat up and looked into Jack's eyes. "He always goes for the junk. Pies and cookies, stuff like that, but it makes him happy." She grew quiet. "You know, Jackie, as long as I tell myself this is just temporary, I feel okay about going, you know, about leaving the kids."

"Yep, temporary is right."

She peered up at him and took hold of his arm, then rested her head against him.

He thought about the breakfast at Clifton's that morning. "If I'd have known it was going to be our only meal I would've asked for the works," he said, half joking. He palmed at the wallet in his back pocket.

"Grab your stuff." He stood up and slung the duffel over his shoulder.

"Where we going?"

"We gotta figure out plan B."

They shimmied down from underneath the overpass and started up Colorado Place. In the distance, a billboard glowed: *Pines Coffee Shop.*

They went in and set their bags down at a booth, and Bea disappeared into the ladies room. A waitress brought two cups of black coffee and placed them on the table, along with a menu. Bea returned with her hair pinned back and a fresh coat of lipstick on. She eyed the coffee. "Can we afford these, Jackie?" she whispered, lifting a cup to her lips and blowing off the steam.

He flagged the waitress down, and when she came over he handed back the menu and glanced at Bea. "We're gonna have two plates of fried eggs, some of those country-style hashed browns, and two sides of toast with butter." The waitress jotted the order into her notepad and took the menus and headed toward the kitchen.

"How much money have we got, honey?"

He spilled a handful of sugar cubes into his cup and twirled the spoon. He stopped and took a sip of his coffee.

"Jackie?"

He lifted an eyebrow at her. "You're just gonna have to trust me on some things, baby." He took another sip. "Things have a way of working themselves out. I can't explain it but they do. For now we gotta fuel up or we'll never make New York."

"What next?"

He leaned back in his seat and scraped his hand over his unshaven jaw. He rolled his head side to side and then looked out the window and took another sip. She could see him turning ideas over in his mind. His look was stolid and focused.

She thought about calling Alex and seeing if maybe he'd wire her some money, but she knew very well that he was hardly making enough to stay afloat in the first place. Plus, she didn't feel right putting him in that position, knowing that if her father found out, he'd take it out on him. After sitting like this for nearly fifteen minutes, she felt Jack's eyes fixed on her from across the table.

"What is it, Jackie?"

He sat up and leaned in close. "I think I have an idea," he said. "I mean, it's a possibility at least. But you gotta hear me out on this before you say anything, alright?"

She sat up straight. The waitress arrived with their meals, and a delicious steam wafted up from their plates and lassoed their attention for a second.

"Go on," she said.

Jack unfolded his napkin and placed it on his thigh. "Before we can really hit the road, even if we hitch, there's gotta be some change in order to last us, right? It don't have to be much at all, but damn, anything is better than what we have now. Wouldn't you agree?"

She speared some eggs into her mouth.

He took a forkful of potatoes and stuffed it between his teeth before continuing. "Of course, seems like all of L.A.'s on permanent vacation." He spoke through his food. "So, here's what I'm proposing. Now remember, you gotta hear me out on this."

"Go on already," she said, jabbing her fork at him.

"Now suppose, just suppose, we head back over those mountains and into that valley of yours—" She felt her stomach turn over. "Stay with me now, baby. Say we head back to Selma, alright, work a little there, just enough for some food money and two tickets east, that's it. Suppose we do that first, then hit the road." He dropped his fork and took her hands in his. "Listen, Bea, two tickets, I'd say run thirty, maybe forty bucks. Food money, another twenty, easy. We'd only have to stick around long enough to earn a good sixty bucks, then we blow outta that place, and then it's New York bound."

Bea pulled her hands away and slumped back in her seat. She looked out the window. The rain was fading, and strings of water dribbled down the glass. Minutes passed while she wrestled with her thoughts. She watched him chew his food and bat his blue eyes like it was a decision that hardly needed any pondering. He sipped his coffee and waited for her to respond. She pushed her plate away and started to open her mouth to speak, but then hesitated.

"Two weeks," she muttered.

Jack leaned back in his seat.

"That's how long it'll take to make that kind of money, picking." Her voice was tepid, gray. "But I'm asking myself, right now, if I got it in me to last two weeks, back in that hole. Fourteen days. God." She shook her head. "You just have no idea, Jack. None at all. Fourteen days might as well be all of goddamn eternity." She glared at him. "I'd rather strike out on nothing."

"It's impossible, Bea, trust me on that."

She lowered her chin and stared at the table. Her eyes flexed.

"What's your worry?"

A faint ray of lightning flashed in the distance. She breathed deeply through her nose.

"It took him half a day to find me one time. That's it. Not even twenty-four hours. I was in the next county over, about sixty miles, and he knew exactly where I was. I made sure none of his friends saw me, didn't even tell little Albert where I was going. I had it all planned out, was leaving him once and for all. This was two years ago, if you can believe that. I was sick for weeks trying to figure out how the hell he knew where I was. Just who did I know that coulda given me up like that. I only told two people, my mom and my brother Alex, and neither woulda said a word. I went crazy trying to figure that one out." She dropped the fork and it fell beneath the table. "It was my ol' man. Yeah, my father, if you can believe that. He told Beto where I was. Beto said he didn't even hesitate, just gave me right up. There's just no way." She stopped talking and decided it was enough. The waitress came by and refilled their coffees. Bea placed her hands at her sides and looked away. Jack took another sip of his coffee and stared at her for several minutes. In that time, she could feel the fire draining from her throat. Another minute passed and now she was picturing herself at the end of those two long weeks.

"Everyone there talks. The whole valley's got eyes, and big ol' mouths too. You gotta know that." Even as she was saying this, she couldn't believe it was coming from her own mouth. "We stay in the camps, I mean in our own tent, and get outta there in two weeks. That would be the only way. But Jack, if we do this, I'm getting little Al. I mean, we go back there it's 'cause I'm getting my baby too. Then back through L.A. we'll stop for Patsy."

"Might be easier if we get to New York first, then send for the kids once we're settled. Wasn't your brother handling them?"

"I can't put that on Alex, Jack."

"No, of course not. Alright then, we'll make it work."

He reached across the table and lifted her hands and kissed her fingers.

"You know, Bakersfield isn't such a bad idea either," she said. "I know this family there, old friends of my folks. I bet they'd know of some work. Besides, it's close enough to Selma, and at least we won't have to deal with anyone."

"Fine by me," he said, picking up his fork and polishing off his meal. He pulled a napkin across his mouth.

"We might even see about working in Lamont."

"Where's that?"

"Near Bakersfield, right up against the foothills. You can go up there and practically look down at the whole valley. It's a sweet little place. I think they got a hoover there too, if I'm not mistaken."

He squinted.

"It's a labor camp, just a bit fancier is all. Small houses is what they really are, but they got running water and bathrooms. It's nicer than Selma's, that's for sure. Not like I need a hoover, just would be nice is all. Two weeks would be a snap in a place like that."

Jack wedged a toothpick in his teeth and a contentment fell over him. "The San Joaquin Valley," he said. A curious smile spanned the width of his face.

The waitress shuffled past and dropped the bill down on the table. Jack turned the piece of paper over.

"Three sixty eight?" Bea said in a low voice. "That's robbery. A plate like this, two coffees, no way it comes to that."

He reached for his back pocket, and just then Bea saw his mouth straighten and his eyes go dull. He checked his front pockets and then patted his coat.

"Did I hand you my wallet?"

She shook her head.

He cussed under his breath and stood up near the table and checked the mouth of the seat. "Shit, last I checked I had it. You sure I didn't give it to you?"

"Quit playing around, honey."

He pulled his duffel up onto the seat and rifled through it. "Fuck," he muttered.

She noticed the waitress staring at them from behind the counter. "Jackie, sit down, honey, the lady's watching us."

He clipped his bag shut and sat down and looked Bea in the eye. The waitress walked over to the table. "Can I get somethin' for you?" Jack coughed into his fist, while Bea averted her eyes toward the sugar dispenser.

"No ma'am," he replied. She began to walk away. "Uh, miss," he called after her, "on second thought, yeah, can we get some flapjacks . . . and uh, another plate of eggs." She glanced over at Bea before heading back to the kitchen.

"What're you doing, Jack?"

He scanned the coffee shop, eyeing the few patrons that were strewn about, elderly folks mostly. The place was sparse. The only real threat was a large man seated at the counter.

"Hand me your bags."

She fumbled with the straps. "Jackie?" She passed them beneath the table. He looked toward the kitchen.

"Listen, Bea, don't go thinking wrong of me, alright? Remember what I said, about their being nothing to hold on to?" She looked confused. "Listen, just do exactly as I tell you."

Her palms turned clammy. "Jackie, geezus Christ—" He hushed her and she fired back in a whisper. "What are you asking me to do?"

He wound both bag handles around his left fist, then took hold of his duffel in the right and inched to the edge of the seat. "I'm the only one of us who'll be breaking the law, you hear me? All you've got to do is walk out when I tell you." Bea took a drink of water. "See that building across the way?" Jack nodded his head toward the parking lot. She shifted her eyes. "When I give the word, you just walk out the front door and aim straight for the back of that building. Don't look back either, just walk right out and hurry over. But don't run, just walk fast, otherwise you'll draw attention to yourself."

"Why don't we just explain to the lady that you lost your wallet?"

"She's liable to call the cops, you saw how she's been eyeing us since we walked in. That hag's just waiting for an excuse."

Bea took a quick nibble at the skin of her thumb before scooting closer to the edge of her seat.

"You ready?"

She angled her legs out from under the table and positioned herself. They stole one last glance at the kitchen and could see bodies shuffling about.

"Go on," he whispered, shifting his eyes from the kitchen to Bea and back to the kitchen. "Hurry."

She stood up and headed for the door. Her small slender legs pumped eagerly and she wanted to look back at Jack but kept on, just as he'd told her to. When thinking back on that moment later, years later, all she would remember is sitting at that table and then suddenly, almost miraculously, finding herself in an alleyway. The rest, she'd recall, felt something like flight.

When she exited, the small bell that was tied to the door handle rang out, and a second later the waitress emerged from the kitchen. She spotted Bea through the window, walking away, and she called out to Jack.

"Where's your girlfriend off to?"

He gripped at the bags and pretended not to hear.

"I'm talking to you."

"What's that?"

"Where's that one off to?"

"She's coming back," he said.

"Yeah, well those flapjacks'll be up in a minute."

He nodded and turned his eyes toward the window. He could see Bea skirting across the parking lot and eventually turning the corner of a building until she was no longer in sight. The waitress shuffled around the café collecting dirty dishes. Jack's foot bounced with anticipation. She made her way to the kitchen, and when the door swung shut behind her he leapt up and made a beeline for the door. Hearing the bell clang behind him, he lifted the bags above his head and bolted across the pavement at full speed. The adrenaline surged from his chest to his feet, and his legs pumped fast and haphazardly. He glanced over his shoulder, and when he did he saw the waitress emerging from the kitchen and staring at the empty table. His duffel slipped from his grip and he fumbled with it, but was able to hang on long enough, until he turned the corner of the building. He dropped both bags to the ground and caught his breath. He peeked around the corner and could see the waitress waving her arms at a short bald man who must've been the manager. He turned back toward the alleyway and called out for Bea.

"Baby?" he whispered loudly.

An opossum stirred behind a stack of crates; he watched it scale a pine tree and amble its way along a telephone wire. "Bea?" He felt a pinch in his side and gripped his rib for a minute. He could hear voices coming from the direction of the diner. He took another look. The waitress and the bald man were standing out front, tangled up in an argument. He turned back to the alley and was about to call for Bea again, when he saw her step out from behind the pine tree. There was a quiet and removed look in her eyes. He threw his hands up and went to her, grinning.

"Promise you won't be mad, Jackie," she said, barely able to look at him.

He stopped where he was. "Mad?" He continued walking toward her. "It was my idea, wasn't it?" He went to wrap his arms around her but she wedged her purse between them. Confusion settled around his eyes. She reached inside her purse.

"Bea—" he began saying.

She pulled her hand out, and he could see that she held something. He looked again and recognized his wallet.

He lifted his hands in the air, then let them fall at his sides. He took another step toward her, and then stopped again and ran his fingers through his hair. "You had it all along?"

She'd never felt so distant from him as she did right then. She nodded subtly. He tilted his head back and looked straight up at the sky, as if asking something of the universe. She moved closer to him, until she was only a few inches away, close enough so that parts of their bodies grazed one another. He lowered his gaze and tried making something out in the depth of her eyes. She wanted to say something but felt it was pointless. He took the wallet and crammed it into his back pocket. Small noises scuttled among the trash cans, and somewhere nearby they could hear voices again, laughter.

"Jackie," she said, fastening her arms around his waist and pressing her ear to his chest. "I don't want you thinking I'm a thief 'cause I'm not like that." He kept his arms at his sides. "I was just looking out for our money is all. Really, honey, I swear." She looked up at him. "You believe me, don't you?" She hesitated. "You trust me, Jackie?"

She thought she saw him nod. The clouds had returned, and a sprinkle of rain began to fall again. She waited for him to say something. She kept her ear to his chest and stared off at the gray haze of lights glowing over Los Angeles. "Jackie?" she said, an exhausted lilt in her voice. His silence was unnerving. She held him tighter. It went on for another minute. A moment later his hand rose up and rested on the back of her neck. His other hand met up with it. He anchored his chin on the crown of her head, and she buried her face deeper into the fibers of his coat. She thought she heard something that sounded like a chuckle. She looked up and saw his mouth bent slightly upward, and there it was again. He couldn't help himself. A spurt of laughter seeped from his lips. She laughed too, and had to press her mouth into his chest to stifle the sound.

II

The San Joaquin Valley

16

Wednesday, October 15, 1947

A wave of clunky trucks and old wagons spilling with families flooded Interstate 5 and washed back down over Tejon Pass, winding their way toward the open cusp of the Grapevine and pouring down onto the flat valley floor. When their bus leveled out, the air was wet with low clouds glommed up at the Tehachapi ridge, where the great tule fog sprouted and laid itself down over the valley like an immense ball of soggy cotton. Entering from the south end of Bakersfield, they could see the wilted peaks of canvas tents jutting up from the campos beyond the cotton fields. They passed a sign that read *Weedpatch Highway*, and Jack turned giddy and pointed it out. "Has to be the Weedpatch of that good ol' Steinbeck book," he said. Bea shrugged her shoulders and enjoyed watching him grow kid-like over it.

Even though she couldn't taste it, just looking at the sky, knowing the air held a distinct combination of mud and ferment, made her cringe and want to reconsider the whole thing. She recalled the last conversation she'd had with little Al, while she was bathing him.

"Mijo, you know that whenever mama leaves, she always comes back, right?"

"You leaving again?"

"No, I'm just saying, that if I ever do leave, you know I'll come back, don't you?"

"I know."

The look on his face was of disappointment.

Passing the open fields and irrigation banks, she thought about the two weeks ahead, and it seemed like an eternity. She wondered if Angie had already spread the word about her being with Jack, and if so, if it had reached the campo yet. Which is to say, had it reached her father yet. She tugged at the skin of her thumb and peered out the window, suddenly grateful for the cloak of fog. She touched the window and it was practically ice.

"We'll be lucky if everything ain't frozen," she said to Jack. "It isn't like the summer. Summer there's all kinds of work. But late October is tough. Only thing bad about summer is the heat. Last year a little girl died from it."

Jack took Bea's hand in his and continued listening.

"She must've been sixteen barely, pregnant too. Laid right beneath a row of grapes and never got up. Guess she fell behind, that'll happen if you aren't quick enough, you just get left behind. I mean you have the mayordomo saying stuff like *el tiempo es oro*—time is money—and so everyone just moves on without you." She stared down into her hands. "When they found that poor girl, she was folded up over her belly, just like a baby herself. Couldn't have been there more than an hour, but by the time another worker found her she was dead. They said her tongue was swollen, that's what happens when you don't get enough water you know. That's one thing about working the fields, you gotta drink lots of water, so you gotta pee a lot too, and they don't have outhouses, except maybe one, and it's always too far away so you gotta squat under a bush or something. They said that's what she was doing when she passed out. Worse thing is they said her mouth was parted open, like she'd been trying to call out for help."

"A damn shame," Jack whispered, unfolding his arms and pushing himself up in his seat.

"Only reason I'm telling you this, honey, is 'cause that's just how it is here, and I don't want there to be any surprises. Sure we're gonna make money, but the valley just isn't pretty."

He gave the passengers a once-over and noticed how they looked exactly the same as the last time he passed through these parts. Same old Mexican with cowboy hat. Same Japanese brothers slouched against one another. Same family with worried eyes huddled in the back. He glanced at Bea with a subtle complacency on his face.

"To think we'll be back east in a few weeks, though." Her eyes shimmered. "I've always wanted say *back east*. Isn't that what people there call it?"

"Sure do," Jack replied.

The bus blew past a gas station where clusters of vehicles had just come off the long drive from places like Blythe and Deming, New Mexico. Men tinkered beneath propped hoods while moms and kids stood around and watched their breath curl up in the chill. They passed tiny motels that looked as if they'd been put together from matchboxes, and then railroad tracks emerged and sidled along the highway; miles down the road, houses and buildings cropped up, and before long a stop sign appeared at every corner. The bus shifted gears and belched down the main strip that was Union Avenue, inching past boutique windows and giant billboards for Maison Jassaud's place, advertising *Marx Brothers Live, Tonite!*

She pulled lipstick from her purse and dabbed some on. He watched her apply a few quick strokes and then pinch her cheeks until the blood rose just beneath the surface.

"Why haven't you written in your little notebook today, honey?" she asked, jamming her makeup back into her purse.

"I wrote some last night," he said, "when you were asleep."

"You ever gonna share any of it with me?"

He smirked and patted his pockets for a cigarette. The bus jerked to a stop, then jerked again and continued on.

"Can I ask you something, Jackie?"

"Sure," he said.

"All that writing in your notebook, does it help you remember things?"

"Of course it does. I can come back to it whenever I feel like."

She closed her purse and placed it on her lap. "I write letters all the time, mostly to my sister Angie. She keeps 'em in her underwear drawer, but never looks at 'em again. I tell her what's the point? I mean, why keep something like that if you aren't ever gonna look at it again?"

"I can't say for Angie, but I can tell you that's how a writer gets things down. Not sure why anyone else might keep a letter if they aren't going to look at it ever again."

Bea thought for a moment. "But if you write something in one of your books about me, shouldn't I get to see it too? I mean, what if someone a hundred years from now sees it? They could think all sorts of stuff about me going by what you say, couldn't they?"

The bus loped over a curb and pulled into the station. Jack shifted in his seat and watched the rest of the passengers filing out. He turned to Bea. "Yeah, I guess they could. Depending on what it is I say about you, sure." He stood up in the aisle, then took hold of her bags and offered his hand. Seconds later they stepped off the bus and out into the frigid air. He pulled his jacket off and draped it over her shoulders, and without uttering a word they walked across Nineteenth Street, past the barber shop and the empty lot, and past Hank's Place, where it seemed like only yesterday they'd crossed paths as strangers.

They started the long trek across town, toward the east side, where the family that Bea knew lived. Driven by the possibility of work and a bite to eat, they huffed along at a steady pace, crossing one intersection after the next: Kern, Baker, Kentucky Street. They passed a string of people eating popcorn and standing in line beneath a theater marquee announcing *La Diosa Arrodillada*, the names *María Félix* and *Arturo de Córdova* emblazoned in red neon. They hurried on, skipping the pool halls and inching toward St. Joseph's Church, where they stopped to sit down on the steps. Jack took his shoe off and gave his heel a rub, while Bea went over to the rose garden and stood before a statue of the Virgin Mary. Quietly, without Jack knowing, she shut her eyes and mumbled the tiniest prayer. She thought of Angie, and how smug she'd be to see her sister at that moment pleading for a little faith to trickle back into her life. They hitched their bags up and continued on, cutting north, over the tracks and up a long slope, past Niles Street and up Haley.

It was still afternoon when they entered the barrio. All morning the sun had been trying to plow a rut through the fog but had fallen short. Their stomachs rumbled when they hit a wall of aroma that sailed out from all the tiny kitchen windows and collided in the middle of the street. A group of kids were kicking an empty soup can and hollering at one another in high-strung voices. Jack took it all in.

"Sure smells good, don't it?" she said.

They walked a few more blocks, cutting through an empty lot and shuffling along the banks of an irrigation ditch, past houses and narrow streets.

"I think that's it," Bea said, starting off toward a yard with a sagging wooden fence. Jack dragged their bags behind, and a few neighbor kids looked on.

A woman in overalls stepped out onto a porch and shouted, "Javier!" A short chubby kid peeled away from the group and went to her. From the corner of his eye, Jack watched as they vanished into the house.

When they reached the front yard, Bea turned to him. "Wait here, alright?"

He dropped the bags and was glad to sit down and do nothing at all. She went around the back yard and didn't emerge again for an hour. At one point Jack wondered if he should go find her. Evening was slowly setting in and bodies had begun to populate the streets. He grew uncomfortable at all the passing eyes glaring at him. He wished he had a cigarette. A whole box of them. He pulled his notebook out from his duffel and passed the time jotting things down. He observed the dirt-ridden yards and patchy lawns. The famished dogs barking at the fattened chickens that roosted on the tops of roofs and cars. He saw a truck down the street letting out a half-dozen workers, women and men, toting lunchboxes and canteens, hats back over weary faces and proud twinkling eyes. A chorus of *Ahí nos vemos* and *Hasta mañana* buzzed in the air. Like clockwork they kicked mud off their shoes and headed inside, where he imagined a humble feast was in the making. Peasant life, he said to himself, the real deal. He sharpened his pencil against the pavement and took note.

When Bea finally came out, she had a drag about her. He noticed this right off and put his notebook away, waiting for her to say something.

"You won't believe this," she mumbled.

He propped his elbows on his knees and spat.

"They've been picked up."

"What're you saying?"

"Deported. To Mexico."

He glanced over at the house, at the rickety door and broken shingles. A chicken coop made of busted fruit boxes sat barren in the front yard. Bea pulled a brown bag from her pocket. "The folks living here offered me some food, so I ate. Hope I wasn't too long, honey."

He lowered his head.

"These are for you."

He grabbed the bag and wasted no time tearing into it. He pulled off a chunk of tortilla and stuffed it in his mouth.

"These are the best damn things I've ever eaten," he said.

A truckload of workers putted past, and from the back a dozen or so long faces, women mostly, peered out. Bea nodded at them and a few heads nodded back.

She watched Jack finish off the last tortilla and stuff the paper bag into his pocket.

She rested her hands on her hips. "They were a nice family too. The man especially. He was friendly to us kids, always smiling, even when there wasn't much to smile about. I remember that about him. Wait'll Alex hears about this."

Jack picked at his teeth. "Now what?"

She looked back over her shoulder at the sun, which was now hanging like a cut of tangerine above the earth. "Let's head back into town, check out the spots over on Baker Street. Should be someone there who knows of some work."

The idea lifted Jack to his feet. He muscled the duffel onto his back and started up the road. Bea stood still for a few seconds and watched him walk away; she waited until he got nice and far before letting him know he was headed in the wrong direction. He laughed at himself, and two kids across the street laughed too and pointed. He waved at them and caught up to Bea, and together they cut through the winding barrio streets, racing the sun as they trudged further into the gut of Bakersfield.

When they reached Baker Street, it was six in the evening, and the tule fog had choked out the light entirely. Up and down the strip, regulars were congregating around the pool halls while fresh-faced solteros zigzagged in and out of flashy bars. Families with tired eyes rolled through on rickety trucks, eyeing the Saturday-night frenzy among the glowing window fronts, while the crabby Basque vendor whistled along, selling fried treats from the old country. Each face contained a varying degree of brown: Armenia, Guadalajara, even Retrop, Oklahoma, after a long summer.

Jack loomed in the shadows as Bea dodged in and out of doorways, hollering in Spanish at clusters of men, inquiring about work. One after another, they shook their heads no. A few names were given, but otherwise their efforts amounted to nothing but sore feet.

Down on their luck and feeling the nag of a mostly empty stomach, they started out toward the highway again, neither of them with enough spirit to lift a thumb. At the eastern rim of Bakersfield, lights from the Lame Duck Motel blinked against the fog, and with nothing more than a nod, they agreed on using their last few bucks for a room. A freshly painted sign hung above the entrance door:

NO MEXICANS, JAPS, OR OKIES

Bea grabbed Jack by the shirttail and ushered him to the back of the building.

"Hand me my stuff." She set her bags down on the floor and then fixed his duffel onto his shoulders. "Hurry on in and get us a room. Tell 'em you need something with a window, something out back."

He looked at Bea affectionately as she buttoned up his coat and straightened his collar. She ran her fingers through his hair quickly.

"What if they mistake me for an Okie?"

She laughed out loud. "They won't mistake you, trust me on that. They'll probably ask you where you're headed or something. People around here don't like stragglers either. Not even motels, if you can believe that."

"What should I tell 'em?"

"Well, don't you write stories? Make one up."

And with that he leaned over and kissed her on the forehead before starting off.

After a dinner of shelled peanuts, which she had lifted from one of the bars, and lukewarm water from the faucet, they enjoyed half a cigarette for dessert. Jack had pulled it from an ashtray on the office counter.

He unfolded a copy of the *Bakersfield Californian*, also swiped from the front desk, and fell on the bed and propped his head against the wall. Bea soaked in the tub while he read to her.

"Listen to this," he called out. "Says here in 1863, Colonel Thomas Baker himself, the man this town's named for, wrote in his diary," he changed his voice to that of an old man's, "This wide hunk of land could have well been lifted up from a cut of gray earth below the Mason-Dixon line, Harlan, Kentucky, perhaps. Yokut scalps now go for $5 a head, up from 25¢ just a year ago, and bloodshed now paints these tule marshes crimson. Indeed, history will always justify a man who means to do right, only right. God bless this sallow piece of earth which I myself can hardly step foot, for there is too much hardpan and gloom, like an aged matriarch who's lost everything but her last good breath . . . not much to the cultured eye, only good for two things really—gold and black gold." He fluttered the newspaper in his hands. "Wish we had us some of that gold right now."

The water from Bea's bath rippled and fell over the sides of the tub as she moved.

"Looks like they need two thousand hands up in Oregon to pick blueberries next month, guess it looks like Oregon's got this valley beat."

"I hate picking berries anyway," she called back.

"No wonder everyone around here's keeping their mouths shut. There's no work, Oregon's got it all."

"Wait'll we get to Selma, honey, there'll be work, just watch."

"Damn, I could use a drink," he said, turning the page and reading on.

"Tulare needs workers. Cattle ranching, says here. Looks like decent pay. Plus they got rooms."

"That ain't easy work, Jack. My brother Alex does that kinda stuff. You should see him. That kinda work will break you. What we need is some regular picking. Cotton might still be around. Walnuts for sure, those are in. Walnuts don't pay much but at least it's something."

"What about grapes? Didn't you say grapes were decent?"

He could hear her stepping out of the bathtub. "Yeah," she said, "if grapes are still around that's what we'll do. They can't all be picked yet."

She came out barefoot in a fresh set of clothes. Jack put his paper down and gazed at her, taking in the way the blackness of her hair contrasted her pale skin.

"I miss Patsy," she said, brushing out her tangles. "Just can't believe Angie would do such a thing. She knew I was coming, after all." She tugged at her hair viciously, then pulled a wad of loosened strands from the brush. She stood quiet. "I wonder if a kid can tell how long their mama's been gone." She cocked her head to one side and continued pulling the hairbrush through it. "Think they have a sense of time like that?"

"No, kids don't have any sense of time. Only adults are that dumb. Kids sleep and wake up when they're good and ready and that's it."

"Think when they see me again they'll feel like it's been an eternity?"

"How long's it been?"

"Not long really." She stopped brushing her hair and looked at Jack. "I know it's only been about a week since you and I been together but it sure feels longer, don't it?"

He looked up from the paper. Bea tossed the hairbrush onto her bags and made her way to the bed.

"First thing I'm gonna do when we get to Selma, honey, is make you a real Mexican meal." Jack moaned. "Spanish rice, refried beans, more of those tortillas you like so much. A cold beer. Don't that just sound good?"

"Are you trying to kill me? I can't think of food right now, it'll drive me nuts."

"You wanna go to sleep already? What time is it anyhow?"

"I've no idea, the fog's got me mixed up."

She lay down beside him and kept to her thoughts for a few minutes. "I've been thinking, Jack, about us picking and all that. Have you ever done this kind of work? I know you said you don't mind doing it, but . . ."

"I've done my share of hard labor, not picking necessarily, but I'm no stranger to getting my hands dirty if that's what you're asking." He ruffled his paper. She decided to change the subject.

"Tell me about New York, honey, would you? What'll the plan be when we're there?"

He let the paper drop to the floor and rolled on his side to face her. "Where will we stay?" she asked, a serious expression on her face.

"I know plenty of folks in the city, decent people we might be able to stay with."

"What about your mom's place, can't we stay there?"

Jack shook his head. "Her place is too small, besides, we want to be in the middle of it all, don't we? That's where the action is. Empire State Building, Central Park, that's the New York I'm talking about."

Her eyes lit up.

"You're going to love it," he assured her. "Might never want to leave." He pushed a strand of hair away from her eyes.

"I can't wait, boy, I wish we were there already."

He ran his fingers over the arch of her hip. "You planning on seeing your old man, once we're back in Selma?"

She rolled over and looked up at the ceiling. "If he's around, I'll get little Al. Probably have to settle a few things too." She paused. "But I won't see him no more after that. Once we're off to New York I won't care if I ever see him again."

This put him at ease and he got beneath the blankets and pushed his body against hers. She placed her leg over his thigh and he drew her in closer, and then she shut her eyes and sighed.

"What is it?" he whispered.

"Promise me we won't stay in Selma more than two weeks, Jackie, can you promise me that? I'm just afraid we aren't gonna go anywhere like this. We need to find work right away."

He kissed the lobe of her ear gently. Once. Twice. Then her neck. "Tomorrow, baby," he said. "Tomorrow's gonna be our day."

17

Five minutes after they stepped out onto the frostbitten pavement of the Golden State Highway, a truck rattled to a stop. Jack heaved their bags into the back and they climbed in and cuddled up to one another for warmth. At the gate of the truck a brown speckled piglet rested in a cage. It stunk horribly, but even so, they couldn't help but smile, knowing that the day had already begun on a good note.

In the distance, mist hovered above the Kern River. Bea spotted a few egrets standing knee-deep in the water, and she pointed them out to Jack. He looked at them in silence. "Reminds me of the Merrimack," he said, a longing in his eye. The cold wind roared and was whipping Bea's hair, so she pulled her coat up over her head. Jack continued, "We used to fish a lot when I was a kid and we'd spot those birds everywhere. I can look at 'em all day. Kind of quiet, mostly keep to themselves." He eyed the egrets and the narrow river, while Bea fussed with her hair. "Hold me, honey," she said, drawing closer. He dragged his gaze over the land to the east, up near the Sierra Nevada foothills, near a wide bluff, and watched the oil pumps as they rose up, then bowed down to kiss the earth. They looked holy, he thought, ominous even, and he mentioned this to Bea. She observed them for a moment before a memory surfaced. "Don't know why, but they kind of remind me of the Indian ladies back in Irapuato." Her voice was low, and Jack had to put his ear closer to her mouth to hear. "They'd make these pilgrimages to El Templo, you know, they'd asked God for some big favor and then have to make good on their promise. So they'd walk miles on their knees, dressed in black, bowing and praying the whole way. Never saying a word to anyone." She paused. "I used to tell myself, man, I hope I never gotta ask for something that big, just couldn't imagine it."

The truck climbed a low hill and then sailed down and away as they watched Bakersfield disappear into the landscape. They rolled on, making good time, flying past the towns of Delano and Earlimart, stopping off in Pixley for gas. Bea went to see if the filling station had a restroom with hot water, but she returned a minute later unsuccessful. The tips of her fingers were glowing red. She climbed into the truck, and Jack, seeing the shape her hands were in, grabbed them and stuck them under his shirt against his skin.

"Woooo!" he cried out. She giggled. The gas station attendant shut the tank and shook his head at the two.

Forty-five minutes later they were climbing off the truck in Tulare. They waved good-bye to the driver, who didn't return the gesture, except to kick up mud as he set back out on the highway. Jack wondered why they'd call this the Golden State Highway when it had been nothing but a gray hue since the moment he laid eyes on it. Bea was too cold to come up with an answer.

They were about to sit down on their bags when out of the fog another truck appeared. It missed them at first, but then ambled onto the shoulder a hundred feet away. And if they hadn't felt lucky before, now they were certain that the universe was on their side. A Japanese man stuck his head out the window and yelled for them to get inside. He leaned over and unlocked the passenger door, and the heavy thing swung open.

"Get in!" he shouted. "Before you freeze to death!"

"Thank you, mister," Bea said, climbing into the cab and scooting over next to him. Jack jumped in and shut the door and the truck lurched forward.

"How long ya been out there?" the man asked, hassling with the gearshift.

"Not long," said Bea.

Hanging in the window behind them, mounted on a gun rack made of deer antlers, was a double-barreled shotgun. At every bump the truck lurched and the gun rattled. The man was wearing a cap with an American flag patch stitched on, and when he gripped the steering wheel, they saw a fuzzy tattoo on the back of his right hand that looked like a coat of arms. The man saw Bea's fingers; he reached into the armpit of his coat and pulled out a hot water bottle and passed it to her.

"Thank you," she said, cradling it like a baby.

"Where ya headed?"

"Selma," she replied.

"Unless you know of some work around here?" Jack added.

"Naw, ain't much around here. The freeze came in early, messed up a lot of crops. It's gonna be a short harvest this year. The oranges are done for but you might find a few grapes left. You say Selma's where you're headed?"

Bea nodded. She could feel her hands thawing out, and she passed the water bottle to Jack.

"That's probably the best place to find anything right now anyway," he said. "Selma's got plenty of grapes, that's for sure."

"Didn't I tell you, honey?"

"Where ya all from?"

"Los Angeles," Bea replied. "Selma too. But mostly Los Angeles."

"That's nice," said the man, lifting his cap off to scratch his bald head.

"I can get ya to Kingsburg, if that's alright?"

"We're grateful for any bit," she replied.

Jack noticed a small picture wedged into the radio dial. It was a military photo. The Japanese man dolled up in uniform, posing with a gun next to Old Glory. Bea noticed it too, and she wondered if it was a fake. She'd heard about how some guys, braceros usually, would get themselves military tags, or photos of them donning some soldier's coat, in hopes of avoiding being deported. It was pointless, she thought. She'd had yet to hear of any raid where some Juan was let go because of the tags dangling around his neck. But folks at the campo needed any bit of talisman they could get hold of, and she couldn't blame them for it. For the next twenty minutes Jack and Bea stared out the windshield at the long icy road unraveling before them.

When they finally reached Kingsburg they scraped together some change, and Bea made a call to Alex. He was busy, but promised to come get them before midnight. With nothing but a good ball of pocket lint between them, they arranged to meet up at the abandoned grain silo near the Conejo Street tracks. It was still daylight when they reached the place, and they sat down to a feast of four partially frozen oranges, a tangerine, and two pomegranates they'd plucked from a nearby grove.

The silos had been gutted at least twenty years past, when the tracks were relocated to make room for that part of the highway. Still, the whole place reeked of rancid chicken feed, and two decades of pigeon droppings had turned the ground white. When they were younger, Bea, Alex, and Angie used to follow the Kings River out to the silos, where they'd stay late into the night drinking a bottle of wine, or else smoking their father's rolled cigarettes. She pointed to the top, where a long iron catwalk jutted out over the domed peaks.

"We must've climbed this thing a million times," she said, angling her head back.

"How'd you get up there?"

"There used to be a ladder, but when the farmer found out we were getting up there he tore it down. Probably for the best, we used to get awful stupid up there." She held her gaze. "The best part of all was that you could see clear out to the ends of the valley, all the way up to Sacramento and clear down to the Grapevine. Around January, when those mountains got snow, you could see right up to Yosemite too," she said, pointing eastward.

The stink inside the structures was so bad that they had to wait outside for Alex. They pulled some garments from their bags and layered them on, hunkering against the walls of the silo and waiting for the night to pass.

"Sure wish we had a bottle of some of that wine," Bea said.

"No kidding," replied Jack, breathing warm air into his hands. A thick white cloud slipped through his fingers and sailed a few feet above his head and vanished. "You think your brother's going to be okay about me?"

Bea nodded. "You don't have to worry about Alex," she said. "He's gonna like you just fine."

"I take it he don't get along well with your old man?"

"Let's not talk about my old man, Jackie, I don't feel like thinking about any of that right now."

"It was just a question. I didn't mean anything by it."

"That's fine."

He lifted a rock up from the ground and hurled it at an irrigation pipe, and it rang out, stirring a family of black birds from a nearby tree.

18

Some time later Alex's truck bounced up the dirt road toward them. Bea asked Jack to wait behind while she spoke with her brother. When Alex pulled alongside the silos he saw her talking with a gabacho. And then he watched the guy duck beneath the shadow of the silo while she approached.

From his position, Jack could see Bea and Alex clearly through the rear window of the truck, and from that distance, he thought Alex looked like a nice enough guy. He was wearing a short-brimmed hat cocked on his head, and he had a cigarette in his mouth.

He saw too that Alex nodded calmly while Bea waved her hands out in front of him.

"Where we dropping this guy off?" Alex wanted to know.

"He's a friend, Alex, he's coming to work la pisca."

He looked over his shoulder, out the back window. "Bullshit."

"He is, I swear it. We're just friends is all."

Alex glanced back once more. Jack could see him now nodding at Bea. They exchanged a few more words, and then Bea looked at Jack and waved him over.

"Friends, you say?"

"That's right."

Jack lifted the bags and made his way to the truck.

"Just pray dad don't catch you with your *friend*," Alex remarked. Bea scooted over to make room. "Or Beto," he added, sucking his teeth. She rolled her eyes.

Jack tossed the bags into the bed and climbed into the truck.

"Alejandro Renteria," he said, sticking his thick hand out for the gabacho to shake. "Good to meet you."

"Same here. Name's Jack."

Alex reached over Bea's legs and unlatched the glove box. He pulled a bag of tobacco out and some rolling papers and flung them onto Jack's lap.

"Bet you could use a smoke?"

"Man, you bet right," he replied, smiling over at Bea and catching a whiff of fresh tobacco. The truck hobbled up the dirt road and wound back toward the highway. Jack busied himself with licking the cigarette paper and sealing it shut. He pulled a match from the small box and lit up, then took a long drag.

"Man, that's exactly what a guy needs after a long day, isn't it?" He took a few more puffs and handed it to Bea and got busy rolling another.

"You two up for a drink?"

Jack jumped right in. "You bet," he said, nudging Bea with his elbow.

"I could use a little something, I guess, but I gotta eat first." She gave her brother a look. "All we had today were oranges. Isn't that right, Jack?"

"Panzón's supposed to be waiting for us at the campo. Says he's got a whole crate of wine, and not the cheap stuff neither." He lifted his cap and set it back down on his head. "That pinche Panzón, man, he's always got some kind of connection with someone. The guy don't do shit but somehow everyone owes him something. I just don't get it."

"Well, I still can't stand him," Bea mumbled.

"That's 'cause he's got eyes for you." Alex looked over at Jack and teased. "Panzón'll do anything for Bea. Man, one time when we were younger I told him if he drank raw cow milk, ya know, straight from the tit, I'd get him a date with her."

Jack puffed on his cigarette. "And the poor bastard did it?"

"Oh yeah, he did, got down on all fours and took that hairy titty in his mouth and gnawed on that thing like it was his own mama's. If only I had a camera, God, I bet I coulda wrangled a sack full of cash off him, that's how pitiful the guy looked. Man!" He slapped the steering wheel and Bea and Jack chuckled. "You'll get to meet him here in a minute, just don't say anything about what I told you. Not that I give a damn, just that he's liable to get his feelings hurt and wind up not wanting to drink some of that good grape he's got."

"You won't hear a peep outta me," Jack replied.

Bea interrupted, "It ain't like Panzón has a lotta friends anyway."

Alex looked at his sister from the corner of his eye, and was genuinely happy to see her. She took another drag of her cigarette and then gnawed on the skin of her thumb.

"How's little Al?" she asked.

"He's fine. Was at Mom's yesterday. Looked happy enough." He turned to his sister. "Probably 'cause Freddy wasn't around to bother him."

"Will you take me to see him first thing tomorrow?"

Alex nodded. "Sure thing."

The truck turned off the highway and started up a dirt road, cutting through a long row of low persimmon trees. Jack rolled the window down and flung his cigarette, then leaned his face out and let the cold air wash over it. He looked back at Bea and Alex.

"Every place has its own kind of air, you know that? That's one thing about traveling a lot, you get to taste the different air each place has." He stuck his hand out the window and let it sift through his fingers. "For instance, New York air don't taste anything like Frisco air, 'cause in Frisco you got the sea salting it all up. Nah, New York air is dense, suffocates you almost. This Selma air, though," he leaned his face back out for another whiff, "there's nothing else like it."

"Roll it up already, Jackie, would you? I'm shivering. Besides," she added, "you'll catch pneumonia like that."

The truck inched over a wooden bridge, and in the headlights, splayed out before them, they saw a small city of gray tents strewn sloppily in mud, separated by heaps of trash and discarded mattresses. Every five feet was a deep rut where the rains had carved canyons into the pathways, and the truck banged clumsily along, while eyes glanced up from bonfires. Dark, shiny faces glowed orange with flames that poked against pitch black. The truck hit a puddle and mud sprayed the carcass of an old truck. A mutt lifted its jowls from the dirt and yawned and went back to dreaming. Wood burners flickered behind canvas walls where shadows of families shifted around. Jack sat with an unflinching gaze, taking in the details, a hard and serious focus pulled over his eyes and mouth.

"This is the campo," Bea said.

Jack was silent.

They turned a corner and another section of tents spread out for several hundred feet. And then another corner, and another row. More trash, discarded mattresses, more mud, and signs of life within it.

"It never ends," he said.

In the headlights a short round man with curly hair stood at the foot of a tent, waving.

"That's him," Alex said. "That's Panzón. Look at 'im standing there. What I tell you?"

Bea yawned and leaned her head on Jack's shoulder while Alex got out. He went over to Panzón and shook his hand. They exchanged a few words before Alex pointed toward the truck and waved the two over. They got out and Bea eyed Panzón.

Alex introduced the men. "Panzón, Jack. Jack, this here's Panzón."

Panzón took the gabacho's hand and shook it, then glanced over at Bea. "Vámos adentro," he said, scratching his oily scalp and turning back around to give Jack another look-over.

It was a bachelor's dwelling, even for the campo. Panzón's only necessities were the clothes on his back, a slab to sleep on, and drink. A small cot was tucked into a corner next to a makeshift wood burner, with the smoke vent jutting up through a hole torn in the ceiling. Two blankets placed on top of the cot. A small table and a couple of fruit crates that Panzón kept in case company stopped by.

He scooted the crates over for his guests, while Alex sat down on the cold, hard earth. He looked at his sister and saw a limp hunger in her eyes.

"Got any grub?"

Panzón twisted up his face.

Alex nodded, "It's for them, they've been on the road all day."

Bea looked directly at Panzón, and he lowered his head a little and glanced up at Jack before reaching beneath the cot and pulling out a small box. He opened it and lifted out a brown grease-stained bag and jammed his plump hand inside. A long curled slab of pork skin with a hunk of blackened meat clinging to it slid out. He snapped it in three places and tossed each of them a chunk. While the gabacho chewed away, Panzón eyed him closely, and then stuck the leftover piece into his mouth and gnawed on it. The crackle of pork rinds filled the small tent.

Alex lit up a cigarette. "So where's this grape you were telling me about, man?"

Panzón bent over and pulled a wadded-up blanket out from beneath the cot. The pork rind hung out the side of his mouth while he unraveled the blanket. Lying there before them were four rotund pickling jars filled with crimson liquid. Alex reached for one. He was trying to unscrew the lid when Bea spoke up.

"You know where there's any work, Panzón?"

Panzón stuck his fingers into his mouth and loosened the chunks of rind that clung to his back teeth. He licked his fingernail clean of it.

"Anything around here?" Alex added, unable to open the jar. He passed it to Panzón. Panzón gave the lid three hard slaps and then wrapped his fat fingers around it and pried it open.

"Nah, not around here," he said. "You just missed the algodón." He threw back several gulps and wiped his mouth on the fat of his bicep, then passed the jar to Alex.

"What about Big Rosie? Think she's got something—for my sister and her friend."

Panzón eyed Jack suspiciously.

"The uvas are still going," he said, with a hint of apprehension. "Supposed to be some work there, but a lot of trabajadores are counting on it." He looked straight into Alex's eyes. "Did you see all them guys standing out there by the fire? They're next in line."

Bea grabbed the jar from her brother's grip.

"Think you can ask Rosie for us?" Alex pressed.

Panzón pried open another jar. He took a swig and passed it to Alex before answering. His eyes shifted around the tent. "Her and I ain't together no more." A dog barked in the distance. Panzón heard it and raised his finger to his lips. They all stopped talking.

"What's the problem?" Alex whispered.

Panzón cupped his hand to his ear.

"It's just that ol' dog."

"No it ain't. Sounded too far away."

"Man, you're paranoid," said Alex, taking another swig from the jar and passing it to Jack. He took the jar and drank a few gulps.

"Good, ain't it, güero?" Panzón said, lifting his chin at Jack.

"Sure is."

"Just forget about it," Bea said. "I'll ask Rosie myself. I know where to find her."

Alex could sense Panzón's mind stirring. He realized in that moment that it was a probably a bad idea bringing Jack here, this late in the season. A gabacho poking around the campo on the cusp of November was never a good sign. Alex caught Panzón's attention with his eyes and motioned him outside.

They walked toward the canal, passing the jar between them, when Panzón started in. "Oyé, how well do you know this gabacho?"

"Just met him today. But listen, I know what you're thinking, so don't go getting all crooked on me, hear? The guy's mellow. Just some gava who's been helping my sister out."

Panzón spit a wad of phlegm to the ground. "I know you ain't that stupid, Alejandro." He swilled from the jar and a line of red liquid ran down the side of his chin. He wiped it with the back of his hand. "You know how the trabajadores get around here, especially this time of year. There's all kinds of tranzas going on, and these guys won't take it. If shit breaks loose, you know the first one they'll blame is the gabacho. You too, probably. Don't matter if you all have nothing to do with nothing. Just how it is."

"Cálmate," replied Alex. "You're getting busted up over nothing, man."

Panzón breathed through his nose. "The guy looks like a lechuza if you ask me."

"Don't go throwing that word around, not while we're standing by this ditch, hombre." Alex spat. "The guy's aces, man, give 'im a break."

Panzón grunted and looked out past the canal. "I gotta take a leak," he said, passing Alex the jar and making his way over to the embankment.

As they approached the tent, Bea and Jack could hear them.

"So what happened with you and Big Rosie?" Alex asked, pulling the door flap back.

Panzón took a gulp from the jar. "That broad's too celosa. Gets jealous if I ain't kissing her ass all the time. Worse part is she's sangrona too. Has to get even for everything. I told her I ain't playing her games no fuckeen more."

"*You* left Big Rosie?" Bea blurted.

Panzón gave her a look. "I did," he replied. "Had to teach her a lesson, 'cause I know she can't live without me. She needs me."

Bea couldn't help herself. "What the hell you talkin' about, Panzón, isn't this *her* tent you're staying in?"

The guys busted up, and Panzón lifted another jar and pried the lid off. He glared down at Bea, then over at Jack. "Where you from, man?"

Jack lowered the jar from his lips. "Back east," he replied.

"Oh yeah? Mississippi or something?"

Jack didn't feel right correcting him. "Around there," he said, standing up and moving toward the door. "Wine's working through me good. I gotta step outside for a minute."

"If you're gonna piss, walk out past the tree line," Panzón called out, "'bout a hundred feet, there's a canal there somewheres. Don't fall in."

Jack stepped out and they could hear his footsteps fading away. Panzón looked at Bea, and didn't waste a second. "Oyé, Beto wanted me to tell you he split for L.A. and that he left Albert with your folks."

"Son-of-a-bitch," Bea said, setting the bottle on the ground. She looked at her brother. "Is this why little Al's over at Mom's, Alex?"

"Cálmate," he replied. "I just heard this right before picking you up. Panzón barely told me. I didn't know."

She stood up and accidentally kicked a half-filled jar of wine over. "I can't believe him," she said. "Tomorrow, first thing we're doing is getting him, you hear me, Alex?"

"Of course," he said, waving his hand for her to sit.

She began pacing the tent and picking at the skin of her thumb. In that instant she recalled the driver of the truck back in Los Angeles. Was it Beto? It had to be. But no. Beto would've never let her go on like that, knowing she was with some white man, traipsing all over L.A.

"Drink up!" Panzón said. He polished off what liquid was left at the bottom of the spilt jar, and then reached for another and pried it open.

Bea sat down on the crate and crossed her arms.

"Look at the bright side," Alex said. "Least he ain't in Selma right now." Panzón said nothing. She looked up at her brother and realized he had a point. Maybe he'd be gone just long enough for her to handle matters and strike out before he returned. It was unlikely, but possible. She swiped the jar from Panzón and took a drink.

The door flap opened and Jack ducked into the tent. He sat on the crate next to Bea, and the rest of the night was filled with conversation that flowed well beyond the four jars of wine. And when they polished those off, Jack pulled a bomber from his duffel, and this perked the guys up pretty quick. The tent rattled with soft laughter and they shushed each other. And when someone from across the campo hollered out for them to shut their faces, they squinted their red eyes at one another and only laughed harder. Meanwhile, Bea rested her body on Panzón's lumpy cot and tried getting some sleep, but it was impossible. All she could do was think about how in a matter of hours she would get to see little Albert's plump face and hazel eyes, and feel his small puckered lips pressed against hers, after what felt like a year of being away. She wondered if Patsy was back with Angie by now, and just the thought of her little girl alone almost made her fall apart. She writhed on the cot and shut her eyes tight, and balled herself up, hoping the rooster's early morning yawp would come sooner than later.

19

That morning, while on the way to their parents' house, Alex assured his sister that everything would work out. She felt good when he talked like this, because if anyone knew the gravity of a situation, and how her father's temper weighed in, it was Alex. Throughout the years he managed to remain the neutral one, keeping to himself, even as a boy, constantly dodging the belt more than the others. As the middle child, it was easy for him to get lost in the drama. Often, from a safe position, tucked away in the corner of the kitchen, he watched his brothers and sisters take a beating while he stood practically invisible. Alex, the well-behaved son. Alex, the hard worker. The responsible one. Which is why it came as a surprise when he enlisted with the army. No one saw that coming. Alex himself could hardly believe it. But he did it. Before the last burning ember vanished on the shores of Pearl Harbor, he had enlisted for the big leagues. He was the first in line, boots shined and hair tightened, *Alejandro Renteria reporting for duty, sir.* But then somewhere along the way something snapped, a mean streak got in him. Three weeks out of boot camp he got into a tussle with his sergeant. Both took a good beating, but in the end only Alex still had his feet beneath him. The family's pride was short-lived. It was for the best, they reasoned: finances were dismal and they needed all the help they could get back home.

When they approached the dirt road that led to the house, they let Jack out.

"You understand, right, honey?" Bea said, as she started to lean over to kiss him. She glanced back at the truck and caught Alex eyeballing them through the rearview. She held back.

Jack stepped away and waved before ducking beneath a canopy of grapes. She hopped back in the truck and sat quietly as they made their way to the house. Her nerves were a wreck, and she yanked at her thumb skin. She thought about the days she'd been gone, counted them in her head, and even though it had only been a week, she was aware that it was still a chunk of little Al's childhood that was irretrievable. She wondered if he'd appear any older than when she left. Alex's voice interrupted her thoughts.

"Don't worry," he said, "Dad probably ain't even home."

"I wasn't thinking about him," she replied. "Was thinking about little Al," she paused. "I just gotta get us outta this place."

He nodded but said nothing.

As the truck pulled up to the front yard, things seemed quieter than usual. They both noticed this right off. Usually chickens could be found clucking about, or else some tractor engine growling past, but there was nothing of the sort. Only a loud stillness in the air. They stepped off the truck and stood in the front yard, trying to make sense of the uneasiness. They fixed their eyes on one another, and just as Alex was about to open his mouth and say something, little Albert's high voice broke open the silence. "Mama!" he hollered, barreling out the front door and flying down the porch steps. Bea knelt down in the balding grass and was almost bowled over by the weight of him smashing against her. She held him tight and breathed in his little-boy scent, every last nook and fold, and pressed her nose into his curly hair and was glad to find it still smelled like dough.

"You miss me, baby?"

He tucked his head under her chin and held on, his small body trembling.

"Grandma told me you'd be coming home soon, she was right. She said any day now, that's what she said. I missed you too much. Mama, I've been helping Grandma a lot . . ." The boy went on, and listening to him, Bea decided she was a horrible mother. To think she'd almost gone off to New York, just a day ago, without him. Seeing her son's plump, round face put a stone in her throat and made her feel unworthy. The boy stopped talking and whiffed deeply at her neck. She held him back at arm's length and took him in once more. He peered over his shoulder, back at his grandmother Jessie, who was now standing on the porch. She fixed her eyeglasses on her face and waved at her daughter. Alex went over and put an arm around his mother, and she leaned over and whispered something into her son's ear and he laughed, and everything felt good in that moment.

"Todo bien 'amá?" Bea called out.

Jessie folded her thick arms across her apron and a satisfied mask enveloped her.

Bea lifted little Al's chin and let her eyes stare into him a bit longer, long enough to search out any noticeable changes.

"You have grown," she said. She ran her fingers through his hair and pulled him again into her. She thought of Patsy right then, and how her poor baby hadn't felt her mother's touch in weeks, and she had to stand up to fend off the tears.

"You've been good for Grandma?"

He looked back at his grandmother, and then over at his uncle. Alex motioned to Bea. She lowered herself once more, eye level with little Al.

"Listen, baby, I got some things I gotta take care of today, but as soon as it's done I promise you I'll be right back here to get you, and then you'll come with me, alright? Boy, you're gonna love where we're going, I just know it."

"Where, Mama?"

"It's a surprise. I'll tell you when I get back, okay?"

The boy scratched at his armpit and looked over at his uncle and grandmother, and could see them smiling.

"How long you going for?"

"Not long at all. Just a day, I promise. And then I'll tell you about the surprise. Oh, you're gonna love it. It's gonna be better than anything you ever dreamed of. But for now you stay with Grandma, okay? Just one little day is all."

His eyebrows bunched up.

She leaned close to him. "Has Freddy been messing with you?"

"No."

"You'd tell me if he was, wouldn't you?"

Just then the screen door squealed open and Jesus stepped out in plain view. He walked past Alex and Jessie to the edge of the porch and squared his shoulders and looked down at Bea.

"You taking him with you?" He spat.

Bea looked over at her mother.

"I'm asking you something, Beatrice. You taking Junior?"

"Not now, Dad."

"He hasn't seen you in a week and you says not now?"

Jessie turned her body toward him, and Alex stepped down off the porch and started toward his truck.

Bea hugged little Al and kissed him on the cheek and ordered him into the house. She stood up from the grass and patted her knees off. "I hafta take care of something, 'apa, but I'm coming right back to get him soon as I'm done."

Jesus looked at Alex and called to him. "Alejandro, a dónde vas?"

Alex stood by the door of his truck. "Just gonna take Beatrice to find work is all, a buscar trabajo." He climbed into his truck and fired up the engine and nodded at Bea to hurry up.

Jesus charged down the porch and paced over to his daughter, his short gaunt frame no longer disguised by the height of the porch. He pulled the tattered work hat off his head and clutched it in his left hand, then leveled his narrow eyes at her.

"You should be looking for Beto," he said, firmly.

Bea scoffed. She looked back at Alex and saw him lighting a cigarette. Jesus pressed on. "Es tu marido, Beatrice . . . you're still his wife." He paused out of frustration. "Junior needs you here . . . no allá de callejera."

Bea could see little Al peeking through the screen door.

"Go inside, mijo," she called out.

Jessie turned around and shooed her grandson away. Bea angled her eyes at her father and tightened her jaw for fear that if she opened it, fire might emerge from her lips.

"Vámonos, Bea!" Alex called from the truck.

She kept her gaze on her father for several seconds before turning and walking away. He called behind her, "Nomás quieres andar de zorra."

His words caused her spine to stiffen. She stopped in her tracks and could feel a tide swelling from the pit of her stomach, making its way up her throat and resting on the back of her tongue. Her mother spoke out, "Déjala." Jesus held his ground. The word *zorra* stuck in that part of her brain, just behind the eyeballs where memories are stored. Back in Irapuato, she'd heard him use that word to describe the Indian girls, especially the younger ones who let their boyfriends grope them in public. She looked back and found him standing still, unflinching. He stuck his hat back on his head and started up the porch, pushing past Jessie and letting the screen door slam behind him.

Bea got in the truck and Alex backed out and sped away, kicking up mud. He could see the anger in her eyes. "Don't worry about him, you know how he is. He's just messed up over the raids. He gets like this every season, tu sabes. He's afraid they'll deport his ass. Just forget him, Beatrice."

On the way to Madera, Panzón told them he knew a guy in Fresno, a Oaxaqueño named Mingo who had the inside on some high-quality manure. According to Panzón, manure sales were happening, and Mingo was gaining a reputation among local farmers as "a guy who knows his shit."

They exited at Calwa, a hovel on the south end of the city, where Panzón still had a running tab at one of the few five-and-dimes that carried mescal. The guys had been buzzing about it since the night before, and now Jack was anxious to try some.

Bea spoke up, "C'mon, Alex, we gotta get serious about finding work. You guys can drink later. Let's see about that manure while the sun's still up."

Panzón ran his hand over his face and shot Alex a glare. Jack kept his gaze on the rolling landscape and said nothing.

"Hell, it's already way past noon," Panzón said, writhing in his seat.

Alex piped up. "Naw, she's right, let's push on, see about this job. We'll have plenty of time later."

Panzón groaned and rolled down his window and stuck his face into the wind.

The truck rambled through Fresno's south side, hobbling over the train tracks past the Greyhound station and entering Chinatown. They passed an Armenian bakery and could see a line of pudgy women gripping canvas satchels overstuffed with bread, yapping like nobody's business. Farther down the street was El Tecolote Restaurant & Cantina, where a man stood out front primping his thin moustache and puffing on a cigar. He watched them as they cruised down the road and around the corner. The whole scene was populated with wary faces heading to or from some kind of market. Bea was growing anxious. She could see the sun quickly inching itself down toward Raisin City. She looked at Jack and wondered how he could be so casual about it all.

The truck idled to a stop in front of a large window with a sign that read *The Asia Hotel*. Across the street was Central Fish Company, where old Chinamen smoked cigarettes in the back alley and gambled on fruit crates, their white aprons smeared with red abstractions. Panzón leapt out of the truck and went to the window and hung his stubby arm over the door.

"I'm gonna see if Mingo's in there," he said, pointing up the street to La Cucaracha.

"Just hurry it up," Bea snapped, "and don't take too long, Panzón," she said, rolling her eyes. She looked at Jack. "You watch, he'll come out half drunk, forgetting why he went in there in the first place."

Jack chuckled. "You sure are hard on the poor guy."

Alex adjusted the side-view mirror.

"Panzón's a parasite. Isn't that right, Alex?"

Alex turned his gaze up the street and nodded. Bea sensed a strange frequency in the air between Jack and her brother. She leaned over and fidgeted with the radio.

"Tell me something," Alex said, staring at his sister. "How'd you two meet again?"

"We were on the same bus, going to L.A."

"Aw, that's right," Alex said, sucking his teeth. "Like that song goes, first time strangers, second time friends, third time . . ."

"It's not like that," Bea interrupted. "Don't be sour, Alex."

"Is that right?" He looked over at Jack and waited for a reply.

Jack shrugged.

Alex tapped the steering wheel with his fingers and scanned the rearview for Panzón but there was no sight of him. He whistled for a minute and then paused. "I ain't blind, little sister, so don't go making me out to be some pendejo." He turned and stared directly into Bea's eyes when he said this, and the intensity was penetrating.

She glanced up at Jack. "Fine, you wanna hear the truth? I don't have to lie about my business," she said, pausing to collect her thoughts. "So I like him, so what?"

Alex cut her off. "Let 'im talk for once." His voice was void of anger and his words rolled out in a calm tone.

Jack hung his arm out the window and angled his head at Alex. "What Bea's saying is right, we met on the bus, sat right next to one another and hit it off. Being new to L.A., she was just helping me find my way around—"

Bea stopped him. "Hell, Alex, he don't need you questioning him like some jerk." She caught herself and stiffened up.

Alex chuckled. "Lord almighty," he said. "If I'd a known this would piss you off that bad, I'd a just kept my mouth shut. C'mon now, I'm only giving you two a hard time, you're right, it don't matter to me either way. It's you I'm worried for."

"Well, I don't need you worrying for me," she said, lifting her knees to her chest. "I do enough of that for myself." She sighed and looked over at Jack, who had a nervous grin about him now.

Several minutes passed before she spoke up again. "Where the hell's Panzón?"

"Give 'im another minute."

"It's been almost a half hour."

Alex didn't respond.

She leaned her ear on Jack's shoulder, and this made him fidgety. She rolled her head back upright and tugged at a small piece of loose skin on her thumb. "I gotta tell you something, Alex. I mean, I don't got to but I feel like I do. Just gotta promise you won't say anything about it, not even to Mom—especially not her."

"Christ, Beatrice, you gotta tell me first."

Jack glanced at her from the corner of his eye. "We're gonna leave for New York." Jack looked over at Alex and saw his face turn serious. "Only reason we came back is 'cause we gotta make some money to start off. Well, and for little Al too, of course."

Alex sat still and stared into the side-view mirror. In the distance he could see Panzón making his way back to the truck. He was clutching his belt loops in one hand and waving a piece of paper in the other.

When he approached the truck Alex wasted no time, "What's the word with Mingo?"

Panzón was out of breath. "He wasn't in there," he said, taking a few gulps of air. "But I met this guy, a Mexicano, says he knows of some picking out by Fowler." He took a few more breaths. "Starts tomorrow morning, though—walnuts."

Alex smacked the steering wheel. "You can't make shit at walnuts, Panzón, everybody knows that. You asshole. What about Mingo?"

"He ain't in there, man, I told you." Panzón scanned the streets. "But he should get here soon, like everybody else." He placed both hands on his hips and jutted his stomach forward. "It's Friday, man, people are getting off early, tu sabes."

Alex glanced over at Bea and Jack. He could see his sister was pissed.

"Hell, I bet if we wait here, the fulano will show up any minute. Then we can talk all we want about that manure."

"Probably ain't no manure at all, Panzón," Bea sneered.

Alex could feel the back of his throat foam slightly at the thought of a beer. "He's got a point, Beatrice. I mean, shit, it's Friday, going on two o'clock, the day might as well be over. Our best shot is to wait for the guy here."

Bea shook her head.

"We can have us a drink while we wait for him, shoot some pool. You shoot stick, Jack?"

Jack looked at the men but was reluctant to nod.

Alex opened the door to step out. "C'mon, Bea, I'll buy you and your friend a round." Panzón moved away from the truck, scratched his neck, and glanced over at La Cucaracha. Alex slammed the door and looked back at them.

"You two comin' or you just gonna sit there like a coupla crows waiting for a worm?" He turned his back and started up the street with Panzón.

Jack rested his hand on Bea's lap.

"I just knew it. I'm so stupid. I knew coming back was a dumb idea."

"Christ, Bea, we've only been here a single day, twenty-four hours—"

"You think tomorrow will be any different? Panzón ain't nothing but trouble, I know him, he's worthless to us."

"Let's just see this day through. If it don't pan out, then tomorrow we'll hit out on our own." His look was sincere. "What do you say?"

Just like the insect from which La Cucaracha took its name, there were hissing sounds from within the depths of the walls, many legs in perpetual motion. The front door was a slab of iron propped open by a cinder block. Inside, a long bar spanned the back wall, which was cluttered with posters of bands—traveling duets, country boys, and Mexican cowboys, mostly—two-bit acts that had been playing the valley since before the Depression. In the center of the place stood four wobbly pool tables, riddled with cigarette burns and beer-stained felt, a speck of blood here and there. Tucked away in the corner was a small stage, and sitting below the only window was a fat shiny jukebox stuffed with every tune from the Andrews Sisters to Xavier Cugat. The place had all the ingredients for a good time, and because there were no clocks or stools, you either partied until you were dragged out by the bouncer, who happened to be a gargantuan Armenian with arms like hay bales, or you were one of the smart ones who scuttled out while you still had all six legs beneath you.

Alex bought a round of beers just as he'd promised, and they all stood around eyeing the crowd and throwing back suds. After a few minutes Bea went to use the restroom, and Alex took the opportunity to pick up with Jack where he left off.

"I always wanted to see New York, you know that?" He lifted the beer to his lips and hesitated. "Almost had a chance, too, but ended up right back here." He took a drink and ran his hand over his mouth.

"Why would you want to leave this place?" said Jack. "Seems like a man's got everything he needs here, especially you. Bea tells me you're in good at the dairy, you're making money, so things can't be half bad."

"That's what she says to you, huh?"

"I know plenty of city folks who'd kill for a little bit of quiet like this. A little room to stretch your legs. Buy your own chunk of land, set things on fire when you want."

"That easy?" Alex steadied his gaze on Jack, then lifted his beer to his mouth. He paused. "You taking my sister?"

Jack lifted his chin. "That's what the plan looks like."

Alex could see Panzón hovering around a pool table, cue stick in hand, pointing at a corner pocket.

"She say anything about the kids?"

Jack stared down into his half-empty mug.

"And you're good with that? I mean you hafta be good with it, otherwise you better get moving along, right?"

"Yeah, I know about her old man too—"

"Aw, don't get me started on that son-of-a-bitch. Man, soon as I see that bum I'm gonna bust into him, simple as that." His jaw quivered and he stilled it with a long guzzle of beer.

Bea came out from the bathroom and was heading back.

Alex put his beer down and spoke quickly. "Listen here, man, you wanna take Bea to New York, fine by me, I get it, but she ain't like you or me, I mean, she can handle her own, but what I mean is she's a good girl, and I'd hate to see her go through more hassle just 'cause you think you got yourself a little prize there. You hear me?"

Jack could see that he was serious. "I hear you."

And with that Alex polished off the last of his beer and passed Bea on his way to the restroom.

She had put on some makeup and was quickly loosening up to the idea of a good time. She drank her beer and rocked her head slightly, and then she took Jack's hand. They stood side-by-side like that, giddy and invincible, chatting away like old friends.

"Kinda wish we were still back at that hotel," she said.

This put a smile on Jack's face. "You and me both."

The jukebox turned out one song after another, hardly pausing between tracks. The music spilled out and tangled up with the rowdy voices that began to populate the sidewalks. Bea swayed her hips to the music and Jack took notice and pointed it out; when he did she became too self-aware, and so she stopped.

"Go on," he said. "You wanna dance, cut loose with me." He set his mug down on the counter and threw his arms up. "C'mon," he clapped, nodding his head at her. He pushed his hips out then clapped some more and made a turn on his heel. "See there, c'mon now, baby." Her eyes darted around to see who might be watching; he grabbed her hands but she pulled away.

"I just don't feel like it, Jackie, honest."

He lifted his beer and polished it off in one swig, then took her hand and led her over to the jukebox, where they flipped through records.

"They gotta have something here you can move to," he said, clicking the button.

"It's not the music. I'm just not comfortable dancing here, not in this place." She looked around and noticed a couple staring at them. The woman smiled at Bea and winked. Alex brought over three shot glasses filled with tequila, and they stood in front of the jukebox and tossed them back. Bea's face twisted. She turned around and stared down at the records.

"They gotta have Pérez Prado, don't you think?" She clicked the button and watched the records flip past.

"Yeah, he's on a streak right now." Jack ran his finger over the jukebox glass. The records shuffled and then stopped at Peggy Lee. Bea laughed.

"Don't you like her?" Jack said, wiping his mouth with the back of his hand.

"You kidding me? Peggy Lee?" She cocked her head sideways at him. "She's a phony."

"She's got something, you have to admit."

She slapped his chest. "You just like her blonde hair and good looks. All men like Peggy Lee for that reason."

"Just as bad as a woman not liking her for the same reason, isn't it?"

"You went to college, didn't they teach you anything? I know you got better taste than Peggy Lee."

"I think she's alright. I don't have any of her records or anything like that, but the girl's got pipes you gotta admit."

Bea grabbed his beer. She took a drink and set it atop the jukebox, staring down at the gray photo of the singer smiling up at her. Her eyes were glazed over now.

"You actually buy all that *Mañana, mañana* junk? I mean, she ain't even Mexican, and every time I hear her voice pretending like she is with all that *caramba* and *ehs* and *ahs*, oh, it just makes me sick. Makes me feel like ripping that mole off her face." She paused, and they looked at each other and broke out in laughter. He slung his arm over her shoulders, and she wanted to tell him how good it felt, just being there, but at that moment Gene Krupa blasted from the jukebox. Jack couldn't help himself, and this time he took her by the shoulders and tried giving her a spin. People standing nearby cheered them on, but Bea clammed up and instead grabbed his beer and took another drink. The drums thumped, and every last toe in the place was tapping now, except for Bea's. She stood by the jukebox watching Jack make a fool of himself as he twirled and slid his feet along the floor and snapped his fingers, bouncing like his kneecaps were giving out.

"C'mon!" he shouted at her.

The music rumbled on, and he shut his eyes and let his body do its own thing, folding front to back like he was possessed. Arms up, he spun and gyrated and didn't care at all how clumsy the whole thing looked, only that the music was moving him now. A leather-faced woman with bad skin and wiry hair looked at Bea with concern, and she nodded and waved at her to go on. Bea turned red at the gesture. The woman fidgeted and looked as if at any moment she might leap right into the gabacho's arms herself. The tequila was quickly taking effect, and now Bea could feel the pulse tugging at her pelvis, branching out to her thighs and fingertips. It was taking more effort to contain herself than to give in. Jack was clapping his hands over his head and his eyes were still shut. She stepped toward him and reached her hand out for him to take. He opened his eyes and saw it there and yanked her into the eye of his tornado, zipping her around; and she let him, blushing, covering her face with both hands, giggling out loud. She wiggled her hips slightly and snapped her fingers and laughed some more. Alex saw them from across the room, and he didn't realize until that very moment just how good it felt to see his sister smile like that, free from worry, no scowl threatening to steal the joy from her face. Just Bea, plain as ever, getting her kicks like she hadn't in too long. And when that song ended, another kicked on, and now she stayed there, in front of the jukebox, hanging on to Jack, another drink, another step. With each new song she added a new move, a twist eventually. And the longer the night went, the braver she became. Dancing moved to the middle of the pool hall now, arms in full swing, hair a wreck, it didn't matter, the dam had cracked. The louder the horns, the higher on her toes she went, the more contortions her body took on. Jack stood back a ways to give her some room. Sweat flew off the ends of her ears and washed over her cheekbones. She made eye contact with him, and he held her gaze like she was staring off the edge of the world. Her bra straps inched down her shoulders and her face glistened in the glow of the jukebox while she danced and had herself one last shot. A black woman whooped and hollered at her, and now Bea's eyes were wide open, and she saw Alex clearly from across the room. He was looking hard, studying her, and the look on his face was pure glee. He'd even forgotten about the woman he'd been trying to make, if for only a minute. He wiped the blur from his eyes, took a step closer, and watched her go. And go she did, song after song, while Jack's own engine was puttering to a near standstill. He'd quickly become nothing more than a point of reference for Bea's spins and maneuvers, her safety net in case she lost control of it all. And then, in the split second it took for the record to flip over, between songs, someone dropped a coin in the jukebox and selected a slow number; it felt like the life-force had fallen out the bottom, and everyone in the place let out a big sigh of relief.

They went out for some fresh air and found the Chinatown streets alive with activity. It was a perfect autumn night for being out. The fog hadn't made an appearance the whole day, and the sky was clear, the stars whiter than ever. The air smelled like wet earth, and a soft steam rose from their bodies. Slowly they strolled up and down the sidewalks, holding one another, kissing at every stop, all the while talking up plans of New York. Every other sentence, Bea stretched her arms up into the air and hollered, "I just can't wait!"

"I'm telling you, baby," he said, stoking her flames, "you're gonna love the city. And it happens real quick too, anyone who steps foot out there gets trapped by all those sweet little exchanges that take place, practically some type of magical collision on every corner at all hours and seconds, and it never goes away—that's New York."

The green of her eyes reflected the headlights of passing cars. She held his arm tighter and leaned her head against his shoulder. He kissed her face, again and again.

"I read somewhere once that New Yorkers aren't ever really from New York," she said, "but from places like Portland or Kentucky. They go there because it's the only place for a person to get completely lost and start fresh. I remember thinking back then New York must be a million miles away, like a whole other planet. But now, I just can't believe it, it feels like it's just around that corner." She pointed up the sidewalk, and Jack laughed and slung his arm over her shoulder. He waved his hand like a wand over the streets of Chinatown.

"May as well have one last good look at all this, baby, these buildings, the people, the big sky, aw man—trust me, you'll do fine in the Apple. Hell, out here you got bigger apples anyhow, not the same strain, no way, but real apples at least. Take a bite of all this, I'm telling you, Bea, because once we're in the city, you won't be seeing much of this kind of life, no, nothing like this."

She gripped Jack tighter, and wished they were already there. But then, as intrusive as a hiccup, Beto's face slipped in, and it killed the illusion instantly. But this time the image of him was different. His wide face was a mask of defeat. It was as if she could see the pace of his heart slow down, as if his entire world was slipping from the seams. He looked dazed and fatigued, on his way to drinking himself to death.

"Jackie, we really need to get to work, honey, we got two weeks, just two weeks. I can't do more than that, I'm telling you."

"First thing tomorrow," he replied. "Just like your brother said, baby."

"Promise?"

"Of course."

And with that, she angled her eyes upward to find the top of Fresno's highest building, the Security Bank tower, four blocks away. From that angle it was easy to imagine that she was already in New York, and that the yellow light spilling from a single window ten stories high was their home, their little warm glow in the big cold city. Right then she felt like she could skip all the way to New York and make it there by morning.

20

They borrowed Alex's pick-up truck and filed through the towns: Selma, Dinuba, Visalia, and all the islands in between. Each one the same—water tower, packing sheds, same patchworked terrain and backroads as you might find anywhere USA, so long as the land is fertile and water flows. They spent the entire first day, fourteen hours, from six in the morning until eight o'clock at night, zigzagging up and down the Golden State Highway, knocking on doors, rolling in and out of the campos and hoovervilles.

Bea spoke to everyone about work: the Filipinos in Pixley, Okies over in Tulare, and all the leftover braceros in between. It was obvious, by the way everyone kept scrutinizing Jack suspiciously, that the unsettling rumor of a raid had reached every last corner of the valley. Even a soft-spoken woman at a camp in Corcoran demanded Bea leave her alone.

"If you're from 'round here, honey, then you know that anyone seen with a stranger has a way of gettin' hurt."

Bea knew the woman was right, so they got back in the truck and drove off.

"They're not afraid of us," she explained to Jack. "It's because of the farmers. They're afraid the unions might come back. Afraid if we get together like that again we'll start making 'em pay up. I guess they have reason to be afraid, though. Heck, anytime they see a few guys in a huddle they act like it's mutiny."

"Can't believe it's still like this around here. Thought the reds were done with."

"Alex says these farmers gotta all die before we can move on. Probably won't see much change for a long time, though, 'cause a lot of these folks have grandkids even worse than them."

It had hardly been a decade since the valley had plowed itself out of the Depression by sheer will and heart-muscle. And now, once again, it appeared things were veering off path. The end of the war brought suspicion, the kind that made it impossible for farmers and campesinos to trust one another, and so mostly they didn't. They mildly rode out each season, doing what they knew best, remaining civil enough toward one another, with the unspoken agreement that in the days following the last harvest, all bets were off.

"It's a backward arrangement, sure," Alex would later explain to Jack. "But as long as families need work and fruit needs plucking, that's just how it is." Jack had begun to write some of this down in his notebook, but when he saw that Alex grew suspicious, he put it away and never wrote another word in his presence again.

"You see," Alex continued, "people here got it in their minds that if you don't like the left side of a stick, well then you just hack it off and be done with it. Problem is, no matter how many damn times you do this you still got the left side, don't you?"

Jack made a mental note. It was obvious Alex had thought long and hard about this.

Bea and Jack drove slowly. The air had grown cold again, and the fog had returned. It was trapped within the four walls of the valley, the entire bowl filled to the brim with pea soup. When they reached Selma, Bea could no longer contain herself.

"I'm afraid, honey."

Jack listened.

"Time's running out, I just know it." She wanted to tell him about Beto, and how she thought it was him driving that truck in Los Angeles. She decided against it.

"Hang in there, baby," he said. "I have a sense about these things."

In the distance, they spotted Alex standing near the dirt road to her parents' house, waving at them. He had good news. He had spoken with Hadinger earlier that day and managed to get both of them on over at the winery. Bea threw her arms around her brother.

"God, and here I was thinking we'll never find work, didn't I just say that on the way here, Jackie? I was just saying, it's gonna be impossible, and now here you are—"

"It'll be good," Alex said, resting his hand on his sister's shoulder. "You ready to get to work, man?"

"Sure am," Jack replied.

Later that night they went to the campo to speak with Big Rosie about a tent. She reminded them that she usually required the first two days' rent up front, but for Bea and her blue-eyed friend she'd make an exception. Big Rosie had always thought Beto wasn't good enough for Bea, and she didn't hesitate to say this right then and there.

"Ese Beto ain't no good. He might have looks but let me tell you, Beatrice," Big Rosie said, puffing on her cigarette. She eyed Jack. "You deserve yourself a good man, un trabajador, me entiendes?" She stepped forward. "Where you from, güerito?"

The corner of Jack's mouth lifted.

"He's just a friend, Rosie," Alex spoke up, slapping Jack on the shoulder.

"Just a friend," Jack echoed.

"Oh yeah? I got friends too," she said. She lifted an eyebrow suspiciously and smoked her cigarette, then reached for a cigar box. "Any a you seen Panzón today?"

They shook their heads.

"That desgraciado owes me three weeks' rent already. If you see his face around, tell 'em I'm looking for him, would you?"

They agreed, and then went to their tent and started making preparations for their first workday.

Sitting on an old mattress, Bea explained to Jack how picking grapes worked. She took the knives and gloves that Alex loaned them and placed them on the dirt.

"See here," she said, lifting a knife and turning it over. "See how it's gotta hooked nose?" Jack nodded and lifted the other knife up and gripped it in his hand tightly. "You're gonna have to squat low, like this." She demonstrated. "But you gotta do it quick. Sometimes they got pacers out there, guys who pick faster than anyone else, and if you don't keep up with the pacer, you'll get canned."

"You mean a guy can't go at his own speed?"

Bea wanted to laugh but saw that he was serious. "You sure you wanna do this, honey? I mean this here's hard work, really, but good thing for us it's only two weeks. Well, less than that now, but it'll go quick if we work hard."

"Go on," he said, fiddling with the leather strap of his knife.

She kept on, demonstrating for him the best way to check grapes, weed out the bad ones, how to grip the knife to make a clean cut, how to always keep it sharp and hold it away from the body, never close.

"One slip up," she said, squinting her eyes. "Man, I've seen guys lose whole fingers 'cause they weren't paying attention."

Jack took everything she said seriously, practicing his grip, sharpening the blade to a clean edge; he did this for several minutes while Bea prepared their lunch for the next day. Eventually he yawned and stuck his knife beneath the mattress; he laid his head on his coat and was soon out. Outside, a nearby fire crackled, and voices murmured from the other tents. Bea stayed up a little longer to hem an extra layer of material over the knees on their pants; it was a trick her mother had taught her. Use the thinnest needle, fine thread, and when the season's over the patches come right off and you still got knees. She took pride in the way her stitches were perfectly aligned, freehand—even her mother would've been proud to see such threadwork.

The very next day they picked sunup to sundown. At first, Jack couldn't help but pick slow, so transfixed was he by the sight of it all. The endless row of huddled bodies. The crook-backed beasts of burden; many didn't speak a lick of English, and looked to him as if they were built solely for the purpose of picking. Their arms were long slender things with massive hands fastened at the ends. Each man, woman, and child squinted beneath sun-chafed cheekbones the color of wet adobe, and they had a permanent look of terror on their faces as they worked. It was a mask of hunger. And he realized at that moment that this was a serious way of life, and that he better get moving on it.

Besides the occasional stop for water breaks, he filled his boxes at a decent pace and managed to stay only a row behind, while Bea chugged ahead, looking back every so often to make sure he was still at least visible. She thanked God they didn't have a pacer for the time being, as it was obvious Jack was falling short, and there was no telling how much longer the mayordomo would let him go on like that. All Bea had to do now was figure out how to keep it going for the next two weeks. She hated the idea of having to put little Al to work, but it was the only way. They needed the extra hands.

That afternoon Alex brought little Albert to Bea, and when she told him about having to work in the fields, he responded happily. "I could be Jack's helper," he said, staring up at Jack. Of course, Jack delighted at this, and so did the boy. They hit it off instantly. Jack opened his notebook and tore a page out and taught him how to fold a paper airplane. While Bea cooked dinner, the two went outside to test their invention, and she could hear her son's lilting voice rising with excitement as the plane launched for several yards, and then his short steps shuffling to retrieve it. Their laughter put her thoughts to rest, and she slowly stirred the pot of beans and felt the warmth of the fire glowing against her thighs. Except for the sound of a few dishes being tinkered with in the distance, the campo was quiet, and when a string of cool air floated in and grazed the back of her neck it all felt like a dream. She wondered why life wasn't like this always. Eleven more days, she thought to herself. Tomorrow she'd pick harder and faster than ever before. And now with little Albert helping out, they'd be on the road in no time.

Not having something to worry her mind with in that exact moment was a new experience. She wasn't sure what to make of it. In some ways it was uncomfortable. After pondering it a few minutes, it became flat-out unbearable. So unbearable in fact that she had to conjure Beto to mind just to anchor her feet to the ground. She wondered where he was exactly. Or more importantly, who he was with. She considered whether or not she should ask Panzón next time he came around. She hated that she thought about him. As a way to erase Beto from her mind entirely, she forced herself to remember all the things she hated about him. The way his eyes glassed over and looked through her whenever they made love. How he often smelled like perfume and whiskey. She might've even overlooked this last one, except that he never denied any of it. Whenever she asked him about it, he'd get this smug look on his face and then throw his hand in the air, as if to say, you're crazy. Suddenly little Al's giggle erupted outside, and it brought her back to the tent. She could hear his voice, his sweet pleading, begging to see the plane fly once more.

"Please, Jack, please," he squealed.

She could hear Jack himself grow childlike too, cheering for the plane, yelling out to little Al, "Launch that thing to the moon!" And when they finally came back to the tent, their giddiness took an hour to settle.

They ate their meal of papas con frijoles and washed it down with tepid water. Bea felt bad about not having flour to make tortillas but neither of them complained about it. They sat on fruit boxes and ate with their plates on their laps and listened to little Al go on about making a hundred more planes come tomorrow. The whole time Jack held his eyes on Bea; she could feel him studying her, and she returned the glance, only lowering her gaze to check on her son, or when the sweet fluttering in her gut became too overwhelming to bear.

Later that night, Jack complained about his back. After she put little Al to bed, she rubbed him down with a horse liniment, assuring him that the body, no matter how many days or months or years, never gets used to fieldwork. He winced at the bony knots of her knuckles bearing down into the joints and across the shoulder blades, and then he smiled when her touch lightened up and her fingertips grazed his skin. He rolled over onto his back and pulled her down onto him and they kissed, but Bea pulled back, too aware that nothing more than a sheet of canvas curtained them off from the eyes and ears of the campo.

The next day Jack awoke, whistling; things were coming together finally. That day he pushed himself to a decent pace, and by noon he'd fallen only half a row behind Bea. The whole time, little Al was bouncing vine-to-vine like a busy bee. He took from here and leapt to there, crisscrossing the berms, ducking beneath to nab the low-hanging grapes, jabbing that curved knife at the end of his tiny hands, in and out of the hard-to-reach places where vines knotted up and leaves cloaked whole clusters of grapes. Every few yards he'd shadow the vines that Jack had just worked on and dig out half a box full of grapes, and smile up at Jack, and then pass him like it was all in a day's work. Jack wiped his face and watched the boy run off toward the fig tree, where he'd found a tall bush to pee behind. He came out latching his overalls and clutching his knife, making his way back to where Jack was hunkered over in the dirt, rubbing his knees and flexing his knuckles. As his assistant, little Al made it his personal duty to cheer Jack up too, and so he washed off a cluster of grapes and gifted it to him. Together they sat beneath a low-hanging canopy of wide leaves and wolfed down every last tender bit of fruit until their faces and hands were sticky. Little Al took him to the canal, and they washed off in the stagnant water and went right back to work.

Later that evening, after they counted out the day's take, Alex drove Jack to the store for groceries. On the way, Alex relayed the news about the blackouts.

"Some of the farmers don't like to take chances when they don't have to, so when they catch wind that a raid's coming, they tell their workers to stay home. Nobody shows up for the day. That's called a blackout. It really ain't a big deal. Just can't get paid is all, but at least you don't lose your job, or worse, get deported. Not that you hafta worry about that part."

Jack looked confused. "So no work tomorrow?"

Alex nodded. Jack reached into his pocket for a smoke. It was the first one he'd had in days. He could afford them again. He put it to his lips and ran his hands through his hair.

"Isn't it the farmers who call the raids on?"

"That's right. Gets confusing, don't it?" Alex attempted to make sense of it for Jack. "See, the farmers aren't stupid. At least Hadinger ain't, he's probably one of the better ones anyway. Farmers only call on themselves once they're damn certain all the fruit's been picked. If it ain't picked yet and they hear a raid's brewing, well then, they call a blackout. The only exception to all this is if they think workers are organizing. Now that's a whole other ball game."

Jack took a drag of his smoke. "I guess one day isn't much if you're alone, but hell, we've hardly earned enough to have a decent meal tonight. At the speed I'm picking . . . ," he paused.

Alex gunned the engine to keep it from shutting off. He angled his eyes in Jack's direction. "Look, man, you're a stand-up guy. At least it looks like you are from what I can tell." He pulled two folded-up bills from his pocket. "If I know the kinda man you are, you'll probably turn this down, it's just how us working men are. But before you do that I want you to hear me." Jack looked at the money trembling in Alex's hand. "The way things work around here, is, well," Alex sucked his teeth, "you just never know how things'll work out. You could be living good one minute, and shit, you better enjoy that one single minute 'cause really that's all you got. Right? I mean things could always be worse." Alex set the money on the dashboard and continued. "You could be out on your ass, alone, scraping pennies. No job? Too bad. Kids? Fuck you. It's just how things are. Especially around here." He cocked his head at Jack. "You're a traveling man, right? I mean Bea says you've been all over the place. So tell me then, man, how many people have you seen, now really think about this, how many people you seen push themselves, wanting to do right by man, knowing damn well no matter how loyal they are, no matter how much muscle they put into something, something they thought worth trying for, a dream, a hope, and at the end of that long day, they ain't got shit to show for it? Worse than shit, really. They just got the odor of shit, the stink, the offal," Alex waved his hand in front of his face. "Worst part is they still put up a smile. Meanwhile that man don't give a rat's ass. I mean, really now, how many folks in all your travels, you ever seen like that?"

Jack smoked his cigarette and thought about it. He shrugged his shoulders. "Guess that's why Bea hates this valley so damn much," he replied.

"Valley hell! I'm talking about *her*, man, about Bea." He pulled his hat off of his head and sighed. "Shit, look at me, I'm giving you this sermon. Look, all I'm trying to say is about you taking her and the kids back east. I want to trust you, Jack. Can I trust you?"

Jack's face harbored a far-off gaze, as if he was looking into the future, his life with Bea and the kids stepping into the mangle of New York. He saw the sternness in Alex's eyes.

"Dammit, I want you to make this happen, man. Don't shortchange her, alright? So, this here's my little contribution. It's twenty bucks, all I can afford."

Jack finished his cigarette and tossed it out the window. The truck pulled into the store lot, and Alex threw it into park and turned his shoulders toward Jack.

"Look man, you ain't gotta be a chief, just take the damn cash. I'd give it to Bea myself, but I'm afraid she'd flat-out refuse." He paused. "Listen here, if what I'm hearing is true about a raid coming down, then you both better get outta here soon as possible. Trust me on this, man, I know what I'm saying."

"Sorry," Jack replied, reaching for the door handle.

"Fuck, man, there ain't no sorrys about this, I'm telling you take the cash."

Jack saw determination on Alex's face, a look he knew well, and knew that when a man's face had that certain bend to it, there was nothing you could do to change his mind. He lifted the cash from the dashboard and buried it in his pocket, and nothing else needed to be said.

21

If there was one thing that the blackouts were good for, it was fueling anxiety. The next morning some of the workers rose earlier than usual and got busy outside, posting themselves around the perimeter of the campo. A few men rallied together to fix some of the odds and ends that had been ignored for too long. A small team started digging holes to bury the excrement that had piled up from the spillover of the outhouse and hadn't been tended to in over a month. The churning of it alone had them gagging, and they were forced to take turns. Every so often a small wind kicked up and carried the stench out over the entire camp, and you could hear the children yakking and yawing about it. Another group took on the role of filling the potholes that riddled the dirt road, where each week at least one truck or another found itself wedged and blown out. And so the men piled stones and dirt into the holes and took pride in their necessary role, and threw back a tin cup of coffee spiked with whiskey now and again to keep their muscles loose and minds agile. Meanwhile, mothers were slapping work rags down on slabs of stone by the canal, or else in ratty wash basins, elbows up and down like jackhammers, scrubbing out two weeks' worth of sweat, pulp, and mud. Muscles knotted up in the forearms of these women as they flexed and twisted up denim overalls with a relentless rhythm, until every tree limb and flat rock and berry bush was strewn over with garments. Children adventured along the misty banks of the canal, skipping rocks, teasing out garter snakes with twigs. Or else they made up songs and sprinkled them up and down the rows of tents, sloshing along in shallow pools of mud, dirtying up their faces and legs. Jack stood at the door of the tent, observing it all, keeping an eye out for Alex.

When he arrived, they threw a few buckets into the truck and then a small tool box with knives, some fishing line, and several hooks, along with burritos made from leftovers and, for the sweet tooth, homemade grape jam sandwiched between crackers. And with this, Bea, Jack, little Albert, Alex, and Epi hopped in the truck and rattled northbound on the Golden State Highway. As they pulled away from the campo, some of the workers cocked their hats back on their heads and wondered out loud to one another why the Renterias trusted this gabacho, this lechuza who suddenly appeared in their midst.

Bea looked back and saw Epi hunched over little Albert in the bed of the truck; their hair was whipping around but they were all smiles. She placed her hand on Jack's lap. Alex saw this, and angled his eyes at her. She could sense him staring. Tension bloomed and she decided to end it there once and for all, but when she turned her eyes toward her brother, instead of bitterness, she saw that he was grinning.

"So where's this place again?" Jack asked.

Alex lit a cigarette and held it between his two fingers as he spoke. "Skaggs Bridge. It's a little spot on the other side of Fresno, up near the Madera line. A friend of mine said the Chinooks are running. So thick all you gotta do is stick a knife in the water and fillets practically jump in your lap, man." Jack smiled at the way Alex spoke. He had his own flair, his own way of gesturing and getting words out. Jack looked down at Bea's hand and put his own on top of it and kept it there.

"You ever spear a salmon?" Alex prodded.

"Naw, but I did quite a bit of fishing growing up. Never really caught much. The river we had was so wide that unless you were serious about it you end up with nothing but mudsuckers, really. We mostly did it to get out there, in the wild, give us something to gut and bloody our hands a little. Kid stuff mostly."

"Well, this here ain't kid stuff, let me tell you, you're gonna love it, man."

Alex adjusted his rearview and saw Epi and little Al huddled up. The day was overcast but once in awhile the sun would peek out and then slip behind the big gray cotton balls that sailed over.

When they arrived at the river, they unpacked their things and made a cozy spot in a small clearing. Epi and Alex squirreled away, snickering like two little boys. Jack took little Albert by the hand and led him to the river. From a distance they could already see silver flickering in and out of the water, as if the river itself were churning up diamonds. Together they scurried to the water, and Bea called out behind them, "Careful, honey, please keep Al close." Jack waved her off, and followed behind the boy as he began leaping boulder to boulder. Now and then he accidentally dropped a foot into the water and yanked it out quickly, and Bea put her hand over her mouth and called out again. "Jackie, honey, please keep a close eye on him, would you?" Jack grabbed the boy and lifted him up onto his shoulders and strode through the shallow end of the water. Little Al roared and laughed and pointed down at the rushing blue, and called out, "Fish!" And Jack called back, "Look at that, would you! Geezus, I never seen anything like it. These fish are the real deal." The water roared and frothed, and soon the sun triumphed and broke through the clouds, spilling down over that small part of the valley, warming up everything in its path. Epi and Alex emerged from the bushes, cracking branches along the way, with huge toothy grins, their eyes reddened like cut watermelon. They peeled open a beer each and wedged the rest of the cans in the stream beneath a felled tree stump to keep them cold. They sat on the bank next to their sister and watched Jack maneuver across the rocks with the boy on his shoulders. Jack turned and called out, "Alex, aren't you gonna show us how it's done?"

Epi slapped his brother's shoulder, urging him on, and that was all Alex needed. He leapt up and kicked his boots and socks off and rolled his pant legs to just below his knees. He looked back at Epi.

"You coming?"

Epi shrugged, then lay back and rested his head against a rock and calmly swilled his beer. Bea stood up and kicked her shoes off and went into the cold water after them.

"Look here," Alex said, making his way toward the middle of the river. "Pay close attention now."

"I never caught a fish before," little Al said giddily. Jack lowered him down onto the embankment, and the boy cheered and clapped his hands and watched his uncle make his way closer to where the great streaks of silver were pummeling his legs.

"Goddamn, these things are big as hell," Alex yelled out.

Jack peeled his shirt off and flung it to the shore.

"Go, Jackie!" Bea hollered.

The two men stood in the middle of the river, looking down at their feet and skimming their eyes at the shimmering beneath them.

"There!" Alex pointed at a bolt of silver darting away. "Damn, these things are fast."

"Toss me that stick, baby, would you?" Jack called out.

Bea reached for a felled branch and flung it at him, and he grabbed it before it drifted off in a current.

"Yeah, that's right," Alex said, "that's how it's done. It's all coming back to me now."

Little Albert moved over to his mom. Bea took his hand and pulled him alongside her, and the two stood close to the bank and watched the men go about their hunt. Epi let out a stony laugh and chugged his beer.

"Trucha, Alejandro," he said, "one of them fishes is gonna pull your ass under. Haw!" He grabbed a jelly cracker and stuffed it in his mouth. Jack and Bea laughed, and Alex kept his focus on the water.

"They're all over, man. Christ! Hand me that stick of yours, would you?"

Jack passed it to him, and Alex pulled his Buck knife from its sheath and began cutting away the bark from one end. When the tip was sharpened to a spear, he put his knife away, gripped the thing with both hands, and drew it far back and waited. Jack turned to Bea and saw her giving little Al a kiss on the forehead. A second later Alex jammed the spear into the water and cried out. "Almost had that son-of-a-bitch!" He drew the spear back again.

"I think you're supposed to throw it at the fish," Epi hollered.

"That's how I've seen it too," Jack agreed.

Alex glanced at both of them and turned his head away. A silver arch peeled out of the water and dove back in. Little Al pointed at it. "Fish!"

Alex turned his head. Another pounced, and then another.

"A whole school of 'em," said Jack, pointing and looking over at the boy. Little Al lifted a rock and flung it at the flashing water.

"Look, mijo," Alex called to his nephew, "your tío's gonna show you how it's done." He aimed the spear, drew it back, and hurled it into the water. It crashed into a stone, then lay flat on the surface and sailed away. Everybody had a good laugh, including Alex. He threw his hands in the air and looked like he was about to give up altogether when his red eyes nabbed an idea. He hurried farther out among the slabs of leaping silver and squatted low. Lower still. Until his back pockets dragged in the water. He stuck his hands in up to the elbows and in a flash was pulled under the current.

Epi jumped to his feet and raced over. "Alex!" he called out. He could see his brother tumbling downstream, hanging on to a bolt of silver like it was the last meal on earth. His legs jutted in the air as he wrestled with the slippery beast and curled his chest around it. A thousand fins slapped his face but somehow he managed to hang on. He jammed his thumb into a gill and punched it on the nose. He gagged up water and continued rolling away. Bea and Jack laughed, and Epi chased Alex alongside the banks, pointing and hollering. "Hang on, man," he said, jabbing his finger at the air, "You got it, man, hang on!" And Alex did just that, the whole time his body slipping away, down past the curve of the river, until he was out of sight. Epi followed his brother, and when he reached the curve of the river, he looked back at Bea and Jack and waved. Alex had made it.

Bea and little Al climbed out of the water, and Jack followed, cold and wet. They pulled a blanket from the truck, and all three wrapped themselves in it and waited for the guys to return. Huddled against one another, they pecked away at their sandwiches, digging their cold wrinkled feet into the soft grass, listening to the hush of the river swirling around them.

Minutes later Epi appeared in the distance, holding one end of a long stick while Alex held the other end. It was speared through a hefty Chinook, angrily twitching out its last efforts. Little Al leapt up and rushed over to his uncles for a close look. He ran his small hand over the chrome scales, and awed at the sight.

"We gonna eat it?"

Epi nodded. "Damn right," he said.

Besides a few scrapes on his arms and face, Alex wore a proud mask. They filled one of the buckets with water, crammed the giant fish into it, and watched it lay there jerking lazily. Now and then little Al would walk over and poke the monster with a stick just to watch it jump, and he'd giggle his heart out over it.

The day was turning out to be exactly what they all needed, time away from the campo and the fields, away from everything and everyone. Jack and Bea took little Al adventuring around the site. They climbed up onto a ledge and could see the river shimmering below. Later they chased squirrels around a large sycamore tree until they were all exhausted. Back at the site, Jack drank his beer, and at Alex's request he recounted a few stories of his own. He told them about the places he'd been, his time away from home, and then slipped into a gripe about his own mother, and how the woman was more or less a rash of guilt.

Alex nodded and offered Jack a suggestion. "Man, one time I bought my mom a sewing machine. Remember that, Bea? And trust me, she ain't never forgot that. We must've had new pants that whole first year, no?" Bea and Epi nodded. "Just buy her something is all, man. Mothers eat that stuff up, let me tell you."

Bea slapped her brother's arm playfully. Epi stood up and vanished behind a bush to smoke a joint by himself, only to return later with eyes that looked like they'd been glued shut. Before long, little Al had fallen asleep on his mother's lap. Jack turned his eyes toward him.

"Poor kid, all tuckered out, isn't he?"

"Look at him," Alex added. "Hell if he don't look just like a Renteria."

Bea stared down affectionately at him and ran her fingers through his curls. She smiled and was lost in him, but then suddenly her grin fell.

"What's wrong, baby?"

She cupped her hand over her mouth. Little Al adjusted his body and she turned her head away and caught herself. "I just miss Patsy is all. God, I miss her." She paused. "I just don't think I can wait another week before I see her."

Jack sipped his beer. "Won't be too long now," he said, resting his hand on her knee.

Alex flung his empty can into the river. "If you two bust your humps for five more days, I bet you can make enough. It ain't impossible." He looked at Bea.

Jack tossed his empty beer can at the river too. "It's settled then. That's what we'll have to do." He jumped up and went over to the truck and returned a minute later with his coat in his hands. He crouched down and unfurled it on the grass. There, wrapped neatly in its plastic, was a large piece of chocolate cake. Bea and Alex weren't sure what to make of it, but it didn't matter. He took the cake out of its plastic and broke it into a few pieces and handed them out; they couldn't have been happier about it, especially Epi. Little Albert awoke and rubbed his eyes. He stuck his head in his mother's armpit, and she fed him a morsel of cake and he was satisfied. Her immense green eyes hung on the frame of Jack's face, and he stilled his gaze on her, until she turned away toward her brother. Alex was sucking on a cigarette; he nodded his chin and waved his smoke in the air, and then looked out at the river, at the flashes of light charging upstream. He nodded to himself, "This right here's what it's all about."

With the night came a cold scrim of fog that spotted stretches of the highway back to Selma. All four were crammed into the front seat, while Epi sat with the fish in the bed of the truck. The whole way back not a single word was said between them. The strange ease of the day was still playing out in their heads. The solitude. The flowing river. A sprig of sunlight. Cake. Fish. All of it had come and gone, peaceful, undisturbed, like a slow-moving blue cloud that never broke a single thunderclap, much less a drop of rain.

They let Epi out by the grape fields near their parents' house and waved him off as they started up the road. When they reached the campo, they passed the small crew of men circled around a bonfire. Alex nodded at them, but they didn't nod back. At the tent Jack gathered up little Albert in his arms, went in and laid the boy down on the narrow mattress, and placed his coat over him. Bea and Alex ducked in through the flap, and Alex pulled up a crate and sat down. He watched his sister move about the tent getting things ready for the next day.

"I was thinking," he said, "about you two going to New York." He ran his hand over his face. "Did I ever tell you, Bea, that I almost went there myself once?" She shook her head. "Well, I did. When I was in the army. We were supposed to ship out of the East Coast. Man, was I looking forward to that." His eyes lowered.

Jack took his shoes off and tossed them toward the door flap. He wedged himself next to little Albert and let his head rest against his duffel bag. "What happened?" he asked. Bea folded her overalls and stared at Jack.

"He got kicked out, if you can believe that. Got into a fight with his sergeant." She shook her head.

Alex looked proud. "How many guys you know can say that?"

"Not many," Jack replied.

"Man, I let that son-of-a-bitch—" Bea shushed him and he lowered his voice. "I let that son-of-a-bitch have it, man, let me tell you. Sergeant Dowdy was his name, a testy bastard if I ever knew one. You know the type, right? Poor ol' boy from the sticks, but soon as they get themselves a uniform they think they're high society and wanna start bumping guys like me around." He broke into a cackle. "Hell, he messed with the wrong guy, let me tell you. I used t' box back in Los Angeles, man, trained with Roscoe Navarette over on the east side." He rubbed his knuckles.

Bea dipped a rag into a bowl of water, wrung it out, and scrubbed her face and arms. She watched her brother leaning toward Jack, relishing the story.

"So this guy Dowdy's been giving me hassle since the day I arrived, right. Supposedly he'd seen all kinds of combat and now he don't have much sensitivity for things, and I'm supposed to be good with it. Well, I wasn't. No one really was, just no one had beef enough to bring it to him. So one day, in front of some buddies he calls me a greaser, and man, I just had enough of it. I get up and walk over to him, and I'm about as still as the San Andreas Fault, man, I'm trying to keep it together, I am. But soon as I get within a foot of that knobby nose of his, all I see is a bull's-eye. God! I don't think I ever had a single punch ever felt so good in my whole goddamn life. It was worth every bit of hell I took for it." He slapped his knee, and then checked his shirt pocket for a cigarette. Jack dug one out of his coat and passed it to him. "I tell you, man," Alex continued while lighting up. Little Albert coughed and rolled over on his side, and Alex got a worried look.

Bea yawned, "I'm tired, Alex, we gotta be up early tomorrow."

He took a drag of his smoke and nodded, then looked at Jack. "I better finish the story another time, before I get an earful." And with that he stood up and said his good-byes before ducking out the door flap. He paused to look back at his sister. "Five days, Bea, that's it."

22

The workers couldn't stop talking about it. Especially that whole first day after it happened. According to the paper, a "wetback" was found strung up in a sycamore tree near Raisin City. From his neck dangled a cardboard sign:

PARASITE

The Fresno County coroner confirmed that because nowhere on the body were there bruises or scrapes the only logical explanation was suicide. A common occurrence among braceros. Naturally. They missed their families back home. Depression was inevitable. Fear was constant. The food too bland. A bottle of whiskey was found half emptied nearby. And for Xixto María Martínez, all the signs were there. On this very day his contract was up. As for the brief poem found on his person, the paper offered no explanation, except to say: Mr. Martínez had a way with words. It was imminent now. Xixto dying the way he died was only a suggestion.

The workers knew this, and thought hard about it as they bent over their vines that morning in a solemn daze. The fields were gray with dew, and each grape wore a thin veil of film so that its sheen was hidden. So quiet were the rows and the shuffling of feet that swallowtails perched themselves on the branches of the vines and plucked the smaller tart grapes at will. And as if things weren't bad enough, a cold snap was creeping in over Devil's Ridge from the north and settling down into the valley, sure to cripple whatever bits of fruit were still unharvested.

That morning, Bea's hands moved faster than anybody else's. Box after box was filled and carted off to be weighed and counted, and within seconds she was right back where she'd left off, on the very same tendril, making sure the job was done right and that every last grape was accounted for. She passed other workers as if they were standing still, and for the most part they were. It seemed everyone was busy scratching their heads, worried whether today was the day it would all go down.

They eyed Jack suspiciously, wondering if the rumors were true. A *lechuza* they called him. A white owl in their midst. For the most part he got good at ignoring their accusatory glares. But off and on he'd feel something, a pebble, smash against his neck. He shrugged it off and kept his hands moving. Meanwhile, Bea kept saying the words *New York* in her mind. And while her feet were sunk firm in the wet soil, the rest of her may as well have been in a subway, barreling down the spine of Manhattan, a purse slung over her shoulder and both kids clinging to her arms. She thought about what her brother had said. "Five days," she mumbled to herself, "just five more little days." She passed the time picturing their new life, imagining the big smell of New York City, and watching the kids monkey around the playground of some brick schoolyard tucked between high-rise buildings. She lifted another box of grapes and hauled them off to be counted.

Meanwhile, Jack trailed one row back, cutting away viciously with his curved knife all the knots and tendrils that cradled the grapes deep in their clutches. His gaze was stern and removed, and his pink face glowed in the cold. Little Albert nipped at his heels, raking out whatever clusters went overlooked and plopping them down into Jack's box like the handy assistant that he was. Each time he did this he looked to Jack for approval, or a smile, anything to erase the worrisome look on his face. Jack watched the way the boy handled his knife and shot around the whole field effortlessly, offering a hand here and there, calling out to the other workers in Spanish, whistling the whole way. He was a little man doing big man's work, and Jack had taken notice that the fields had an army of these little men workers, boys, whose small hands were crucial to the whole operation. Every last one of them wore a defeated mask. And if you looked at them from a distance, he reasoned, you'd think they were full-grown men by the way they stood, hips squared and shoulders back. The only way you could tell the boys apart from the adults was at lunchtime, when they'd all gather around a hole in the dirt to shoot marbles.

Jack observed this and shook his head, remembering a line from one of the great scribes of this territory, William Saroyan, who said it best about such children of the valley: *I was a little afraid of him; not the boy himself, but of what he seemed to be, the victim of the world.*

Later that day, Panzón found Bea and handed her a small envelope. It was a letter from Beto. He made sure Jack wasn't around when he gave it to her. She stuffed it in her back pocket and kept right on cutting grapes without missing a beat. Panzón stood there, with his gut out, expecting a thank-you that never came. He went back up the row, and Bea watched the hams on his back shift side to side, and from that angle, in that moment, she felt genuinely bad for Panzón. If only for that single minute.

When it came time to count out the day's take, which was done in front of the entire crew of workers, Jack stood quietly as he watched his meager pickings pale in comparison to Bea's and little Albert's. The men snickered and so did some of the women. But money was money, and nothing made Bea happier than to see things moving along.

That evening, he walked to the store for some flour, lard, and a pack of cigarettes, while Bea stayed behind. She had taken on sewing overalls for Big Rosie in order to make some extra money. While little Albert sat on the mattress doodling in the dirt, she laid the large tattered garments over the small wooden table and ran her hands over the material to smooth them. At that moment, she remembered the envelope in her back pocket and pulled it out. She looked at it, and noticed that the flesh on her thumb was healing. She went over to the door flap and tied it shut. She looked at the letter once more. It felt frail in her hands. She unfolded it.

Beatrice,

I'm in LA now with my brother. I don't even know if your back in Selma yet or if your still over here. I left mijo with Jessie and told Panzón to tell you. I came here to find some work. I need some money though so send it to the address on this envelope. Also, I heard some things about you that I hope better not be true Beatrice. If it is true than I think your trying to hurt me aren't you? I hope not. I'll be wating for the money and see you real soon.

Beto

She folded the letter and stuffed it back into her pocket. She stood over Big Rosie's pants and tried hard to steady her hand in order to get the piece of red thread through the needle's eyehole. Her fingers quivered. She couldn't shake Beto from her mind. She tried humming a song, little Al's favorite, and he smiled and hummed along. It worked for a little bit. She lit a cigarette and focused on stitching. What exactly did he know? She turned angry and cursed him under her breath, but that only lasted a few short minutes, until she heard footsteps approaching the tent. Her heart raced. But then she heard Jack's voice, whistling.

She went over and untied the door flap, and when he walked through, she held him.

"Everything alright?"

"Yeah, it's fine." She paused. "Jackie? We really need to pick faster. I mean being here is getting to me. I don't know how much longer I can take it."

"I hear you. We'll give it an extra push tomorrow."

She looked into his eyes, and hoped that he meant it. When he looked away, she reached for his chin and held it steady. She looked into him once more.

For dinner they had themselves a good meal of potatoes and refried beans with tortillas. Once little Al was asleep, Bea suggested they go over the plan again.

"On the road we'll have to be resourceful about everything," Jack pressed. "At some point we'll have to hitchhike." His eyes calculated. "Don't know how that'll work. Never hitched with kids before." He shrugged.

"It ain't impossible, I bet," Bea countered.

"Right, it'll sure as hell be tough, though."

She dug out the small box she'd been keeping their money in, and it rattled with coins. They opened it and started counting. This took all of sixty seconds. Twenty-two dollars and twelve cents. Bea scrambled to her other pair of work rags, and so did Jack, and they rifled through each pocket carefully, and this produced several more coins. They dropped those in the pile and added it up.

"Twenty-three dollars and nine cents," Bea said.

Jack stared at the money.

"It's better than nothing." She picked up the cash and set it back into the box. "We can make it, Jackie, just a few more days, honey. Like you said, we'll just have to push extra hard tomorrow."

He reached over and stroked her hair. "Right," he said.

Outside, the sound of men's voices churned, and it sounded as if the lookout crew was assembling by the canal. Wide shadows cast over the tent walls, and some of them were toting rifles. Jack took the box and handed it to Bea to put away.

She did, and then walked over to the door flap and peeked her head outside. In the distance she spotted a large figure standing, squared off at the front gate of the campo. When the figure turned, she saw that it was Big Rosie. Big Rosie spotted her too and waved the butt of her rifle for Bea to get back inside. Bea waved back at her, and Big Rosie walked over to their tent.

"Go inside, mija," she called out. "It ain't nothing to worry about."

"What's going on?"

"Nada, just a couple of pendejos having it out, you know how men are," she said. She turned and headed back to where the commotion was.

"Come on back inside, baby," Jack said, rubbing his hand over her shoulder. "It'll be fine, just like Rosie says." He leaned over and kissed her neck.

"Not now, honey," she forced herself to say. "I mean, I want to, I just . . ." She sighed and stood up, then went over to the mattress and lay down beside little Al. Jack went and lay down on the other side of the boy and pressed his face into his duffel bag. She turned in his direction and could see the outline of his body in the blue dark. She whispered.

"I told my mom, Jackie."

He groaned.

"I mean about going to New York." She paused. "She thinks it's a swell idea. At least it's what she told me. I can't believe it myself, I mean, that she'd say something like that. Guess moms are funny that way. Always telling you something unexpected like that. I didn't say anything about you though. But I think she knows anyhow."

Headlights shone through the canvas walls of the tent, and a truck rattled down toward the canal.

"I hope everything's alright out there," she said. "Sounds like something's going on, don't it?" Jack didn't reply. "Honey?" Little Al jerked in his sleep and coughed. His voice sounded hoarse and he coughed again. Bea touched his forehead but it wasn't feverish. She pulled the blanket up over their bodies, all three of them, closed her eyes, and fell asleep worrying about the voices.

23

By the next evening little Al's cough had worsened, so Bea went to her parents' house to see if she could leave him there.

"It'll only be a coupla of nights, mijo." Little Al understood, and though he was reluctant to be left there again, he knew it was for the best.

For the first time since they'd arrived at the campo, Jack was left alone. He decided to make a fire, so he went out to gather some twigs over by the canal. He walked past the rows of tents, keeping an eye out for anything that might make good kindling. A few rows over he saw a group of men huddled around a bonfire. One of them spotted Jack and motioned to the others. They eyed the gabacho and began whispering in Spanish, loud enough for Jack to know they were talking about him. He hurried back from the canal, wood in hand, and slipped into the tent.

He got on his knees, opened the stove's mouth, crammed the twigs in, and tried lighting it up. The wood was moist and it snapped out loud. Black spurts of smoke rose up, and he inhaled the harsh scent of plum wood. He rubbed his hands together and pulled the pint from his coat pocket and drank, watching the flames slowly rise and lick through the cracks. He polished the last of the whiskey off, and then reached for his notebook and thumbed at the pages. After a minute, he glanced over at the empty bottle. Across the campo he could hear soft voices, children whispering their good-nights in Spanish, then a child's song echoing, and a mother's voice carrying a light melody over the snapping of the flames. Jack rested his head on the pillow. Just then a spider scurried over his wrist, and he watched it duck under the canvas before making its escape.

Lying there, he thought of Bea and how she'd fare in New York. He could already see her eyes darting to and fro, like all the hungry tourists who saturated Fifth Avenue. Sooner or later, the shape of her body taking on the posture of invincibility that all people get after living in the city for a year. He'd show her the real side of it all. Grab some greasy dogs down on Bleecker, then take her up the narrow stairwell to a friend's place, show her off, watch them study her like a rare specimen. He could feel his neck loosen up, and his mood lightened at the thought of it. And then there were the kids. He tried picturing how they'd fit into it all. They'd need space for one thing. He was restless.

The sound of truck tires rolled over the soft dirt road, and he tucked his notebook away and peeled back the door flap for a look. The vehicle kicked up mud and made its way a few rows over. He could hear the excitement in men's voices as they piled in. It sounded like a small group of guys revved up for a night on the town.

He thought of his friends back in New York, and how, earlier that day, he'd spoken with Carlo over the phone. It felt good to hear his voice. It had been too long, this he was sure of, and he couldn't wait to return home now, with his new girl on his arm. Suddenly, the idea of spending another week in the fields weighed on him like it hadn't before. Five days now seemed excessive. They needed the money now. He sat up and decided he needed to find Panzón.

When she arrived at her parents' house, Jesus was still not home. Her mother helped her tend to little Al's nagging cough by giving him a tea made of ground ancho, vinegar, and honey. It was an old recipe that she swore by, and so little Al was forced to drink it. Afterward, Bea sat on the living room floor and watched her mother cradle the boy against her warm body and sing to him old songs that Bea remembered from her own youth. Little Al looked content there, tucked against his grandmother. She took notice, and realized she hadn't seen that look on her son in a long time, that peaceful gaze that sprouted from something so stable. She marveled right then at how her mother always managed to make a home feel like a home, regardless of how often they had moved from place to place.

"You better get going," Jessie said.

"I know. I will. I just wanna stare at mijo a little longer."

Jessie pecked the boy's forehead and held her mouth against his flesh. "His fever's not that bad, he'll be better mañana."

Bea nodded and went over to little Al and whispered into his ear. "Be back for you tomorrow, baby, promise."

Little Al opened his mouth and took in a breath of air.

Jack walked to the opposite end of the campo, where Big Rosie's cabin sat, but saw that her lights were off. He made his way over to where the men were standing around the bonfire, and when they spotted the gabacho coming their way, they fell silent.

"Any of you fellahs got a match?" he asked, waving his cigarette in the air.

One of the men lifted a branch out of the fire and stuck the hot flame in his face. He eyed them and lit his cigarette. They took inventory of his size. Jack puffed on his cigarette then took his pack out and offered them each a smoke, but they refused.

"You guys know where I can find Ponzo?" The men looked at one another. He repeated, "Ponzo?"

"Panzón?" the man holding the branch replied.

"That's right, Big Rosie's man. Know where he'd be?"

They stood silent. Jack scanned his eyes over the crew of them and looked out at the darkened field. Silhouettes darted in and out of tents. He looked down the dirt road that led to the highway and puffed on his cigarette.

"Forget it," he said, starting off toward the road.

When he got to where it met the highway, he spotted the store in the distance. He ran across the wide lanes over to it.

A few men he recognized from the fields were stocking up on powdered milk and lard. They nodded and Jack waved them over.

"You fellahs know where I can find Ponzo?"

"No, we haven't seen him," replied a kid of about fifteen. He spoke English with a thick accent. He translated for the others. "Está buscando a Panzón."

Jack didn't like the way one of them was looking him over.

"What's his beef?"

The young man turned to his friend. "Dice, qué te pasa?"

The man didn't reply. He only kept his steel gaze on Jack, and then walked to the icebox and pulled out an ice cream. Jack looked at the young man. "If you see Ponzo, let 'em know I'm looking for him, would you?" The kid nodded.

Jack scanned the liquor shelf behind the clerk and pointed to a pint of whiskey. He set his money on the counter. The clerk stuffed the bottle into a paper bag and took his money. They exchanged a glance.

Outside the store he unscrewed the cap and threw back a long gulp. He looked up and down the highway, took another swig, and then remembered that he'd left the woodstove burning. He took another gulp of whiskey and started back.

When he got to the dirt road, he could see in the far-off distance the light coming off the bonfire where the men were huddled. Silhouetted nearby were the peaks of the tents, and he tried bringing his eyes into focus. He ducked beneath a row of grapes and stood in a rut for a second, before deciding to avoid the men altogether. He was sure they were out for him. He made his way around the back of the campo, out to where the canal was. The nearby farmer's dogs yelped in the distance. The air held a strange energy. He pulled a cigarette from his coat pocket and lit up. A blade of headlights cut across the darkness, so he moved deeper into the fields and watched to see if maybe it was Panzón. It was too dark to tell. When all was clear, he continued on, down the row of grapes, high-stepping puddles of mud, weaving beneath the low canopy of vines. It was cold out and he could see his breath unfurling in front of him. A light steam hovered inches from the ground. He guzzled more drink to keep warm.

Bea was halfway down the front porch when she saw the headlights of her father's truck approaching. As she stood waiting for him, the words *New York* came to mind, and she could feel the skin of her thumb itching to be poked at. The truck engine rattled to a stop. Jesus got out and shut the door, then reached into the bed for his lunch sack and walked over to the porch.

"Where's Junior?"

"Inside," she mumbled, "con 'ama."

Jesus stood expressionless.

"A dónde vas?"

"Nowhere. Pa'l campo."

Bea could see the muscles turning over just beneath the skin of his jaw. He lifted his tattered hat off his head and pointed it at her.

"You know what people are saying, Beatrice?" He paused. "No me hagas pendejo. The whole campo knows about you." His face seized up and he couldn't get another word out. He took a breath. "What you do is your business, you wanna run all over Selma, como una zorra callejera, I don't give a shit, but you wanna bring Junior here, to my house—"

Bea couldn't resist. "Your house?" She spat. "You don't own this place, you never owned a damn thing in your life, 'apa. Never gave nothing to us, except . . ." She hesitated. Jesus stepped within two feet of her, and up close she could see that the gaunt flesh of his face was weathered, and his pale eyes looked as if they'd shut permanently any second. He was tired and could barely muster the strength.

She wanted to finish what she was saying, but instead found herself staring into his face. She could only recall one time in all her years when she had stood so close to him. It was on the train, when she was only ten, moments before the sight of Irapuato came into full view. Back then it was a smile that enveloped his entire face, and whether or not it was intentional, he had aimed it in her direction. Right then, a small part of her wanted to throw her arms around him, to feel his rough hands gripped across her back and around her shoulders.

"Eres una sinvergüenza," he said, the bags flexing under his eyes. "Beto told me que andas con un gabacho."

"When did he tell you this? Before he slept with another woman? Or after he spent all our money at the cantina?"

"I heard it from Panzón too, everyone knows!" He gritted his teeth and exhaled through his nostrils. A gunshot echoed in the distance and they froze for a second. Another rang out. Jesus looked out past his daughter, and then spat on the ground and stepped away. "You better not be with another man, Beatrice," he threatened, waving his thick finger inches from her face. He fumed and turned away, before looking back again. "I hear you're with another man—" His hand quivered in the still air, and that was it. Those six little words dangled, like a noose just waiting for a neck.

Bea folded her arms over her chest, and suddenly remembered that Jack was alone back at the tent.

⌒

As he circled the east perimeter of the campo, he could hear voices arguing inside one of the tents. Shadows flailed on the other side of the canvas walls, and it looked as if a dozen men were inside. The farmer's dogs yelped again, and this time, because of his proximity, they seemed close by. When he reached the canal, he leapt over a thin trail of frozen water and nearly slipped but caught himself. He stopped, suddenly remembering there were armed lookouts posted everywhere. He heard footsteps. Or thought he did. He stood perfectly still and tried listening, but could only hear the raucous voices coming from the tent. It got louder as the men began stepping out of the door flap one by one. Dogs yelped, and would not shut up. He moved alongside the canal, quickly, before ducking under another row of grapes.

"Who's there?" a voice called out.

Jack moved quickly away from where it came. A gunshot fired out and lit up the night. He could hear men's voices shouting, and they were headed in his direction. He reached the fence and could see now that the whole campo was stirring.

"La migra!" cried a woman, as she barreled down the mud road holding her infant.

Another shot rang out. Men spilled out of their tents, toting shovels and wielding grape knives, pointing fingers in all directions. Far off, he spotted Big Rosie clutching her rifle. She aimed it upward, toward the Sierra Nevadas, and blasted a round into the sky. Bodies scattered. Jack scrambled up the fence, and when he reached the top, something yanked at him and brought him to the ground with a thud. Before he could let out a single word, a bulky fist found its way to his face and then his jaw. He ducked and it jackhammered against the top of his skull. "Gava," he heard a voice snicker, right before a flurry of boot heels stomped on the meat of his back. He thought about calling out for Big Rosie, but when he raised his head, that same fist cracked the side of his mouth. He doubled over and clenched every last muscle in his body and could feel something leaking out the side of his head. It was warm, and he gripped at his face with both hands and waited for what felt like hours before it all came to a halt. A fist gripped at his collar and tore him back and away. He wiped at the mud in his eyes, and though he couldn't see, he recognized the voice. It was Big Rosie. A man blurted something at her; it was a rapid fire of Spanish that Jack couldn't make out. She tugged the gabacho to his feet and then stopped to glare into the eyes of the men who were responsible for the beating. More words were exchanged. He tried opening his right eye to get a look but it was useless. Big Rosie's voice bellowed. One of the men cursed her. She leveled her rifle at them, and that was that.

Back at her place, Rosie laid him down on a cot and gave him a cold slab of beef for his face. He tried saying something, thanking her, but his words came out slurred and incoherent. She shushed him, and then went to her door and stood out front, rifle in hand. He could hear her calling out to a few of the workers. It sounded as if she was attempting to bring some order back to things. A couple of men hollered, and he could hear the rush of footsteps hurrying about. It went on like this for some time. Through it all, he faded in and out of sleep.

When he awoke again, Bea was there, kneeling beside him.

"Honey?" she said, wiping the mud from his face with a wet rag. Big Rosie stirred behind her. She was smoking a cigarette, and Jack waved his hand for a drag. She passed it to him, and he put it to his lips and inhaled. He reached into his coat pocket and pulled out the bottle of whiskey and threw a swig back. Big Rosie grabbed it from him and took herself a swig too.

Bea looked up at her. She wanted to know the details of what had happened, but the expression on Big Rosie's face suggested the timing was bad.

"He'll be fine, mija," she assured Bea. "Just got a little roughed up is all. He'll manage."

Back at their tent, Bea lit a small fire and had a good look at Jack. His right eye was swollen red, and his lip was split. His left eye cocked and slid over in its socket, and she lifted his face up. Staring at him, she felt bad. Like somehow she was to blame. He groaned and rolled onto his belly. She helped him unbuckle his pants and slide out of them as far down as the knees, before he went completely motionless. She lifted his shirttail and found his back was the color of squashed grapes. It was swollen too. She wanted to say something to him, to ask questions, but knew it was worthless. The odor of whiskey emanated from his clothes, combined with a sharp stink of urine. She sat down next to him and listened to his shallow breath ebbing in and out. Voices continued to stir around the campo, but they were light, emotionless almost. The sound of a truck approached in the distance. She went to the door flap and tied it shut; she could see the headlights cut across the wall of the tent before turning away. She crept onto the mattress and pressed her body against Jack's, then cradled his head with her arm gently. The smell was rank, and she had to roll away from him almost instantly. She pulled the blanket up over both their bodies and shut her eyes, certain now that returning to the valley had been a bad idea.

24

The next day Bea arrived home from the fields and found Jack sitting on a tin bucket outside the tent. He was smoking a cigarette and scribbling in his notebook. When little Albert appeared from behind her, Jack broke into a smile and waved the boy over.

"What're you drawing?" asked little Al.

Jack showed him a small sketch of a man's head.

"That you?"

He nodded, then turned over a new sheet of paper and handed little Al the pencil and notebook. "Why don't you go inside and let me have a word with your ma."

The boy looked back at his mother.

"Draw me some animals, baby," replied Bea.

He liked the sound of that, and he took the book and pencil and ducked inside. Bea pulled two pairs of work gloves from her back pocket and flung them onto the ground next to the tent. She took the wide-brimmed hat off her head and adjusted the soiled handkerchief underneath. Jack stared at her. "That other set of gloves belong to the boy?"

She nodded.

Jack looked away. "Sweet kid like that really has no business being out there, ya know."

"I know, but he's alright. Besides, he's excited about New York too," she paused. "Says he wants to see the Pistachio of Liberty. Isn't that the cutest thing?"

Jack traced his fingers over his eye. "I've been thinking about how to say this to you, Bea, about last night. I mean, thanks for not hassling me about it too much. There's nothing a guy hates more than to be reminded of how bad he took it." He hesitated. She could see the crease between his eyebrows. "I've been sitting here half the day wondering who or what to blame, but I guess, in the end, who the hell knows?"

Bea looked confused.

"It could just be this whole damn universe is to blame. Everyone and everything in it, all of us in the same boat. Just how it is, and there's no use complaining about it." He touched his lower lip. "I'm not sore, if that's what you've been thinking. I just needed you to know this. I'm grateful, actually. If you can believe that." He angled his eyes up at her and smiled. The swelling in his face had hardly gone down, and the skin around his eye was still flushed. They could hear little Al's voice inside the tent, making animal noises as he scratched away in Jack's notebook.

Bea stepped closer to Jack and stood, hovering over him, his head about even with her hips. She mussed up his hair, gently, and then bent down and kissed the crown of his skull.

"Jackie—" she began to say.

He stopped her. "This don't change anything, if that's what you're thinking. You know, the whole time I was lying there taking those hits, I kept saying to myself, Bea's right, we gotta get out of here. Shoulda been gone already."

She squatted down in front of him and looked into his eyes. She wondered if it was possible that somewhere, lost in all that blueness, he was kidding himself. There was no real way to tell. All she had in that moment were his words.

25

They agreed that from now on Jack would stay in Hadinger's barn, and Bea and little Al would stay with the folks. It was an arrangement that Jesus seemed to have no say in, so he made himself scarce, much to Jessie's content. Even so, it wasn't an easy decision, but in the grand scheme it was a small, worthwhile sacrifice.

The next afternoon Bea went over to Big Rosie's place to return her overalls and collect the money for the sewing job. Upon entering, she noticed a look on Big Rosie's face that she had never seen before. Her eyes had lost their authority, and her posture was like a deflated balloon. She wore only a loose-fitting cotton shirt, and her unbridled breasts spread wide over her belly, pointing down at the cold earth. When she walked they swung side to side, and when she lifted her cigarette to her mouth Bea could see the skin beneath her arm drape like a broken wing. She set the overalls down on a table, and Big Rosie pointed to a small stack of coins.

"You haven't seen Panzón around lately, have you?" she said to Bea, her eyes fixed on the wall.

Such a ubiquitous presence was Panzón that if he wasn't at the campo, or hauling workers around, something felt eerily out of place. Bea shook her head. "Not lately."

Big Rosie wagged her chin slightly.

Bea grabbed the money off the table. "He'll show up," she said. "He always does."

Big Rosie dragged her eyes in Bea's direction and looked her friend square on. She puffed her cigarette and waved the smoke away from her face. Her mouth parted slightly; she wanted to say something but was trying to find the words. Bea rustled the coins in her hand.

"I think Panzón left me," she said, smashing her cigarette out in a coffee can. "For good."

"He couldn't do that," replied Bea. "You kidding?"

"Yeah, yeah, he could, Beatrice. You don't know Panzón. He's a snake, trust me." When she said this, she turned away, as if calling him that had triggered something. "The season's almost over, and then all this mierda with the raids, it adds up, Beatrice. My gut tells me he left." Suddenly, her face twisted in a knot and her lips trembled, but she caught herself and yanked her head upright. "Beatrice," she said. The bags beneath her eyes were round as bowls. "If he left . . . I don't know . . . I just don't know." She shook her head. Her lip trembled again and her jowls tightened. She ran her hand over her face and then got up to find her cigarettes. She lit another and stood with her back turned to Bea. Her words leaked out in a whisper. "You just don't understand. I know he's no good, anyone can see that, but I have feelings for him." She looked up at her friend and saw a blank stare on Bea's face. "You can't understand. How could you? You so pretty, Beatrice—hell, guys kill themselves practically for you." She slumped back down in her seat. "It ain't like I got a line of caballeros waiting to have a look at me—" She waved her hand across her body and then took a drag of her smoke. Before Bea could respond, Big Rosie buried her face into both hands and began weeping quietly. The bulk of her back shook, and Bea went to comfort her. But when the tips of her fingers grazed the bare flesh of Big Rosie's large brown shoulders, a howling sob spilled from Rosie's mouth. She folded over her belly and heaved twice before catching herself, suddenly, and stiffening back up. "Ay, Dios, Beatrice, you don't need this, you got your own hell to deal with." A couple of tears ran over her cheeks and down her neck, and she didn't bother to wipe them.

Bea felt bad about taking the money right then, and she set the coins down on the table.

"What're you doing? Take the money, Beatrice, it's yours, for fixing my clothes."

"I don't need it."

"Don't give me that," she replied, and then she fell silent. She leaned back in her seat and folded her arms. Her eyebrows bunched in the middle. "Dime mija, is it true you're going to New York?"

This caught Bea off guard. "How did you hear?"

"Everyone knows." She hesitated. "You thinking of going with the gringo?"
Bea turned away.

"Listen, Beatrice . . ." She hesitated. "There's something I need to tell you."
Bea angled her eyes at Big Rosie. "Come here," Rosie said. "Sit down."

"I'm fine."

Big Rosie smashed her cigarette out in the coffee can. She wiped the tears from her face, and then swallowed a deep breath. Her chest rose and fell. She looked at Bea and saw her green eyes fixed on her.

"It was Beto."

Bea looked confused.

"The other night. It was Beto. He was the one who put that chingaso on Jack."

Bea's face turned red, and she felt light-headed.

"I wasn't going to tell you, for your own good, mija, but that's the God-honest truth. I saw him with my own two eyes."

"Jack said it was a whole mess of guys."

"Beto had a couple of guys with him. I didn't recognize them, but I saw Beto. And let me tell you, he saw me too."

Bea turned and started for the door.

"Hold on, Beatrice, that's not all."

"I don't need to hear this, Rosie, not now."

Big Rosie stood up from her chair and stepped toward her friend.

"Listen," she said, scraping the coins off the table. "I've been thinking a lot about telling you this, but you know me, I don't get involved in nobody's business around here. Not unless I have to. Unless someone's not paying rent, or if they're causing un desmadre, pues, then I have to 'cause it's my job." She positioned herself between Bea and the door. "But I do gotta tell you this, Beatrice, and I want you to listen good." She took a step back. "The other night, I can't tell you exactly what happened, but I can tell you what I saw with my own two eyes." She hesitated. Bea felt nauseous. "Like I said," Rosie continued, "I don't know what happened or why things got out of hand, but by the time I got to that fence, Beatrice, where they had Jack, they weren't beating him anymore, mija, no they weren't." She shook her head in disgust. "By the time I got to him Beto had his—" she stuttered, "that cabrón was pissing on him."

Bea stepped back and away from Big Rosie. Even though she wanted to plow right through her, she knew it wasn't her fault. She could only stand there and wait for her to finish.

"Only reason I tell you this, Beatrice, the only reason, is 'cause you need to know the kind of man he is."

Bea let out a hard laugh. "Oh, believe me, Rosie, I know exactly who he is."

"Pues, leave his ass then, mija," Big Rosie's voice hardened. "You deserve better than all this." She waved her hand in the air. "Vete de este pinche valle, get yourself a good life, you're young still, mija, and so pretty. You deserve that gabacho, and whatever your plan is with him, take it, 'cause you never know if this train ain't never gonna come your way again. Some trains only go one way, you know. They only pass through one time and that's it, take it or leave it. Beatrice? Take that money for the clothes. If I had more, I would give it to you." She grabbed Bea's wrist and jammed the coins in her hand. Bea turned and started toward the door. "Mándame una postcard," Rosie said.

Bea jammed the coins into her pocket, and could hear Alex's truck revving. She put her hand on the doorknob and was about to leave when she hesitated. She glanced back at her friend. "Rosie? I hope you don't hate me for saying this, but Panzón ain't nothing but a lying son-of-a-bitch, far as I see it. You deserve better too."

Big Rosie nodded. "Yeah, mija, you got that right. But not everything is about love. Sometimes a man is good enough if he can just get you from one day to the next."

Alex revved the truck engine again. Bea looked at Rosie once more, knowing it would be the last time their paths would cross.

"Ay, te watcho, Beatrice," Rosie called out. "Que Dios te bendiga."

26

That evening she snuck out to the barn carrying a plate of food. She found Jack resting on a mound of hay, scratching words into his notebook. He was excited to see her, and to see a large hot plate in her hands, a tail of steam lightly rising from the calabacitas, rice, and beans. He shut the book and cleared a place for her to sit. She set the plate down in front of him and explained that the mashed green and yellow pulp was squash, mixed in with bits of corn and peppers. He didn't hesitate to dig in and sop up the beans with a wedge of tortilla. She grew quiet at the sight of him wolfing it all down, huddled there in the barn like some feral dog that had gone days without a meal. The skin near where his eye met with the bridge of his nose still bore a slight discoloration, a pale blue sliver of moon. He chewed away, content, hardly noticing the sour note that had taken over Bea's face. She couldn't help but think of what Big Rosie had told her, about what Beto had done to Jack. It made her cringe just to picture it. She knelt down beside him and took his hand and kissed it.

"Honey," she said, "I can't stand the thought of you out here, while me and little Al are over in my folks' house." She ran her fingers over a tuft of hay. "Ever since the other night, just seems like everyone's lost their minds. I bet you're miserable out here, aren't you?"

He chewed the food in his mouth while turning over her words in his mind. He set his plate down and took her in his arms. "Did I tell you I spoke with my friend Carlo, back in New York?"

"Who's Carlo?"

"He's a good guy, a real friend. Says we can stay at his place for a spell, just 'til we get out on our own, a few weeks at most. You're going to love him, baby. Says he can't wait to meet you either."

Bea's face lit up at the thought of it, and she leaned away from his arms and dug into her pockets. She pulled their savings out and set it all down on a piece of wood and began counting.

"How much we got there?"

She totaled it. "Thirty dollars and fifty-two cents." For a split second her eyes glazed with concern. She gathered the change and stuck it back in her pocket. "This oughta be enough to get us started at least, don't you think, honey?"

Jack fell back on the hay and stared up at the roof of the barn. "Who knows, could get us to Denver. Depends on a lot of little things, really."

Bea lay next to him and rested her head on his arm. "Boy, I really miss Patsy."

He pointed up at a rafter. "Look at that! Now tell me that isn't the ugliest creature you've ever seen?"

She looked up and saw a tarantula tickling along a slab of wood.

"What do you suppose it's doing there?" he asked.

"How should I know? It's probably wondering the same about us."

"Hell if that isn't the biggest spider I've ever seen."

"Oh, he ain't harmful. It's probably more scared of us." She looked at Jack. "Two big ol' bodies down here, making a nest in this hay. Imagine what she must be making of that."

"Think spiders are territorial?"

Bea nibbled at his ear. "What're you saying? Like maybe this barn belongs to her?"

"Maybe she thinks it does."

"Well, maybe it does."

Jack relaxed and moved his hand onto her belly and nipped back at her. He slid his fingers under her shirt, and she shut her eyes and drifted back, and he rolled on top of her. She pulled his shirt up over his head and threw it off, and he tugged at the button on her pants. She lifted her hips so that he could pull them off. The dank smell of moist hay and old wood was everywhere. A thread of wind slipped through the cracks in the barn wall and the cold air sent ripples of goosebumps across both of their bodies. Lying there, on her back, she had a perfect view of the gargantuan spider, and watched its hairy legs tremble above them. Jack nibbled at the inside of her thigh and then made his way up her torso. He took one breast whole in his mouth and she gripped the back of his head and leaned over and whispered some words to him. A gust kicked up and the barn shuddered but the spider remained diligent. Bea could see its two fangs tickling the rafter. Its bulbous backside lifted and settled down and lifted again. Their bodies had shifted on the mat of hay, and the black hairy creature repositioned itself, as if peering down, wondering what to make of the commotion below; the four legs entangled, twenty fingers gripping, one body pressing down into the other. She shut her eyes and drew Jack's head against her mouth and whispered to him, "I love you, Jackie." And she waited, hoping she'd hear him say it back to her, until finally, he did. "Me too," he said, and said it once. She pulled him into her and shut her eyes, and she thought about Broadway, and all those lightbulbs going off around her. She thought she could smell New York on his skin as she sunk her chin down onto his shoulder and let the hush of his gentle breath lift the hair behind her ear. And then she remembered the tarantula, spying, palpitating, several feet above. She opened her eyes, and when she did she discovered that the creature was gone.

27

Early the next morning Bea adjusted the strap of her overalls before helping little Albert into his. She wiped his face down with a warm rag and tied his shoes and hurried him out the front door. She clutched his hand as they went through the damp fields out to Hadinger's barn. The first load of workers were already in the truck and shuttling out toward the winery by five o'clock. She could hear the truck's engine growl down the dirt road, past the campo and out onto the highway. The fog was thicker than ever, and only when they were face-to-face with that big decrepit barn were they able to actually see it. She slid the wide door open and poked her head inside and called out for Jack. She stepped inside and called for him again but got no answer. She glanced over to where his duffel bag had sat the night before and was now missing. The place was quiet. She sent little Albert around back to see if maybe he was milling about somewhere, exploring. It was just like Jack, she thought. Probably off petting a heifer, or else befriending one of Hadinger's chickens. She stood at the barn door and scanned her eyes across the fields, scrutinizing the vast fog for any sign of him. It was the kind of ominous blight she had seen year after year, an immobile grim cloud, like the cloak of an old bitter ghost dragged out at the end of each harvest. She stuffed her hands into the front pockets of her overalls, and waited for little Al to retrieve Jack, but the boy returned empty-handed. "He's gone." He shrugged his little shoulders. She cupped her hands around her mouth. "Jack!" she called out, slapping her hands down against her thighs. "Jackie!" she tried again. Little Al called out too. "Jack!" She ran over by the edge of the fields and squatted down to see if maybe she would spot his legs somewhere in the distance, but nothing. She was suddenly nauseous. Little Al looked up at his mother. She hurried back to the barn. She spotted the matted hay where just hours before they had made love, the indentations of both their bodies still present. "Jack," she called again. She tried swallowing but could only manage a dry phlegm. She noticed the worried contortions on little Al's face. He was staring up at her numbly. She composed herself, then grabbed his hand and rushed out of the barn.

They had hurried back to where the workers were gathering, when a faint whistle rang out and caught her attention. She thought it was in her head, until it came again, louder. She turned to where she'd heard it. There in the distance stood Jack. He was waving at her from a hundred feet away. She let go of little Al's hand and ran to him. She could feel the hole in her stomach expanding to her chest. She gripped Jack's body tightly and buried her face into the denim threads of his coat and felt the hard buttons skid across her cheekbone.

"You okay?" he asked, putting his arm around her.

She released him and noticed an easiness on his face. His square jaw and pink cheekbones were framed by a floppy hat, and his blue eyes appeared as aloof as two dangling grapes. He stood with his weight on one leg, and she saw her brother's curved knife hanging from his belt loop, readied for the day's work. He cupped his hand to her ear.

"Bea?"

She rocked back slightly and took a good look at him. Her eyes flexed. She glanced over at little Albert, who was now sitting down on a berm, fidgeting with his knife. The boy coughed and wiped his nose with his sleeve.

"Jackie," she uttered, looking back at little Al to make sure he wasn't listening, and when he looked like he wasn't, she continued. "Honey," she said. The words were lodged in her throat.

"Yeah?"

The look on her face was empty. She stiffened her lip. It took another second for her to collect her thoughts. "Remember what I said last night in the barn? I meant it, you know."

He pulled his hat off and played with the rim a minute, before lifting his pale gaze up at her.

"I love you, Jackie."

He put his hat back on. She waited for a response.

"I need to know, honey. I need to know if you love me." She looked back at her son.

"Yeah, of course I do," he whispered, wadding both gloves in his hand.

"I need you to be straight with me, Jackie. If you don't feel this way," she hesitated, "just come right out and say so. I can take it. I need to know, here and now." Her eyes narrowed and her mouth was a straight line.

He rested his hands on his hips and scanned the landscape.

She gripped at her temple. "It just doesn't make sense. I keep asking myself why a man like you would wanna tangle up in my mess. I mean, you're free to roam wherever your heart desires, but me, hell, I got kids. And you don't have any idea what it takes to raise 'em." She remembered little Al and lowered her voice. "We've been leaving him at my folks, and Patsy's with Angie, but once they're both with us, I'm telling you, it don't get easier. Have you thought about that?"

Jack looked over at the boy and found him staring.

"If you ever thought about leaving, Jackie, I wish you would just say so. 'Cause once we're out there, back in New York, me and little Al and Patsy, we won't know anybody except you. We won't have anybody at all to help out if things go wrong, we'll be a million miles away from anybody. I can't go through all this only to find out you have a change of heart. I can't."

She took a breath, and when it seemed she had nothing more to say, he put his hand on her shoulder. "Sounds like you've gotten cold feet?"

"This is all I ever wanted. But I need it to be real, see? You've grown on little Al too, and if he could say what's on his mind, I bet he'd wanna know the same."

Jack fiddled with the knife. "I meant what I said last night," he replied. "I feel the same way about you. About the boy too."

"God," she uttered, lifting her hand to her forehead. She folded her arms and stared back at little Al. "Hang in there, baby," she said. "Me and Jack are almost done talking, alright?"

"I know," said little Al, squinting up at his mother.

She took a few steps and moved past Jack. She peered up the long row of grapes, into the white shroud that cloaked all of Selma. "I've been giving this a lot of thought, honey." He watched the back of her shoulders rise and fall. "Jackie, I got this crazy idea and I want you to hear me on it, okay? Remember when you had the idea of coming here, back to Selma, and I heard you out, remember that?" He nodded. She looked away for a moment. "Geezus, honey. I think it's just gonna be easier if you go ahead. I mean, on to New York, without us."

He couldn't believe what he was hearing. He stepped back.

"I stayed up all last night thinking about this, and it's really the only way." She wanted desperately to touch his face right then. Instead, she dug her hands in her pockets. "We've been here a week now, and can you believe this is all we've managed?" She pulled out the small wad of cash. "It ain't enough to get us all there, the four of us."

Little Albert was growing restless. He reached up and tugged at a vine and tore off a single leaf.

Jack's face was cold. He looked at her from beneath his eyebrows. His voice was empty of emotion. "What're you saying? I go to New York, and then what . . . you'll come later?" He looked doubtful.

A part of her wondered if telling him about Beto was a good idea, but she decided against it.

"After the other night, honey, it just ain't safe for you here."

His breath curled out in front of him. He peered over at little Al and the boy was shivering now. He cocked his hat back on his head. "Seems you already made your mind up about this."

"I haven't. Hell, I don't know if this is a good idea or if it's coming from that part of me that keeps screwing things up. I just know that this place ain't good for you. Me and the kids, we can manage, at least for a little longer, but you—" She stopped talking.

Jack ran his hand over his jaw. "You're sure about making it back east?"

"In a couple of weeks, by Thanksgiving at least." She hesitated. "No later than Christmas . . . by Christmas for sure." Her green eyes shimmered. "You just be ready for us. Have that sweet little place all warm and cozy, so when we get there, Jackie, first thing I'll do is cook you a good Spanish meal."

"Mama," little Al called out.

"Hold on, baby." She stepped closer to Jack.

He reached out and took hold of her neck. The fresh calluses on his hand scraped against her skin, and damn if it didn't feel good to her right then. She took his hand and placed the small wad of money in it.

"Take it, honey, so you can get back home, safely, to your mom."

"I can't do that, you keep it, for you and the boy. You're gonna need it if you wanna make New York by Christmas." He crammed the money back into her hand.

"I swear on my life, I never met anyone as sweet as you, Jackie." She kissed him on the lips, then stood for a moment, realizing there was nothing else to do now but walk away. She could see he wanted to say something. A part of her hoped he wouldn't utter another word. Still, another part of her needed it. She put one foot in front of the other and went over to little Al.

"Let's go, baby," she said, helping him up. She looked back at Jack and could see the intensity of his eyes was like a stilled ocean.

"Jackie," she said, "promise me you'll leave right away?"

He took his hat off and held it at his side. "Promise you'll make New York?"

"I'll be counting the days, honey."

Little Al looked at Jack. It was all happening too fast for him. He lifted his hand solemnly and waved good-bye.

"See you in a couple of months, pal," Jack said. The boy turned away.

"You will write me, won't you?"

"Of course I will," Jack replied, breathing warm air into his hands.

"You gotta write me, honey, I'll miss your sweet words."

She put her arm around little Al's shoulders, and they started quietly up the row. Jack watched the back of Bea's hair rise and fall with each step, while the boy held his mother's hand and fell behind.

When they were a good distance away, and it seemed like they were in the middle of their own clouded dream, little Al stopped walking. Bea looked down at him and tugged at his hand to continue on, but the boy refused.

"Why is he leaving?" he asked.

Bea knelt down in the dirt. "It's okay, mijo, we'll be with him soon, hear me?"

Little Al looked at the ground and she kissed his face. He turned and peered back over his shoulder, to where Jack had stood only seconds ago. Now there was nothing more than a scrim of white.

"Jack!" he cried out.

Bea hushed him.

"Jack!" he said again.

"Stop that," Bea said, pulling his body tight against her chest.

He called out Jack's name once more, but his small voice was stifled. He collapsed in his mother's arms and sobbed. She buried her mouth into the nape of his neck. "I promise you, Albert, we're gonna see him again real soon. You watch, by Christmas we'll be in New York."

Later that morning, when Jack came to the highway, he backtracked to the post office in Selma and made a call to his mother. She was glad to hear her son's voice, and when he asked her to send him money for a bus ticket, she was more than happy to oblige.

"How long before you're home?" she asked.

He stared out across the railroad tracks, past the dull low buildings of downtown Selma and out across the sad gray skyline, and then he touched the soft tissue of his eye.

"Soon as I get that money," he promised. "I'll be home soon."

III

Mañana Means Heaven

October 30, 1947
Jackie Kerouac
133-01 Cross Bay Bld.
Ozone Park
Long Island, New York

Dearest Jackie, I got your card. It made me very happy and at the same time blue, cause I couldn't go with you. It makes me happy to know that you care about me, cause I feel the same way about you. Hope you're home now & hope you got my letter. Also ans. to my sis house.

Love & Kisses — Yours Bea

28

October 30–31, 1947

On Thursday morning, when everyone had gone off to the fields, Bea quickly packed a small bag with only one change of clothes each for herself and for little Albert, and tossed in a few sandwiches for the long bus ride to Los Angeles. There was no need to call Angie to let her know she was coming; it would only be a quick trip, to pick up Patsy and make amends with her sister, and possibly, depending on how that worked out, to ask her for a favor that could only be asked in person.

By six-thirty that evening she was standing on the steps of Angie's house on Blanchard Street, where kids were playing stickball and sipping water from a leaky faucet on the side of Antonio's Market. She knocked on the door and her nephew Robert answered, and right away he and little Al bolted up the street together, shouting at the rest of the kids. Bea went on in and found Patsy sleeping against Angie's chest. Her sister looked up at her from her worn place on the sofa, and spoke softly to her so as not to wake the baby up.

"What are you doing here? Alex said you were back in Selma?"

Bea set her bag down and went over and gently lifted Patsy away from her sister's grip. She peered down affectionately at her tiny pink face, and then buried her nose into her small chest and whiffed deeply. She stood like that for several minutes before speaking a word.

"I'm not staying long," she said. "I just came to get Patsy." She hesitated. "But I also needed to talk to you."

George walked through the front door, letting the screen snap back and slam against the frame. Angie hushed him, raising her finger to her mouth in scorn. He raised his hands in the air and glanced over at Bea.

"She's here for the baby," Angie said. George nodded, then went into his bedroom and shut the door.

Outside, the kids were gathered on the front porch discussing Halloween costumes. Robert was giddy over a cowboy outfit his mom had made him from a couple of potato sacks, while all Knobby could talk about was how real his gun looked, the wooden toy his father bought him just to match his policeman's costume. Meanwhile, little Albert hadn't thought about Halloween at all, not until his cousins had mentioned it. When they asked him about his own costume he shrugged.

"I don't like Halloween anyway," he replied.

Bea went and put Patsy down in her bassinet and then returned to her sister, knowing there'd be words waiting for her. And of course, there were.

"I have to tell you, Beatrice, you really surprised us this time," she said, lifting a cigarette to her mouth and lighting it.

Bea grabbed her own cigarette, and they went out on the front porch, shooing the kids inside. Angie continued. "Mom's sick over this, you know?"

"I'm not worried about Mom. I spoke to her about it already. She knows all the hell I've been going through with Beto."

"It's not Beto, Beatrice, I mean of course we all understand that. So he's a jerk, leave him then. But this gabacho you been going with, seriously, are you out of your mind?"

Bea puffed her cigarette and stared out at the purple-hued Los Angeles skyline. She wondered how to respond in such a way that her sister might find a seed of understanding in all of it. "Will you just listen to me, Angie, honestly, for one minute?"

Her sister rolled her eyes.

"I didn't plan on things going like they did, they just happened that way. I'm not making any excuses about it. I was coming here to be with you, just like I said I was. I wasn't trying to end up with Jack. I was just minding my own business, right there on the bus, and next thing I know this nice man is being friendly with me. Not regular friendly, I mean, Angie, if you knew Jack, you'd see for yourself, he's a sweetheart, he really is. I never met anyone like him before, and I bet you haven't either."

Angie fired a look at her sister. "George is good to me. You don't know what you're talking about."

"See there? You're blowing a fuse over nothing, that's not what I meant at all." Her face turned sullen. "Look, it don't matter anymore anyway." She looked up at her sister. "He left yesterday, back to New York."

Angie flung her cigarette off the porch. She looked at Bea, and in that instant, seeing her sister sitting there, she remembered the kind of loyalty Bea had always shown her while growing up.

"I ain't mad at you, Bea. Just that all this is creating the kind of fuss that me and George don't need right now. Don't get me wrong, we love Patsy, we do. Just that times are hard right now, tu sabes, and Dad keeps putting pressure on Mom to speak with me, like I'm supposed to set you straight or something." She reached over and touched Bea's knee. A long silence hung between them. "So he left?"

Bea nodded. She finished her cigarette and flicked it off the porch.

"Is he gonna write you?"

"Said he would."

Angie looked concerned. "You know he can't write you in Selma, right? I mean that would just be stupid."

"Guess I hadn't thought about it much."

"I know George is gonna kill me for saying this, but he can write you here, if you want? This Jack guy."

Bea smiled at her sister and nodded.

"He really a sweetheart like you say?"

Later that evening, Angie ran errands and prepared the kids' Halloween costumes, while Bea stayed at the house coddling Patsy to rekindle the bond she was sure had been compromised. That night, they made a meal of pork chops con arroz y frijoles. After dinner, George retired to his room, as usual, while little Albert watched his cousins try on their costumes, one last time, just to be sure they were ready for the next day. Meanwhile, Angie and Bea stood over a pile of dishes, scrubbing and drying, one by one, catching up on so many things, memories mostly, about dancing in their bedroom as kids, and of course bonding over the mutual hatred they had for their father. The whole time Bea waited for the right moment to present itself, when she could ask Angie about that small but invaluable favor that could only be asked in person.

When the dishes were done and the kitchen immaculate and smelling of cleaner, they sat down at the table. The house was quiet now, a cricket's chirp from beneath the stove the only thing audible, and they finally reached that moment of the day when they could drop their shoulders back to their natural position. Bea decided now was the time. Of course, what she didn't know, could not hear, was that little Albert had drifted off to sleep in the hallway, just on the other side of the kitchen door. In that precise moment, hearing a familiar strain in his mother's voice, he awoke, and remained motionless, listening closely. He could hear her pleading with Angie; that much was obvious. But what exactly she was pleading for he couldn't tell. He rolled over, pretending to be doing so in his sleep, until he was close enough to hear.

"I'm not asking for a lot of money, Angie, just enough to get me and the kids back on our feet, you know, the fields are worthless right now. Can't make anything turning trays or picking algodón."

Angie's voice was lucid. "I would, carnala, I really would, I promise, but you see how George is already." Her voice lowered to a whisper. "He'd kill me if he knew I was giving you money."

"I'll pay you back in one month, I promise."

And then a long silence. Little Albert strained to hear. A cabinet drawer opened. Soft footsteps shuffled along the wooden floor. The clink of change, and then his mother's voice shushing his aunt's. And then more footsteps. Back to the drawer.

"It's all I have, Beatrice."

Bea was thankful.

"Look," Angie continued, "George gets his military check in a few weeks, a month or so, maybe. I can send you some more then, okay? But that's all I can do."

A short silence loomed.

"We'll be heading back to Selma tomorrow," Bea replied.

A knot festered in little Albert's stomach. He turned on his side, away from the door, and thought about Halloween. Nothing about it excited him anymore. He shut his eyes and could only think about how lucky his cousins were, and how ace they looked in their costumes, grinning from ear to ear, cowboy and policeman, candy of all varieties awaiting their grasp.

The next day, on the bus ride home, Bea kept to her thoughts, and uncharacteristically, so did little Albert. Patsy sat up most of the time, until the sun burnt out and only darkness enveloped the bus, and then she fell limp in her mother's arms, sleeping with the fragility of a canary. Bea looked down at little Albert, whose tired chin was lifting and dropping into his chest. She had been watching him closely the entire time, quietly wishing away the disappointment on his face. And he might've forgotten completely that it was Halloween had it not been for a young girl, about his age, who boarded back in Gorman, dressed as a witch, cackling the whole way. Bea poked him gently with her elbow.

"Mijo," she whispered. "Albert."

He rolled his head over and looked up at his mother with tired eyes. She leaned over and kissed his forehead.

"Albert, I'm sorry about Halloween." She hesitated. "I promise you it'll all get better. I mean, this little cloud we got hanging over us, that's all it is, just a cloud. You'll see, Christmas will be different."

He lowered his head.

"You believe me?"

He mumbled. She ran her fingertip over the smooth edge of his ear and stared down at the lull of his eyes and mouth.

"You just worry about kid things, alright?"

He nodded, and then adjusted his body, before letting go the weight of his head fully against his mother's arm.

November 2, 1947

Dearest Jackie:

Hope you received my letter by now and post card. Jackie, don't write to my sister's address; address your letters here to the post office at Selma, Calif. I am going to stay here in Selma until it's time to go to New York to see you. I sure miss you and so does little Al. I have little Patsy here with me also now. Boy! How she's grown. I wish you could see her, she would sure love you and the first thing she would ask you for would be a kiss.

She's so sweet, even if she's my little girl, I say that myself. You'd think so too if only you were here. I'll send you a picture of her, soon as I can. Jackie it's been cold & raining here already. How is it over there? Do you still miss me? I'm always thinking of you and the lovely times we two had together even the ride on the truck. I get so blue when I hear your favorite songs on the radio.

Jackie—I came back to Selma on Halloween night so you can see I didn't celebrate at all. We were riding on the Greyhound bus that night (it really didn't matter). Jackie please send me a picture of yourself so that I can look at you every day. I love you so much. Even if we are far away from each other, I still won't forget you. Say hello to your Mom. Ans. soon.

Love & Kisses to you Jackie Boy.
Yours always, Bea. X X X X X X X X X X X

29

New York was the only thing on her mind. Each day she pressed little Al, reminding him, especially during the longest work days, that the reason they picked so hard now—grapes, walnuts, and whatever else came their way—was to make sure they'd get there by Christmas. He didn't mind it so much, and when they were up to their elbows in vines he'd ask her to tell him, once more, about the snow and how it blanketed all of New York City. Of course nothing made her happier than to oblige her son's interest, and so she played along, describing to him what real snow falling from the sky must look like, especially in a city like that and especially at night, with all its skyscrapers and bright lights freckling the dark.

"Great big ol' flakes?" he asked, eyes large as discs.

Bea nodded and let her gloved hand drift slowly down to simulate the way it moved, or at least, the way she imagined it did. "And at night all those city lights make it glow like fireflies," she said, watching her son's eyes follow the path of her hand.

"And the kids can play in it, go sliding down hills?"

"Of course!" she replied. "That's all they do out there."

And from then on, whenever they were among rows of cotton and little Al bent down to pluck the fluffy white clumps from their stems, he imagined each one a ball of snow, and upon placing it into his sack he looked inside and saw not a day's worth of gatherings but the makings of what could very well be the world's largest snowman. He worked harder than he ever had before. Eight, sometimes ten hours a day, drudging mud, clipping vines, his hands and wrists whipped red, and sometimes his cheeks too, but you wouldn't know it by the constant smile on his face. Witnessing this made Bea feel uneasy, but she knew that getting there, to that place where Jack awaited them, would require all the work the two of them could take on.

One Saturday afternoon, after an exceptionally quiet day around the house, she pulled a single dollar from the cigar box and took the kids downtown for some ice cream. Little Al got two scoops while Patsy and Bea shared a cone, and then they all went to the park that sat beneath the water tower and ate until their hands and arms were sticky up to the elbow. It didn't take long for the sugar to do its job, and so little Al raced around the playground, while Patsy clung to her hip and bounced around laughing the whole time.

When she grew tired she sat down on a bench and observed them both closely. They looked happy, and if she could say so herself, satisfied. The last time she'd seen an expression like that on little Al's face was when he was flying paper planes with Jack. It made her feel good to see that she alone could bring the same joy to her son's life, and her daughter too, for that matter. And then she wondered in that moment whether or not the kids actually needed Beto at all. Or any man. It seemed entirely possible that she alone could continue on this way, and things would still turn out as they were meant. She pondered the idea for a minute, until it became too big a thought to get her head around. She scanned all of Selma's short buildings and narrow streets, then looked at the quaint storefront windows and over at the red train tracks. She turned the other way and saw the packing house nearby, and a row of hotels and bars. Behind it all were the barren fields, the waning grapes and felled cotton, plum trees upturned and ground into the soil for next season. By now Patsy had climbed up onto her lap and nestled her cheek into her mother's arm, and then little Al walked over and lifted his droopy lids and angled his hazel eyes up at his mother too. She knew then that it was time to go home.

On days when it rained and no one worked, Bea spent hours writing letters, updating Jack on how plans were coming along, assuring him that she still had every intention of making it to New York and that if things kept on as they were she was sure they'd make it there by mid-December at the latest.

But then, from one day to the next, a freeze crept in. So frigid was it that mud crackled beneath every footstep. The farmers fired up their oil heaters, but even so, half of the fruit that was left hanging froze and became worthless. Even though some light picking went on, it was obvious that the season was over. The campo had nearly dissolved, and already half the workers had packed their jalopies and headed south, to Arizona or Texas, while still others trudged north up the Golden State Highway, to Oregon and Washington. Bea had considered returning to her parents' house yet again, only until the cold snap fizzled, but knew that if she did, receiving letters from Jack there would be impossible.

For the most part her letters had gone unanswered, but this didn't stop her from dragging the kids to the post office each day. Upon discovering there was nothing with her name on it, she'd walk to the nearest payphone and call Angie to ask if any letters from Jack had arrived there. Each time she was forced to do this her stomach knotted up. The calls themselves were not cheap, plus Angie had lost heart and began to despise her sister for making her keep such a secret from the family. For those left in the campo, the news that Beatrice had left her marido for a gabacho was now overshadowed by the freeze.

But then one day a letter did arrive for her. After dinner that evening she sat in the tent, stoking the woodstove with more logs, and while the kids slept, she opened the letter and fixed her eyes on each word, for what seemed like hours. She lifted the paper to her nose and tried catching a hint of Jack, lingering somewhere amidst the dried ink. She stared at each well-crafted sentence, scanning closely, as if investigating for a plump piece of fruit that had gone overlooked. She had no idea that little Al was quietly, discreetly watching her every gesture from his cozy place beneath the blanket. And from there he saw that, each time, after every reading of the same letter, she did something he found strange, curious. She held it to her chest, and sometimes her face, whispering to it, as if it were Jack in the flesh. And then she placed it gently into its envelope and tucked it beneath the mattress. Afterward, she would take out the small cigar box which held their savings, and count how much money they had. The last time she did this—yesterday—he heard her say clearly, tenderly, *Almost there, Jackie.*

30

She awoke with the image of Jack overwhelming her every thought, and could feel her jaw muscles tighten, and a warm saltiness gather in the back of her throat. The days were blending into one another, it seemed, and each morning sounded exactly like the next; a rooster, a dog, an engine. Voices and smoke. A part of her couldn't help but feel trapped in the campo. "This must be what purgatory is like," she said out loud, but only to herself. She closed her eyes and could see and feel his slender body lying next to her, her head propped against his hard bicep. She could smell vividly the tobacco, sweat, and moist denim, that manly aroma that emanated from his presence. She then recalled, with perfect clarity, the way he would lean into her and kiss her forehead softly, and how she reciprocated with pecks on his chin and neck, the smallest sound of the lips coming off the skin. At this vision, her body curled up into itself and she gripped at the bedsheets and pulled them to her chest. She felt their resistance tug at her legs and back, and she knew it would take an act of God to convince her to get out of bed this morning. Her mind was playing reruns of moments and scenarios, of conversations and promises, all the sugary exchanges between them that she could conjure in that instant. She drank a cup of water to calm her thoughts but it was pointless; both hemispheres of the brain were snapping off memories, instances, flashbacks, and she could not, did not, want to control it. With Patsy still asleep and little Al outside, she buried herself beneath the sheets and conjured the force of Jack's square chest and broad torso bearing down on her, the weight of him almost too much to bear. Her heart raced, and she writhed on her back until she could not contain herself. She inched her right hand down over the wave of her hip bone, past the bristly forest of her pubis, with a bit of apprehension at first, before shutting her eyes slightly, and nestling her hand there, among the warm pages of that dark place where all stories begin—the whole time praying to dear God that little Albert would not enter the tent, or that Patsy would not jut up from her sleep as she so often did, unannounced. She quivered, and wanted badly to call out to Jack, and then she did, but only in her head, though a part of it still seeped from her lips. The "a" of his name trembled out and she could feel her womb warm, until suddenly, chaotically, a bolt of electricity shot through her. It sparked in the frontal lobe, the gatekeeper of all memory, and rushed through her limbs and found its exit in a slick and fluid release. When she was done, she leapt up and washed herself with water from a small tin bucket, her face and hands first, and then her body. She pulled a shirt over her head, then went outside, looking for little Albert.

31

That evening, while scrubbing little Albert down with a wet rag next to the glow of the woodstove, she fretted that his cough would not let up. She felt his forehead and it was clammy. She bundled him up with several layers of clothes and tucked him warmly against her body that night. After a couple of hours of listening to him cough, his throat sounding like truck gears grinding, she decided to ask one of the neighbors to drive them to the hospital.

While waiting for the doctor to see them, she phoned Alex and he hurried right over. From down the hall he could hear his nephew's voice, hacking uncontrollably. He arrived with sleep still in his eyes, a worried look gathered on his face. He went to Bea and put his hand on the back of little Al's neck.

"Christ, Beatrice, how long's he been like this?"

Bea picked at her thumb and didn't know the answer. "It just got worse tonight, right after I bathed him," she said.

Alex bent down and lifted his nephew up; little Al's head hung over his uncle's shoulder.

After a few tests, and several needle pricks that little Al was too exhausted to cry about, the doctor concluded that what the boy had was advanced bacterial pneumonia.

"Will he be alright?"

"He's going to have to stay here a few nights. We'll need to keep a close eye on him."

"How long will it last?" Bea asked, glancing over at her brother.

The doctor eyed little Al. "There's no way to tell, really. Could be a day or two, maybe even a week. Just depends on how his body reacts to the penicillin."

The next two nights, Bea sat slumped in the chair at his bedside. Her mother stopped by at one point to bring some soup for her grandson, but he wasn't up for it. Jessie relieved her daughter, and Bea went home to take a bath. Before returning to the hospital, she had Alex drive her to the post office to see if Jack had sent anything.

"Have you heard from him?" Alex asked.

"Yeah, he sent me a letter 'bout a week ago." He could see the excitement on his sister's face. "Says he's ready for us." Bea angled her body toward Alex. "I got enough now, Alex."

It took him a minute to register what she meant. "How much?" he asked, his eyes widening.

"About seventy."

"Is that enough?"

"Yeah, I checked on tickets already, over at the Greyhound. Think I have it all figured out. It'll be tight, but we can make it."

He slapped the steering wheel with the butt of his hand. "Hell, I almost wanna come with you."

"Let's do it, Alex," she replied. "I got the money, you've got this truck, we can make it. Soon as little Al gets out, tomorrow maybe, or the day after."

Alex shook his head, "Nah, no way, I only wish I could, but right now ain't good for me."

"You said it yourself, remember, you've always wanted to see New York—"

He cut her off. "I can't."

She looked at her brother, and fell back in her seat.

When they reached the post office, Bea got out and hurried inside. A minute later she returned empty-handed. As she walked toward the car she caught her brother staring at her and she put up a smile.

"Guess I can't expect one every day," she said, slamming the door shut.

"He's probably got a lot going on right now," Alex replied. "I'm sure that's what it is."

∾

On the third day, after giving him a good looking over, the nurse said little Albert was well enough to go home. Alex went to pick Bea and his nephew up from the hospital and found them in the lobby, waiting to be checked out.

"Just gotta fill out some forms is all," Bea said to her brother. "Then we can get outta here."

While Bea waited for the hospital official to come out, Alex took a seat next to his nephew and made small talk. An hour had passed before she decided to get up and go speak with the woman who sat behind the counter.

"Excuse me, Miss, I'm supposed to be waiting for some papers. My son's getting checked out today."

The woman took down Bea's name and had her wait another ten minutes, while she disappeared behind a wall. When she returned, a man appeared with her. He was donning a brown suit, and he asked Bea to step around to the side door so they could talk.

She called Alex over, and he and little Al followed them into a cramped office.

Bea took the only seat, and Alex stood behind his sister with his nephew propped against his leg. The man introduced himself as Mr. Balakian, and then he shoved a few papers across the desk at Bea.

"You workin' over at the labor camp?" he asked, a curious glare in his eye.

Bea nodded.

"Just gonna need you to fill these papers out."

"What is this?"

"Just gotta provide your work visa number . . . you got one, don't you?"

Bea grabbed a pen off the desk and looked down at the forms.

The man opened his top desk drawer and pulled a small piece of hard candy out. He jutted his hand toward little Al. "You like candy, son? I bet you deserve one of these, don't you?"

Alex nudged his nephew. Little Al took the piece of hard candy from the man's fingers and thanked him.

Bea signed her name and passed the forms back. Mr. Balakian looked the information over. He smiled and pulled a cash box out from the desk drawer.

"Looks like the only thing left is a matter of the bill," he said.

Bea glanced over at her brother. "What's it come to?"

The man rifled through the forms, and then calculated the numbers in his head. "Comes to fifty-three dollars and seventy-nine cents."

Alex stood motionless. Little Al coughed, then went to his mom. He rested his hand on her shoulder and lowered his head onto her. "I'm tired, Mama," he mumbled.

Bea patted his hand, and looked up at Mr. Balakian.

"Is there some way this can be worked out?" asked Alex. "Can't she make payments?"

The man shook his head apologetically. "I'm sorry. We can't release the patient 'less his finances been cleared."

"Are you kiddin' me—"

"Alex," Bea said, thrusting her hand toward him. "It's alright. I got the money. Just gotta go to the house."

The man nodded, and then leaned back from his desk. He glanced over at Alex and then down at the boy.

Bea turned to her son. "Mijo," she said, "you stay here with Uncle Alex, alright? I'll be back in a little bit."

An hour later Bea found herself standing at the front desk of the Selma Sanitarium, purse slumped open, counting out, hesitantly, nearly every last dollar she had. And as if that wasn't bad enough, the clerk took the money and counted it out, twice more, in front of her. The whole time, Alex looked over his sister's shoulder and shook his head at the terrible luck of it all. Little Al stood by, afraid of what this meant.

On the drive home Alex kept both hands on the steering wheel and hardly spoke a word, except to say, "The whole thing's a goddamn racket."

Bea sat quiet, emotionless.

For little Albert, the silence was excruciating. He looked over at his mother and could see her disappointment. He remembered the look on her face when they were picking, and how excited she got when talking about the snow, and how Jack would be there waiting.

"What about New York, Mama?"

Alex looked at Bea from the corners of his eyes.

She pulled little Al closer, against her chest, and petted his hair. She thought about how she'd looked down at him in that same way, on Halloween night while on the bus, making promises about how things would be different come Christmas.

"We'll get there," she said, and that was all.

The boy quieted, and kept to his thoughts. Somewhere inside he knew she didn't believe it. He blamed himself. Had he not gotten sick, they might be halfway to New York by now. He hated himself for it. He rested his head against her arm and listened to her breathing.

Alex nudged his nephew. "Don't worry, Albert," he said. "There's always mañana."

The boy had heard that word used for as long as he could remember. It seemed like the adults said it whenever there was nothing else to say. He'd heard it from his grandmother, Jessie, most often. Whenever Jesus couldn't find work, he'd come home tired and desperate, and she'd ease him off with one word, *mañana*. Almost always, it was used when money was the subject. In fact, so similar were those two words coming off the tongue that for the longest time he suspected mañana meant money. When can you pay me? *Mañana*. And then there was the way his father used it. "You can forget about mañana, Beatrice, ain't no mañana!" And when used in this way, it was like a slap to the face. However an adult decided to use that word, there was one thing little Albert was sure of—the word itself carried weight. But for all the times he'd heard it uttered, spat, or mumbled, in that moment, cruising up the long, dark road, when it came from his uncle's mouth, *mañana*, it no longer sounded like something a person just said. No, in that moment, it sounded like a possibility, a promise of things to come.

November 18, 1947
Selma, Calif.

Dearest Jackie:

I was sure glad to get your letter after so long. It's good to know that you arrived home okay. I was hoping you would. Jackie, I've written more often then you have. I go to the post office just about every day and no "letter" from you is all I get. Jackie, I didn't stay in L.A. at all. I came right back to Selma after I brought Patsy and I haven't left this little town since. Jackie, I'm sorry to say that I haven't been working too steady, you see little Al was sick, I had him in the hospital here in Selma for two nights, he had a touch of pneumonia, he snapped out of it right away though. They gave him penicillin shots. That's what cured him so soon. I was so worried I sat by his bed side for two nights. The Doctor told me I could stay there in case he would wake up.

I am saving what ever little money I have left after I buy what we need here at home. Jackie, Nellie my brother's girlfriend is here with me now. She cares for the children, while I work. I'm sure glad cause now I can work steadier and save a little more money. She's all alone, no family just she & I. My brother Alex is here, just about everyday. Jackie, Alex said he was going to get another car, a sedan and if he did then we could come to N.Y. with him. He wants to bring his girlfriend. I'll let you know what he decides.

Jackie I would like very much to go to that certain Mex. Restaurant, to eat there with you (if I can make it there), I'm trying very hard. I hope you can work like you say, part time—cause, I might need a little help from you. I'll let you know later on how much I've saved. I can't tell you now cause it's really nothing but chicken feed. I'm not going to buy any clothes for myself just stockings now and then. That way I wont spend so much. "Honey Bunch" I miss your company also and I often think of that little tent, where we had to live, it wasn't much but I enjoyed being there with you. We are still living here in a tent, but here we have a gas plate I keep it burning all day & night also. It's been so cold here and the fog comes down just like rain, we haven't seen the sun for two days. Jackie, tell you're mom that I would like very much to cook a Spanish meal for you—all. I can hardly wait to see you, and meet your Mom.

I hope you're Mom does like me. I hope you have a lot to tell me, when we see each other again. Jackie, why do you feel the way you do? Will you tell me in your next letter? Then I'll tell you how I feel since you went away. I'm sorry to hear that you had to hitch-hike and worst—cause you went hungry—just think if I had been with you! Well, we two would have found a way out. Don't you think? Jackie, Please write more often Honey cause I really miss you.

Love & lots of Kisses Sweet, Yours—Bea
xxxxxx ans. soon.

December 4, 1947
Selma, Calif.

Dear Jackie;

Thanks for writing, I appreciate that very much. Although I only got two letters in answer to my several. Jackie, I'm really happy about you joining the Merchant Marines, you know why? Cause I love to travel and if I had the chances you have, I would do the same. (If only I had been born a man.) Or at least if I didn't have any children to tie me down. I really wouldn't mind the children so much if I had a husband to go with them.

Jackie—my husband left his job and no one knows where he is right now—which makes me feel much better. Jackie, I didn't really want very much to come to N.Y. this winter cause I realize just how cold it would be up there. It's been very cold here too. But of course it doesn't snow. Although if you were there I wouldn't mind the cold so much. Yes, I received the letter you sent me at my sis's house she brought it herself.

Jackie I want you to know that the only reason I wanted to go to N.Y. was because of you. I wouldn't want to go otherwise. I'll wait until you let me know that you will be there. In the meantime, I'll stay here and work and save some money whenever possible. Jackie, please write as much as you can cause otherwise, I'll feel very lonesome and blue. You write such cheerful and sweet letters that's why I love to get them. Your letters are very interesting too.

Jackie another thing, I don't want you to think that I'm mad cause you took off. I feel just opposite (I'm glad) As I said before, I wish I were you. (I envy you) Jackie, how long is three trips? Honey be sweet and send me your picture in your uniform. Please do that for me. I'll always think of you, no matter how long you stay away or how far away you'll be. I'll stay as sweet as I can. (But just for you). I've turned down all the fellows around here cause I don't feel anything for them. The majority of them are so stupid and ignorant they just don't know how to treat a gal. I'll say adios for now and I'll be praying to God that you will come back okay and that you will have time to write to me. I hope you'll never forget this poor gal, cause she will always think of you.

I remain as ever,
Bea R. Franco
xxxxxxxxxxxx-oooooo
Kisses   Hugs

IV

I Remain As Ever

32

Monday, February 16, 1948

When she opened her eyes, there before her stood the majestic, craggy, internal mountains of Salida, Colorado. The sky was a pure blue and swept with white clouds that resembled vast strokes from a heavenly paintbrush. The bus drudged over the Rocky Mountains slowly, so as not to slip down the snow-white shoulders into the ravine a hundred feet below. The sun was busy melting off a fresh coat of powder from the night before. Tiny pathways of crystalline water trickled down the sides of the mountains and across the pavement. She held her gaze out the window and for the first time in seventeen years took in a lush panorama that was not imposed by a tractor's will. It felt natural, right, and she sat entranced by it the rest of the way to Denver.

As the bus entered the city, she pulled one of his letters from her purse and studied it. He would be in Denver only a short while, before shipping out with the Merchant Marines. He was living with a guy named Roland, in a small place off Lafayette and Colfax. She searched for clues of his desire to see her, to once again pick up where they'd left off. It had been a little over three months now since last she saw his face, standing there amid those drab Selma fields. Her stomach fluttered at the thought of seeing him again.

Colfax Avenue was unusually sunny for a February. The traffic stuttered past Lafayette Street, where she stood on the corner swathed in a thick coat, anxiously hoping to spot him hobbling up the sidewalk, or else hear his warm voice, tossing words out high into the air from around the corner of one of the cinder-block buildings. She looked again at the address on the envelope, and then jammed it in her purse before scrambling up the porch steps and trying the buzzer once more. No one answered. She sat on the stoop, nervously, watching the sun-chafed faces of people walking past. She thought about how she had considered writing to him, telling him of her decision to come out to Denver, but in truth, she wasn't sure herself until she was on that bus halfway across the state line. Across the street at J.B.'s Pizzeria the neon sign blinked in the window; two Italian men stood out front smoking cigarettes and talking in their native tongue. A moving truck coughed black exhaust from its tailpipe, startling a gang of pigeons that roosted on the white peaks of the Rosenstock Place building. The sunlight was quickly waning, and the city buses were filled with bedraggled workers on their way home. A jovial couple strolled up the block, hand in hand, and they nodded at Bea as they strode past, turning a corner and heading down the long straight slope of Colfax, toward the glaring golden dome of the capitol building. She stood up on the top step, and with the cold tongue of winter lapping at her ankles, she had only enough strength to try the door once more. When she did and no one answered, she hurried down the steps and ran back up Colfax to the nearest vacancy sign that caught her eye.

Pushing open the door of the Lion's Lair Inn, she saw a yellow-faced man stand up from behind his tattered counter and wave at her. His gut threatened to slip from underneath his shirt, and he sipped heartily from a tin mug.

"Need a room?"

Bea nodded, shivering.

The man scratched the back of his neck and leveled his eyes at her. "Cheapest room is two bucks a night."

"Sign out front says one and a quarter." She sniffled and blew into her hands.

The man shook his head. She grabbed her bags and started back out.

"Hold up there," he said. "A buck and a quarter is fine."

She opened her purse and pulled out a five-spot and set it on the counter. "How long will this last me?"

He lifted the bill and then gave her a once-over. "Five nights," he said, ringing the cash box open and cramming the money into the drawer. "But anything after that is a buck and quarter, hear me?"

After unpacking her bags she decided to soak her road-weary limbs in a hot bath and come up with a plan. Lying in the tub she thought about the kids, and how yet again she'd left them. But this time was different, she assured herself. She ran her hand over the scar on her belly and remembered how gently Jack had caressed it during their first night together. She could see clearly the turquoise of his eyes, the shape and sincerity in them. Just as clear was the tone of his voice when he spoke to her in those quiet hours of predawn L.A. But what she could no longer see, no matter how hard she tried, were the precise details of his face. Without realizing it, somewhere along the way, he had disintegrated into a vague image, a mere shadow, that she feared looked nothing like him.

33

Denver was unlike any place she had ever seen. It certainly wasn't like Los Angeles, and definitely nothing like Selma. In either of those places you couldn't walk more than two steps without hearing Spanish flavoring the wind, but here, way up in the Rocky Mountains, people spoke and moved with a different attitude altogether.

That first morning, after she had stopped by Jack's place again only to discover that he still wasn't home, she found herself on the banks of the winding Platte River. There, she gazed toward the scarlet mountains, listening to the soft applause of the Union Pacific trains shuttering in the distance. She stood there for a long while, silent and alone. Of course, it was not the same kind of aloneness that she found while sitting in some campo tent back in Selma, no, this one had a quality of purpose, like she was meant to be right where she was.

She spent the whole afternoon walking the arched spine of Colfax Avenue, ducking in and out of the speakeasy lounges and small diners and cheap whiskey joints, searching for him.

At one point she stumbled upon a park, a quaint spot near East High School where teenage boys huddled around benches and smoked cigarettes. They were red-faced youth, all of them, with shabby clothes and hardened hands. The type that chopped logs on weekends at the family farm, or else taunted bighorn sheep just for fun. They whistled at Bea when she walked past, and she ignored them and clutched her purse, pulling her worn blue sweater up over her chest.

Above her the sky continued to unscroll its dramatic swashes of light and dark, with vast dollops of clouds that practically moaned, they were so obese; they languished across the plains, eastward toward Kansas. They were a melancholy sight, and she couldn't help but feel this way about everything in that moment.

She pressed onward, scanning all corners and cracks of Denver.

At Park Avenue she stopped to watch a young family cross the street. The children's hands were interlinked and they bounced along joyfully, squawking like a row of homebound Canada geese. She wondered what it would be like living here with little Al and Patsy, in a city like this. How very different it would be from the valley, unrestrained and lush, its pastoral innocence still intact. Had it not been for this vision she carried close to her for the rest of the day, she might've allowed herself to feel dismal about the fact that finding Jack was proving far more difficult than she had anticipated.

34

The next day she tried the opposite direction. She traipsed the old pool halls and open dives of Market Street, where she thought she might find him scampering down one of the sidewalks, hands jammed into his pockets, cigarette tucked between his teeth. Or else hunkered near the window of some shoddy establishment, jotting words in his notebook, staring at the pages forlornly, as she'd seen him do so many times before. When this turned up nothing, she walked along the grid, hitting Larimer Street, then Lawrence, stopping to look at the sad display of brass horns in the pawn shop windows on Twenty-First before deciding to quell the grumble in her stomach.

On the corner of Twentieth Street she ducked inside a hole-in-the-wall cantina. It was a gaudy spot with a neon cactus hanging over the door and a sign that boasted *Authentic Mexican Food, Hot! Hot! Hot!* Its name reminded her of a story her father told.

If Jesus had ever imparted any knowledge to his children whatsoever, it was that shred of Mexican history he dished forth whenever he found himself embarrassed by the pocho speak his kids tried passing off as Spanish. Of course, he told the story the only way he knew how, straight-faced.

"El Bosque de Chapultepec is sacred land because that's where los Niños Héroes died. Six children who gave their lives for Mexico during La Revolución. You see, they were cornered by a bunch of gringos and they refused to surrender, so they wrapped themselves in the Mexican flag and jumped. This is an important story. Especially for kids, don't forget it." And that was it, the full extent of his patience and knowledge.

Of course, El Chapultepec Cantina maintained a legacy of another sort. It was a seedy dive that reminded Bea a lot of the Azteca back in Fresno, where her father used to take them on Sundays to talk to men about "work." It had that same musty stink of old yeast, rancid salami, and body odor. The only difference, really, was that instead of pool tables, El Chapultepec had a grand piano, drum set, and microphone perched idly on a short stage, where a banner hung above:

Jazz Every Friday Nite! Otherwise, the people in El Chapultepec were the same breed as the ones at the Azteca. Four men slouched over the bar, chortling small talk about "slapping some dame's ass the other night," and showing her the time of her life. Among them, a pock-faced toothless woman sat grinning, desperate for the company of anyone willing to give her the time of day.

Bea took a booth and ordered a beer and a plate of "Arroz y frijoles." The waitress twisted up her face, and so Bea tried again, "Rice and beans, please."

She took her sweater off and rubbed her hands to warm them. She looked around for a minute, and then got up and went to the ladies room. It had a flimsy wall, with holes in it where voices from the kitchen seeped through, along with the static broadcast of a local radio station. They were discussing the weather, and the pending snowstorm seemed to be the only thing on everyone's mind. She wondered if it was anything she should concern herself with.

Back at the booth, she tried listening to the forecast over the rowdy voices, and eventually she was able to catch enough to know that by morning there would be a blanket of snow eight inches thick. The storm was expected to reach Denver by late night. A few people grumbled but mostly no one cared, and it certainly didn't stop them from ordering another round of whiskey. She thought about that Bing Crosby song, "White Christmas," and how her sister Maggie, the one who made herself scarce these days, used to sing it aloud while picking cotton. And once that song entered her head, there was no getting it out, and so a part of her was now anticipating seeing that white stuff come spilling from the sky. She thought of little Albert too. He would love Denver, she was sure of it.

While eating her food, she noticed a small window leading to the kitchen. Through it she could see the faces of two women and a man. They were wiping their brows over a hot stove and yakking about their lives. They looked content, mostly, nipping at each other's ear, cackling out loud every other minute.

When the waitress came around again, Bea asked if she could speak with the owner. The woman straightened up. "You're looking at her, honey." She was caught off guard and didn't know whether to take her seriously or not. "I do it all around here," the woman said, her voice raspy but sweet.

"Any chance you could use some help?" Bea uttered. "I can cook and clean pretty good."

The woman sighed and gave Bea a serious looking over. "You don't wanna work here, dear, trust me."

"I could use the money."

The woman rested her hand on her hip. "Got any experience?"

"No, but I grew up with brothers and sisters, used to cook and clean for them a lot. I can sew pretty good too," she added, eyeing the tattered curtain that hung over the only window. The woman looked back over her shoulder at the kitchen, and then after a minute she turned to Bea.

"How soon you lookin' to start?"

Later that night, she returned to Jack's place on Lafayette Street and banged on the glass door. When no one answered, she pressed the buzzer and shouted his name.

A crabby man stuck his head out and barked for her to get lost. "Can't you take a hint, ya dumb girl?" he hissed. "Christ's sakes, you got my dogs giddy with your racket."

The man's voice made her skin crawl, and she wanted to give him a piece of her mind right then, but knew that staying on good terms with the old bastard was probably in her best interest.

A frigid wind crawled in over the Front Range and in a matter of minutes the temperature dropped thirty degrees. She raced back to the hotel room, where she filled a tub with hot water and drowned her toes until they thawed out. Meanwhile, she took both of his letters out and studied them closely. The pencil lead was faded where her fingers had run over the lines again and again. If she hadn't almost memorized them, it would've been impossible to make out. *Denver*, he wrote, *I'll be in Denver....* This was all the assurance she needed. She stuffed them back in her purse, and spent the rest of the night trying to put the details of his face together.

The next morning she awoke earlier than usual. Before the sun could be seen on the eastern tip of Colfax, she dressed herself in extra layers, just as Loretta, her new boss, had advised her. According to Loretta, the snow was supposed to be brutal that morning, and Bea was excited to see it for herself. But when she walked out onto the strip hoping to find a clean slate of white, she found instead nothing more than a pale smattering of frost.

On the way to work she made a quick stop by his place, and this time only looked through the window. She'd hoped to at least catch a body moving past, or some other sign of life within that flat. But just as she'd feared, this turned up nothing. Shying away from the building, she spotted the old man peeking out from behind his door, gawking, shaking his head side to side. She hurried off to work, the whole way worrying that she might have missed her small window of opportunity. Was it possible that Jack had already made off with the Merchant Marines? It couldn't be.

35

Now that she had a job, the hours passed like seconds. A few days turned into several. Still, each time she found herself in front of his building, walking up those cold steps, a part of her sensed, knew, that she'd leave yet again with nothing more than scorn from the old man. Regardless, she returned, each time calling out his name, knocking, banging on the door profusely. Until one evening the man did finally stick his head out and threaten to call the cops. She decided to leave a note in the mail slot.

I'm here Jackie, staying at The Lion's Lair on Colfax. Come by soon as you can.

As ever, Bea
xoxo

She agreed to work full shifts, and though this made Loretta happy, Bea soon found herself too caught up in the business of waiting tables at El Chapultepec to look for him. Before she knew it, a single day had passed when she hadn't thought about him at all. And then another. Soon, an entire week had come and gone without so much as a visit to his place. Between all the clocking in, taking orders, and hauling around hot plates of food, she mostly thought about the kids. Nightly, while in her hotel room, she found herself starting letters to them that she couldn't find it in her heart to finish. What could she possibly write that would make her absence seem insignificant? While staring down at the blank sheet of paper, she thought about what Jack had once said, back in Los Angeles, how the gods had created words for every situation under the sun. He was wrong. She broke down and phoned her sister.

"Have any letters arrived for me?" she asked.

"Nothing," Angie swore.

"You sure George didn't get a hold of anything?"

"I'm telling you, Beatrice," she lowered her voice, "Jack hasn't sent anything." There was a long silence on the phone.

Before Angie could say another word, Bea hung up.

∽

That Friday night El Chapultepec was frantic. Musicians were busy setting up equipment while hordes of slick types and working stiffs encroached on the bar and pasted themselves to every booth and wall. Before long the bass thumped in the chests of all those crammed bodies, and the trumpet squealed; every bottle, window, and loose tooth vibrated, and it wasn't long until everyone was hungry and thirsty and demanding of things. Food! Whiskey! Every voice shouting to be heard, emphasized by flailing hands. Bea worked harder that night than she ever had in her life, balancing four, sometimes six mugs of beer over the heads of couples busy tonguing at earlobes, while others blew thick walls of cigarette smoke in her face.

Loretta, a woman whom Bea was sure had been born and bred for the sole purpose of running El Chapultepec, saw the apprehension on her newest worker's face. "It gets better, honey," she hollered, waving a dollar bill from behind the bar.

Bea kept her cool while she darted around delivering drinks and hot plates of food. Now and then a coin flew her way from some happy bindlestiff who'd drunk himself cross-eyed. And of course the longer the night went on the more folks guzzled, and the more they guzzled, the hungrier they got. It was a never-ending romp, and it trailed on until five o'clock in the morning, when finally the piano man fell over and had to be carried off by his bass and trumpet players. The three of them used one another as a crutch as they all hobbled out the back door and into the alleyway where, despite all the forecasting, still not a single fleck of snow gathered.

∽

She stayed in bed most of the next day. While lying there, she thought about little Albert and Patsy again, and wondered what they were doing and how they were faring without her. She looked out the window and saw that Colfax was quiet and barren. Pulling the blankets up over her shoulders, she contemplated the New York number on one of the letters, but after giving it a bit of thought, she convinced herself calling was a sure sign of desperation.

An hour later she found herself perched at the foot of his building, staring disdainfully at her own reflection in the glass door. On the other side of it the

206

crabby man—Walter, she'd discovered his name was—stood snarling at her, refusing to open it, or to entertain any questions of her man's whereabouts.

At one point—though he never mentioned it to Bea—Walter himself went knocking on Roland's door, only to beg that this Jack character make himself known and, for God's sake, handle this lovesick woman of his. Of course, no one answered, which led Walter to believe that Roland, or more importantly, the man of this woman's imagination, had gone on vacation, or else, possibly, never existed in the first place.

36

Days later Bea set out looking for him again, this time amid the dirty hovels and odd rumblings of Larimer Street. It wasn't far from downtown, so when this turned up nothing, she continued walking, and soon found herself standing before the herculean brass doors of the Oxford Hotel. It was the type of place as swanky as her brother imagined—red brick and glass, everything glistening, right down to the wrought iron awning. Two tuxedoed doormen nodded and tilted their hats at her, and she backed away. A black car pulled to the curb and a young, dapper couple got out; one of the doormen dutifully handled their bags and escorted them to the concierge. They shuffled inside, all smiles, disappearing from Bea's sight.

She continued down the street, eyeing the massive windows and clusters of boutiques, passing a barrage of signs announcing the newest winter apparel, expensive wares, gaudy hats, stuff she'd never buy even if she had the money.

She was tired from walking and bought a coffee from a street vendor, and then sat down in the shadow of Union Station, watching the trains blowing steam and come skidding in from the eastern plains. She observed people loading and unloading, family and friends waving so long, hello, embracing to leave, embracing to return, it was impossible sometimes to tell which was which. The Union Station building sat wide and watchful, like a giant gray frog on its haunches, while the clock fixed at the top clicked its minute hand and measured out time for the people of Denver.

She couldn't help but pay special attention to the women. The way they carried themselves out here; small bag, pencil skirt, posture perfect, sure of themselves. They reminded her of all those arrogant little daisies that used to sachet the Selma streets without a worry in the world. A small group of them passed, and she overheard one snickering to the others about her husband, and how his affair was probably the best thing that could've happened to her, now that Chester was in her life. The look on their faces appeared to Bea like nothing more than well-constructed façades; she was sure of it. Another train whistled its departure, and again a wave of passengers made their way to the platform. Women and children stood by, waiting to board, while husbands hauled matching baggage with nametags flailing in the cold breeze. In that moment, quietly sipping her coffee, the whole scene appeared to her phony and colorless, and she assured herself that this wasn't real at all, not one bit of it.

37

On Monday night Loretta decided to shut the place down early. She shooed the only two patrons away, and she and Bea closed up, but not before taking a cigarette break in the alley.

"Think it'll snow?" asked Bea, taking a drag of her cigarette and staring up at the black night.

"Hell, who knows?" replied Loretta, sniffing at a shot glass of whiskey before taking a sip of it.

"I've been here most of February now and still haven't seen one flake fall."

"You shoulda learned already, honey, just because a person says it's gonna snow don't make it so," Loretta said, chuckling. "Especially not in this town."

"Just once, once I'd like to see it."

Loretta dropped her cigarette and lit another. "Careful what you ask for."

Bea looked at her strangely. Loretta drank the rest of her whiskey and sucked on her cigarette. "You're still young, honey, you ain't got much to be so serious about."

Bea thought about little Al and Patsy. She pictured their faces, and in that moment she nearly broke down. It didn't take much for Loretta to see through her.

"Mind if I ask you something, Bea?" She didn't wait for a reply. "Don't get yourself in a tiff over it neither, alright, it's just a question is all. Something I've been curious about since the day you stepped into my place."

Bea stubbed her cigarette out against the alley wall and dropped it to the ground. She could see Loretta was busy trying to figure out how to ask her question.

"Does that man of yours . . . the one you said you came here looking for," she hesitated, "is he for real?" Bea's eyes flexed. Loretta scratched her elbow. "Don't get me wrong, honey, I know he's for real, probably, but I mean, you been looking for him all this time and it's just, well, it's a little strange, I think."

Bea wanted to be mad at her right then but she couldn't. Loretta dropped her cigarette and smashed it out with her shoe.

"I'm not looking for him anymore," said Bea, "so it don't matter." She was shivering and Loretta noticed, so they went back inside.

Bea was quiet for several minutes. She walked over and yanked the jukebox plug out from the wall, then grabbed a rag off the bar and began wiping down the tables. Loretta filled a bucket with water and slapped the mop down onto the floor, slinging it back and forth.

"You ever think about going home?"

"You mean Selma?"

"Wherever the kids are . . . that's home, ain't it?"

Bea finished wiping the last table and turned to face Loretta. She could feel her throat swell up, and she looked away.

"It's late, Bea," Loretta said. "You oughtta get outta here before that snow finds you." She winked at Bea, and then pulled the mop to her chest and began dancing with it. She pushed it across the length of the dirty floor, twirling, until a corner of Bea's mouth turned up and a small chuckle seeped out.

38

The next evening she found herself, reluctantly, in front of his building. She sat on the curb across the street and glanced up at his window. She decided not to bother Walter or his dog by knocking on the door; instead, she just sat there. She noticed a dim light on. It was barely enough to illuminate the window, and she wondered if it had been there all along or not. When she convinced herself it had, she stood up and dusted the seat of her pants off and started up Colfax. Only once did she look back at the window, and when she did she realized, with all certainty, that had Jack's face appeared in that moment, it might not have been what she wanted at all. Not anymore. She turned and hurried away, her breath unfurling in the air around her, racing back to the hotel.

While she was unlocking the door to her room, the hotel manager appeared. "Where's the rent?" The paunch of his gut thrust out.

She opened the door and looked back at him. "I'll have it tomorrow."

"I guess you'll hafta wait 'til tomorrow for this letter too," he said, waving an envelope in front of her.

She set her purse down and pulled her wallet and counted out a few bills. "I'll get you the rest tomorrow," she said, waving the wad of money in his face. This satisfied him, and she took the letter from his grip and slammed the door behind her. It was from home. Lying on the bed, she tore it open and read:

Dear Beatrice,

I hope you are okay in Denver. The kids are doing fine but they miss you a lot, more than ever. Patsy cries a lot but mom holds her and cares for her. Little Al got into a fight with Freddy but he's fine. I'm teaching him how to defend himself now because of it. Beatrice, they really need to hear from you. When you get this letter call us.

Alex

PS: Maybe you can send little Al a picture postcard of the snow falling? I bet this would cheer him up real good.

Because it was February, the end of the month had arrived sooner than she expected. That night she slept with the window curtains drawn back, so that just maybe, with a bit of luck, she'd wake up to a white world on the other side of the glass. At least this way she'd have something to tell little Albert about, next time she saw him. She couldn't shake the image of his face from her mind. She pictured him, alone on his grandma's porch, a sad frump, and it made her miserable. She worried about Patsy too. Once, when Patsy was only a few months old, Bea had left her with her parents, and upon returning the next day she found her little girl lying on the kitchen floor, rolling her body over a plate of mashed beans and rice. The image of it still tortured her, especially when she was so far away.

It must've been one, maybe two in the morning when she rolled on her side and stared out the window at an empty sky. From her place on the second floor she could see the silhouettes of the Front Range jutting up like arrows pointing westward. She sat up in bed for an hour. The city was quiet. Not even the regular murmur of borrachos staggering down Colfax could be heard. She pulled the blankets up over her knees and chest, and suddenly, she felt a world away from everything. She needed to see the kids. They needed her. She was sure of it. And in that dark and solitary moment, fearful, she couldn't help but wonder if all the damage she had done was irreparable.

39

By six the next morning she was standing in line at Union Station, among the big-hatted women and their matching luggage, with her own bags in hand, anticipating the train ride home. The sun had yet to come up that morning, and all of Colorado was beneath an immense sea of gray. As the train chugged away from the cold downtown buildings of Denver, Bea thought about Loretta, and knew that if she was every bit of the woman she appeared to be, she'd understand why her newest employee would not show up to work that day, or any day thereafter. Still, she couldn't help but feel bad about it. Loretta had been nice to her, and if not for her frequent talks over whiskey and cigarettes, Denver might've left an impression on her as the coldest city in the world.

The train rattled and charged up the incline of the Front Range, picking up speed and burrowing through the great divide. As it cut through the gorge town of Morrison, a flotilla of clouds sunk down over Denver, and from within their frigid bellies they let drop a veil of white flakes. At first the flakes arrived slow and sporadic, but within minutes, all the traffic on Colfax slowed to a near halt, and children stood on front porches and sidewalks wagging their pink tongues to taste it. On the small windows of El Chapultepec a pattering of wet flecks kissed the glass and whispered across Market Street, and down onto the Platte River, where each flake dissolved and was whisked away by the slow-moving stream. They fell on the railroad tracks and dusted heavily the eastern plains, and turned the concrete ashen gray. So close was Bea to witnessing this, that had she sat in the last cart, the caboose, and turned her head around to look back, just once, she might've caught a glimpse of it. But she had looked back once before, and was done with it. She slid her body down on the seat cushion, nestled her ear against her sweater, and fixed her eyes out the window.

As the Rocky Mountains scrolled past, she thought about her father and wondered why, with the money they'd made as a family, harvesting all those years, he had never once purchased a home for them to call their own. She vowed to one day confront him about it. The train released a plume of smoke as they rounded an immense cliff, and suddenly, staring out at the towering white peaks that inched past her window, she recalled the look on her father's face. That curious smile that gripped him upon entering Irapuato some seventeen years ago. A warm calm fell over her, and though she would never come to terms with his way of doing things, or understand fully his complete disregard for anything that resembled love, she knew at last the answer to the question that had nagged her ever since that first train ride, when she was only ten. How, in the midst of their own deportation, among the pleading of the herded and the cold stuttering of boxcars, among the prodding boots of immigration officers, the excrement and the wailing, the curses and the prayers—how in God's name her father was able to conjure something that resembled a smile. Back then she could only attribute it to his callousness, and his utter disdain for anything that resembled emotion. But now she knew better. It had nothing to do with leaving, and everything to do with returning.

AFTERWORD

FINDING BEA FRANCO

Saturday, September 11, 2010

Only a month ago I'd returned home from the East Coast, where I'd spent three days at the New York Public Library scrutinizing each one of Bea's handwritten letters to Jack. It was my second trip, in fact, and both times I'd held the same aged scraps of paper in my hands and placed them on the clean green felts of a sterile archive room and ruminated over them, investigating them for clues, landmarks, sediment, sentiment, anything that might reveal who she was, and her whereabouts. The same way I had once seriously contemplated climbing to the top of that big tin water tower in the middle of Selma and shouting out her name in hopes that some passerby, a campesina on her way home from work, might shout back—"Hey, you! You're looking for la Señora Franco? I know where she lives, come down from there!"

But here I stood now, on this street, this yard, sweat tickling the length of my spine and gathering on the skin beneath my moustache. The heat was unbearable this day; it was early fall and still in the mid-90s. I wanted badly to remove my blazer but didn't want to expose the tattoos on my left arm. I was too aware that this was a moment that needed to be handled delicately, strategically. One misstep, one bad move, and it could take months, years, before I'd ever get this family to open their door to me again. I rehearsed my lines once, twice, but it didn't help. I kept forgetting them and had to trust that they'd come back to me in the moment. In the seconds before walking up the steps and knocking on the metal screen door I panicked, thinking about the kind of reaction I'd get with this far-fetched claim. Would they refute the story before hearing me out? Would they slam the door and threaten to call the cops? Not unusual in these parts. Or was it possible that they'd always known and simply didn't want to be found? Which would mean I'd be ruthlessly picking at the seams of an old wound. It was all possible. But there were the glaring synchronicities that kept playing in my head. Like this one: the simple and true-to-God fact that the yard I found myself standing on in that moment, the yard belonging to one Bea Franco, was only one mile down the street from my house.

As I went up the concrete steps, a cat leapt from the stoop and sidled up to my leg. I wanted to bend down and pet it but was too close to the door now to do anything but channel my focus on the strength of the first impressionable knock.

She wasn't expecting anyone, so when she heard the door, she peeked through the window curtain first. Not recognizing the face on the porch, she did what all people on that side of Fresno do, she spoke through the bolted metal screen. I smiled and squinted my eyes, trying to make out her face on the other side of it, but it was impossible. She asked what I wanted. Her voice was light, but with a hint of age behind it. I had to talk fast. I wiped the sweat from my brow.

"Is this the home of Beatrice Franco?"

"Yes, it is," the woman replied. "What's this about?"

"Are you Beatrice?"

"No." She hesitated. "I'm her daughter, Patricia."

Already it was proving fruitful. I fumbled through my lines, tried explaining, painfully inarticulate as I was, that I was a writer. She stood silent, unimpressed. I pushed on, spilling to her this unlikely story that she wouldn't believe for some time. Even as I spoke it and knew it to be true, it sounded absurd coming from my mouth. Finally, I said, "I'm working on a book about a woman, a farmworker from Selma in the 40s." I paused and could feel my legs beneath me again. "She was a character in a book, a famous novel . . . her real name was Bea Franco." I gave her a second to respond, but Patricia had nothing to say. "I've been researching her for three years now. I know it sounds strange, but everything I have tells me that the woman I'm looking for, Bea Franco, is the owner of this house—your mother."

"I think you have the wrong person."

I had to think quick. "Can I ask you a few questions then, so that I can cross your mother's name off my list?"

"If you can ask me through the screen door."

I fumbled through my tote bag and pulled out a sheet of paper and gazed at it. The questions, which seemed so well crafted just days ago, now appeared transparent and forced. I abandoned them and trusted my instincts.

"Do you have a brother named Albert . . . or Alberto?"

"Yes," she replied, timidly.

"And your mother, Bea, was she back and forth between Selma and Los Angeles in the 40s?"

"Maybe."

"She has a sister named Angie, right? Four brothers. Alex was one of them . . . and Freddy."

"Uh huh."

The air thickened. I could tell she was creeped out by what I knew. I pushed on. "Your mother, was she born around nineteen twenty, or twenty-one?"

She hesitated to answer. "What did you say your name was again?"

"Tim," I replied. "Tim Hernandez." I slipped my card through a crack in the screen door and she yanked it from my grip.

"Can I show you some letters?" I brandished the small stack. She hesitated. Her instincts, I'm sure, warned her against opening the door, but another part of her, that curious voice that grips us all, cracked it open slightly. I passed them to her. She stood silently. I could hear the paper shuffling in her hands every few seconds. I strained my eyes, yearning to look through the screen to catch a glimpse of her face, to see for myself whether or not she resembled the image of her mother, the one described in Jack's book. When she was done, she cracked the door open and passed the letters back to me.

"Come back Thursday, you can speak with my brother about this."

I took the letters and thanked her. Still, a part of me was hoping it would be enough to get inside. I had to settle for the invitation to return. As I started off, I realized she hadn't closed the door, so I moved deliberately slow, searching for an angle, any excuse to stay on that porch. What had I missed? The cat walked up to me and I bent down to pet it. And then it hit me. "Can I ask you one last thing?"

"Sure."

"Is your mother—" I hesitated, almost too embarrassed to ask it, for what farmworker did I know ever lived past seventy-five, eighty, if they were lucky? Still, I had to ask. "Is Bea alive?"

"Yes," she replied, "but she's sleeping now."

I looked at my watch. It was two o'clock. The door slammed shut and I turned and went quietly, respectfully, down the steps. Though on the inside it took everything for me not to bound, leap off that porch. I hurried to my car, which, strangely enough, was parked farther away than I had remembered it. I sat in it for several minutes, slapping the steering wheel, reeling at the fortunate insanity of it all. I was speaking to myself for a minute before I thought to grab my handheld recorder and get it all down.

Then came the hardest part—how to live out the next five days and not chew the side of my tongue raw with anticipation. I found myself frequently returning to Jack's book, re-reading the passages about Bea's blue eyes, her lustrous black hair and petite frame, the confidence with which she strode through Selma streets. And I couldn't help but wonder how I'd find her now. Would there be any resemblance between this sleeping woman in the winter of her life, and the Mexican girl of his memory? Would she be lucid enough to recall an illicit affair that happened over six decades ago? And of course, when all was said and done, there was still the singular, most important question of the day—what does she remember of their time together?

To put it mildly, the next several days rolled by torturously. Each night I sat at the small desk tucked in the corner of our bedroom and wrote long-winded speculations, treatises practically, on why this is or isn't the Bea Franco I was looking for. I was convinced I had to be diligent about my questions. I didn't simply *want* her to be Bea Franco, I had to prove it was her.

Over the course of three years I'd compiled a list of one hundred and ninety-six Bea Francos, scattered across the United States, of which only eighty-five were crossed off. Now and then I wondered how it was possible that any person might live so long a life and never once come across their own name between the pages of a book. Why hadn't anyone found her? It was a question that nagged.

A year before I had driven to Selma and met a man, Don Shantz, who was the archivist of the local historical society. Together we filed through school year books, 1935, '36, '38, trying to locate Bea within the pages and indexes but found nothing. Mr. Shantz then drove me to take a look at the building that was once the Selma Sanitarium, the only hospital around back then, he informed me, where a mother might've taken her son had he contracted pneumonia. It was now a convalescent home. Then we went out past Nebraska and Gaynor Streets, and saw the old neighborhood where Bea's folks once lived, but the addresses had changed. We ended our day over on Bethel Avenue, out by the old Selma Winery, where Mr. Shantz parked the car alongside the dusty shoulder and let me out for a minute. I eyed the landscape, the dilapidated siding of the winery, and the sprawling grapevines and gnarled fig trees. It was a familiar portrait, one I'd grown up with and knew well. In the distance the same tired palm trees and sagging fences loomed. The same hunk of land my own family had labored on for three generations. Back then I thought finding Bea would be an impossible task. So in that moment, looking out over the landscape, I had come to a critical decision: I would stop looking for her and write the book, Bea's story, rooted in what little I knew, but mostly, in how well I knew it.

Thursday, September 16, 2010

Five days had come and gone. I returned to her house, and was met at the door by a tall man with hazel eyes, Albert. I played it cool upon entering, though right off my eyes were scanning the room for her. She was nowhere. Instead, I found green shag rug and faux wood panels lining the place from wall to wall. Photos of family, children's smiling faces, old and recent, hung askew alongside military photos, including one of Ronald Reagan poised handsomely before an

American flag. Stacks of old 33⅓ records were piled at the bottom of the wilted china cabinet by which Albert stood. On the other side of a small round dining table was Patricia. She walked over to shake my hand, and I took note of her light skin and wide hazel eyes, just like her brother's; I was finally glad to put a face to the voice behind the screen door.

We sat at the table beneath the dim yellow light of a single lamp hanging overhead. The curtains were kept closed; according to Patricia, it was easier on her mother's eyes. I almost jumped at the opportunity to ask of her whereabouts right then, but I held back, knowing full well that, still, I had to be tactful about the order of business.

Albert is a broad-shouldered man with a bald head, square jaw, and a no-bullshit glare about his eyes. He had been a truck driver, a Teamster for a big part of his life, and I figured the only way to reach him was to talk nuts and bolts, starting from the beginning.

I reached into my tote bag and brandished a copy of Jack's book, published fifty-three years prior. I opened it to the dog-eared page and read a few lines— the part that describes in perfect detail how Jack met a Mexican girl on a bus in Bakersfield, way back in the fall of 1947. When I was done, brother and sister looked at one another and shook their heads subtly. They stared back at me with a look of uncertainty. Albert nodded. "So," he said, "what's this story of yours?"

"I believe your mother is the Mexican girl."

He laughed robustly and ran his hand over his face and breathed through his nostrils. "What makes you so sure?" he asked, glancing over at his sister. Patricia stood up and went into the living room to turn off the television.

"It sounds crazy, I know," I said. I pulled my files out and spread them on the table. Albert scooted closer and fixed his eyeglasses on his face. Beneath the sepia light cast from the lamp, he scrutinized the documents. Minutes passed, and soon it had been an hour. Finally, he removed his glasses. "You're saying my mother had an affair?"

Silence filled the small house. I knew it would come up. I was aware of the possibility from the beginning, but still I had no well-crafted reply. "That's what it looks like," I replied. Patricia's face wadded into confusion. "It was sixty-three years ago." I said this attempting to put some perspective on it. I could feel the silence festering quickly, as if a wedge was forming between us. I tried changing the subject. "Right now there's more than twenty books published, biographies about Jack that also have your mother's name in them." I paused. "They mention you too, Albert."

The news blew him back in his seat, and he got up and fetched his laptop. He returned and fired it up, pecking his mother's name into the search engine. And there it was. He was baffled to see the list of websites, links, and information out there. He spent thirty minutes scrolling through, clicking on various tabs and shaking his head, laughing out loud at the oddness of it all, the misinformation, the speculation, fiction, and straight-out surrealness of that moment. Patricia gently tapped my shoulder. "Show him the letters," she said. I pulled them from my tote bag and placed them on the table in front of Al.

Gripping the letters, his mother's letters, written to Jack when he himself was still only six, Albert's eyes widened. He was speechless. It was as if he knew right then, upon first glance, simply by the curve and slant of her writing, by the way she signed her name especially, that wherever I came from, and whoever I was, I had found something that they didn't know they had lost.

When he was done reading, Albert ran his thick hand over his jaw and leaned back in his chair. He turned his eyes out toward the shut curtains, where now sunlight was slashing in through the blinds. "You're an author, right?" He paused. "How can they put stuff in their books and not tell us?"

"Maybe they couldn't find you," I replied.

"How did *you* find us?"

I shook my head slightly, well aware that there was no single answer. It was an accumulation of alignments. Albert lifted a brow at me, expecting an answer.

"It wasn't until I found your mother's letters at the New York Public Library," I began. He folded his arms and Patricia scooted closer. "Two of them had addresses, one in Selma and one in Los Angeles. I tried the Selma place first, but it wasn't there anymore. I even checked the old Sanborn Fire Maps of the thirties and forties. They only showed where the house used to be, but it isn't there now." I hesitated. "On another letter your mother included her middle initial, 'R.' I wasn't sure if this was her middle name or her maiden name, so I tried everything. For months I checked the Internet—Rosales, Romo, Rodriguez, Ramirez, Rosas—it was a long list, and I kept crossing names off. I tried middle names too—Rosa, Rene, Reyna—but still nothing. I called Fresno County Hall of Records and asked about death and marriage certificates; of course they couldn't find anything." Albert scratched his chin. "I finally decided to try the cemeteries." Patricia let out a subtle gasp. "I called every cemetery in three counties, asking if they had any plots for Bea R. Franco . . . of course you know how that turned out."

Albert breathed deeply; his wide chest rose and he rubbed his hand over his moustache. He glanced at his sister and she adjusted her eyeglasses. I could see they were getting tired. It was all too much to take in in one sitting. I decided to switch gears.

"What about your mom?" I asked. "Can you tell me about her?"

Patricia spoke up. "She's doesn't do much, keeps to herself mostly. She's home a lot."

Albert picked up from there. "She never really leaves the house," he said. "Her eyes are bad."

"How's her memory?"

They looked at one another. "It's alright."

"Does she remember things from her past?"

They nodded.

Their energy waned. Albert looked at his watch. He stood up from his chair and stretched, then lowered his eyes at me.

"Let us think about this for a few days," he said, lifting his hand for me to shake. It was an abrupt ending, but I understood. "You can come back next week." I nodded and pulled my files together. I packed them away, searching my brain for a tactful way of asking to see their mother. Albert hovered for a minute, and I could see that his face was a tangle of uncertainty. Patricia moved toward the front door, and again I had to abandon the idea of seeing Bea. Albert disappeared into the hallway.

"He'll be right back," Patricia said, ushering me politely to the door.

An awkward silence crept over us.

"What's the cat's name?" I asked.

Patricia raised her eyebrows. "It don't have one, I think."

We chuckled over it.

When I reached the threshold, I heard within the old house a door creak open. Albert's voice filtered through the walls, and I could hear him saying something, incoherent. The wooden floors groaned under the weight of his footsteps, and then he emerged from the unlit hallway. He was walking slowly, with calculated steps. I started to wave good-bye to him but he motioned with his hand for me to hold on. When he entered the quiet space of the dining room, there beside him, stepping out of her son's shadow, clutching his arm tenderly, stood Bea Franco.

She ambled carefully into the yellow light, clutching the fold of her sweater shut. She cocked her head to one side and squinted her eyes up at me. Her face was the pale color of an almond shell, and her hair a coiffed entanglement of autumn red, but only at the tips. The roots were pure snow. The tiny domes of her shoulders hunched over slightly, and her short slender legs were draped in loose-fitting cotton pants. She stood there with a puzzled look, as if she was staring at an apparition. Albert stood by his mother proudly, and Patricia moved toward them.

"This is my mother," he said, "Bea Franco."

I was caught off guard and stood petrified. I set my bag down on the carpet and moved to her. I had never imagined how I'd greet her if the chance presented itself. I guess a part of me was always skeptical. I could only do what came natural. I took her warm, frail hand in mine, and set my other hand on top and looked into her eyes.

It was in that moment that I would discover the first detail that Jack fictionalized about her. In his version, he wrote that her eyes were blue, and that there were "timidities inside." Her eyes were not blue at all. They were a vast, brilliant shade of deep emerald. And if ever there were timidities, they had long since been replaced with resilience.

"It's an honor to meet you," I said.

Memory Belongs to the Rememberer

From then on I visited her frequently. We'd sit for hours and talk beneath the dim light of her dining room table, sipping cups of instant coffee that she'd make just for the occasion. Usually either Albert or Patricia hung around, but sometimes they didn't. Especially when the conversation seemed to be going nowhere at all, as it so often did. Albert had to constantly remind me that his mother's memory was beginning to fail. Knowing this, I began asking her the same questions over and over. Sometimes I'd get the same answer, and sometimes an elaboration of the first. But once in awhile, her answers would take a new turn entirely. On one occasion I asked her if she'd ever been outside of California. She replied, "Yes, Irapuato, Guanajuato. I hated it." I asked her the same question again a week later. "Yes," she said, "I lived in Denver once, where I worked as a waitress for a month." At one point, I sensed, even Albert began to find her unpredictability amusing. There was no chronology either. Her memories came as they came. I took notes. And if that wasn't bad enough, her eyesight was getting worse. She had developed cataracts, and so a thin gray veil hung over both of her eyes. She once described it as "looking through cotton balls." If she wanted to read she had to pull a hefty magnifying glass from the china cabinet drawer and position it about two feet away from her face.

Around the fourth visit I knew that, sooner or later, I'd have to find a tactful way of getting to the subject of Jack. With her children around, it seemed in bad taste to even ask about an affair, even though it was, clearly, almost a lifetime ago. Albert and Patricia knew their father was no saint. They'd heard the stories, had lived it, and recalled his memory with much trepidation. Regardless, it was a sticky subject, and so naturally I was hesitant. I phoned my friend Mark, a former investigative journalist for the *Los Angeles Times* and an author who had a reputation for teasing truth out of the most hardened people—politicians. If anyone knew how to navigate around this situation involving an elderly woman and her two retired children, it would be him.

"Look, man," Mark said to me, "ask the lady about her life. After all, it's her story you want, not Jack's. We all know his story already. So, ask her about her life, and really listen. Pay good attention to her. People know when they're being paid attention to or not. So when she gets to the part in her life, right around where you think she meets the gringo, then ask her. You gotta be up front about it too, you can't skirt around it. Just ask her, did you ever have a friend named Jack?"

"You think a photo will help?"

"Forget the photo, just talk with the woman, and be straight about it. You'll see."

On my next visit I had planned on doing just as he suggested. Of course, I still brought a photograph along, in case. My mind was set now. I was going to ask her about Jack. But when I got there, I quickly realized she had other concerns. She began speaking about her ex-husband, Beto.

"He was too fast for me," she said, in a near whisper. "Couldn't keep a job either. That's just how he was." Her eyes bothered her and she rubbed them and blinked profusely. She got up to dim the light and then sat back down and continued. "I left him years ago. I guess he passed away around 1960. Albert," she called to her son, who was busy watching the Dodgers game on T.V., "what year did your father die?"

"Sixty-three," Albert replied.

"Yes, '63. I didn't go to his funeral, but Al did."

All I could do then was go along with it. "What happened in the years after?"

"I got a job working for Greyhound. I loved that job, and I worked there for a long time, more than thirty years. Right here in Fresno. In Chinatown." She sipped her coffee and then grabbed a pack of Skittles and tore them open and swallowed a handful. "That's around the time I met Roy," she said, chewing. "He was a good man. Worked a lot, but he was nice to me." She swallowed her candy, and then quieted. She lifted her hand and pointed to the carpet near my feet. "Roy died right there." I looked down at the shaggy fibers of carpet. "I woke up one morning, this was back in 2002, I think, and I came out here and just found him lying there." She pointed again and her eyelids grew heavy. And this is when I decided, once again, that any talk of Jack would have to wait. I looked at my watch; it was a quarter past nine o'clock, and it was clear she was tired. I thanked her for the coffee and asked her, as was now routine, if I could return.

"Next Wednesday would be good for me," I said. "The thirteenth?"

She smiled. "That's my birthday."

"Are you having a party?"

"If I have company I will," she replied.

She was dressed in a yellow blouse with short sleeves so that her shoulders and slender arms were exposed. She seemed happy that morning, and upon arriving I noticed that neither Albert nor Patricia were around. But before I could get my bag open and pull the photograph of Jack from my folder, in walked Al with a cake in one hand and a six-pack of soda in the other. Bea was delighted to see the cake, and she went into the kitchen to put some coffee on. They stood around and talked about how beautiful the cake was, and what flavor, and how she couldn't remember the last time anyone threw a party for her birthday.

"How old are you now, Bea?" I asked.

She got a faraway look in her eye. "Let's see, I was born in 1920 . . . I think," she hesitated, "yes, so I'm . . ."

Al cut in, "You're ninety, Mom."

She squinted as if the mere sound of that number made her tooth ache, and then she laughed. It felt good to see her face light up like that, and to hear the sweet sound of breath skirting from her chest in such a way. We took our coffee into the dining room and sat at the table. Al followed behind with the cake, lit up now by three candles. She watched him set it down and her eyes beamed. Together, Al and I launched into an off-key version of "Happy Birthday"; all the while, Bea peered down at the mass of chocolate glowing beneath the small flames. When the song was done, she leaned over and blew each flame out one by one.

The afternoon passed quickly, and before we knew it, only crumbs were left on our plates. We'd drunk half a jar of instant coffee, and kept up a conversation that took us well into the evening.

At one point, Albert leaned back in his chair and folded his arms, then shot a look at me from across the table. I knew right then he was wanting me to ask his mother about Jack. I still wasn't sure about the timing. Bea's head hung low, and it was obvious she was tired. She looked at me and winked, and the expression on her face chimed a subtle curiosity, as if wondering, who exactly is this guy? This author, who has taken such interest? She took a handful of Skittles from an open bag and placed one in her mouth. "The orange ones are my favorite," she said. And in that moment, with the photograph of Jack burning in my back pocket, I glanced over at Albert, and we both knew that the time was right. I pulled the photograph out and placed it on the table.

"Bea," I said, timidly, "do you remember a man, a friend of yours named Jack?"

She blinked her eyes several times, then angled her face away from the light and thought for a moment. When the answer did not come quickly enough, Albert nodded at me and pointed his eyes at the photograph.

"Do you think a picture of him would help you remember?"

She nodded. "Maybe."

I lifted the photograph and passed it to her. She took it from my hand and stared blankly at it for a second, then rubbed her eyes and blinked again.

"I need my magnifying glass," she said, rising up from her seat.

Silence filled the dining room. Outside a car whisked past, and then a dog barked after it. Bea tucked the loose end of her sweater under her arm and shuffled to her china cabinet, and from the drawer she pulled out her magnifying glass. She gripped its black handle, then flicked on a small desk lamp and lifted the thick lens inches above the photograph. Her back was to the table where Al and I sat studying her closely. She maneuvered the photo until she'd found the right angle, and then held it as still as she could. Her hand trembled. She fixed her eyes on the image for a few seconds, then looked back over her shoulder at me. "He sure is handsome, isn't he?"

"Do you remember him, Mom?" Albert asked, growing impatient.

She turned the photograph toward the light and stood motionless, fixated on the details of Jack's face. Her breathing was audible but soft. Her chin lifted slightly. She hesitated, and then stared at the photo another minute. Finally, she turned toward Albert, little Al, her son. And had Patricia been there too, she would've looked at her daughter with the same hint of loyalty. She lowered the magnifying glass and gave the photo one last glance. "No," she said, "I've never seen him before in my life."

Clockwise from top left: Bea and little Al, Los Angeles, 1942; Little Albert, age 8, circa 1950; Bea and Angie, Selma grape fields, 1947

ACKNOWLEDGMENTS

For trusting me to write this story out of a shadow, I am forever indebted to Bea and her family, especially Albert Franco, for his many hours of dedication to this project. Also, a big thank-you is owed to the spirit and memory of Robert Welsh, who generously lent his time, sharp memory, and photographs, and who, regrettably, did not get to see the book in print (RIP).

This book was written with the support of many collaborators, researchers, archivists, and friends. To those people I offer my sincere gratitude: Don Shantz, archivist at the Selma Historical Society; Mark Arax, Alex Espinoza, and Kyle Behen; Adreann "007" Allen, Betty Jo Brenner, Rebecca Plevin, Sarah Parkes, Devoya Mayo, Christine de la Hofer, and Estela Sue; Michele Serros; and Jason Mc Donald, for your keen eye and for hosting me in NYC. I am also grateful to the following institutions: New York Public Library's Berg Collection, Naropa University, Bennington College, Los Angeles Unified School District, and Colorado Center for the Book. I owe a special thank-you to my agent at Full Circle Literary Agency, Adriana Dominguez, who believed in this book from the start, and to my literary hermana, Irene Vilar, for her early support of this project. My gratitude especially goes out to my mother, Lydia Zuniga Hernandez, for being instrumental in the relentless pursuit in helping to locate the elusive "Terry." Finally, to my wife Dayanna and my children, Rumi, Salvador, and Quetzani, for making a life with this writer, and then holding down the fort with enduring grace and patience when I'm away. I'll say it again, this one is for you, always for you.

Also, I am indebted to those valley writers, artists, and cultural workers (living and dead) whose creative works, research, images, histories/herstories, and voices I am certain you will find lurking in these pages: Mark Arax, Nick Belardes, John C. Doffelmeyer, Wilma Elizabeth McDaniel, John Spivey, Michael Medrano, Aris Janigian, William Seacrest Jr., Lawson Fusao Inada, Daniel Chacon, John Steinbeck, Matthew Rangel, Pop Laval, Juan Felipe Herrera, Patricia Wakida, William Saroyan, Lee Herrick, the Hmong American Writers Circle, Lance Canales, Sylvia Ross, Maceo Montoya, and David Mas Masumoto.

FINAL NOTE ABOUT THE LETTERS

Bea Franco's letters to Jack Kerouac (which appear on pages 172, 178, 190, and 191) have remained in their original state, with the exception of only minor edits for clarity. This was done with the full permission of her family and estate.

ABOUT THE AUTHOR

Tim Z. Hernandez is a poet, novelist, and performance artist whose awards include the 2006 American Book Award, the 2010 Premio Aztlán Prize in Fiction, and the James Duval Phelan Award from the San Francisco Foundation. His poems and stories have appeared in numerous anthologies and journals, and his books have been widely acclaimed, including a spot on NPR's *All Things Considered*. In 2011 the Poetry Society of America named him one of sixteen New American Poets. He holds a BA from Naropa University and an MFA from Bennington College and currently calls the Rocky Mountains home.